CAPTAIN
SAVE A HOE

BASED ON A TRUE STORY

iiKane

Made of Music

Under the smile of a player

Beats the heart of a lover

Prologue

Philadelphia, 1984

"Oh Baby, you are lookin' good! Didn't I tell you this look would be fabulous on you?" a young Georgie exclaimed, using the opposite end of the comb to fluff the curls on his *"customer."*

"Oh wait, this curl is too tight; it should hug your face...like that," he said triumphantly, tongue hanging out of the corner of his mouth the way it always did when he was at work. *"Now, look at that."* He picked up the doll baby and turned it to face the mirror, standing behind the doll like a proud father.

"Didn't I tell you? You are beautiful! Wait, what's that? You want to kiss me? On the lips? But I'm Georgie Porgie; I make all the girls cry."

He took the doll in his little eight-year-old arms and leaned it back, just like he had seen Billy Dee Williams do in his mother's favorite movie *"Lady Sings the Blues."* He closed his eyes and puckered his lips, leaning in to kiss his doll when he was interrupted by a yell.

"Georgie!"

His mother's voice echoed up the staircase. It seemed like she was right in the room with him.

"What!" he hollered back, knowing she couldn't hear him over the blaring music.

He sat the doll down and headed downstairs.

"Sky's the limit and you know that you keep on.
Just keep on pressing on…"

The sound of D-Train's *"Keep On"* filled the living room that had been converted into a bootleg hair salon, complete with two swivel chairs and three chair hair dryers. Two women sat under dryers and one in the swivel chair as Stephanie danced on long legs, swinging her curvaceous hips and waving a Newport 100 in the air. She bore a striking resemblance to Sade with her light skin and freckles sprinkled across her face, down to the forehead and all.

"Whoa! This is my song! Georgie! Boy, I know you hear——," she spotted Georgie at the bottom of the stairs. "There go my Baby! Georgie, come dance with your Momma!"

"Dag, Momma, every time somebody come over, you want me to come dance," he whined, trying to play as if he didn't love it. He was a natural performer and never missed the opportunity to show off.

"Boy shut up, you know you love it! Now, do the snake!"

Georgie got in the middle of the floor and began curling his body back and forth to the women's delight.

"Now, Michael Jackson! Michael Jackson!"

He grabbed his little crotch, bit his bottom lip, and then kicked his leg as he imitated the legendary pop artist. He wanted to do his moonwalk, but the thick rug didn't allow for a smooth glide across the floor.

"Look at him!"

"He's adorable!"

"Now get nasty with it, Baby!" Stephanie urged, loving the attention that her son was receiving.

Georgie put his hands behind his head, stuck out his pelvis and started winding his hips suggestively, looking directly at the women as he blew them a kiss.

"Oh my God, he's gonna be a little heartbreaker!" one woman exclaimed with a snicker.

"He already is, ain't you? Tell 'em who you are, Baby!"

"Georgie Porgie Puddin' Pie, kiss the girls and make 'em cry," he sang, bobbing his head to the beat.

The women could see why, with his smooth and creamy bronze complexion, grey eyes and long wavy hair that Stephanie kept in a ponytail, he resembled a young Ice T. It was only a matter of time before he would make those song lyrics a reality.

"That's right, my Puddin' Pie," Stephanie laughed. She took his hand and they began to dance together as she sang, "Georgie Porgie Puddin Pie, Georgie Porgie Puddin' Pie, Georgie Porgie Puddin'Pie...."

Ten years later…

"Georgie, what you laughing at?" the girl between his legs questioned.

They were sitting in the bleachers by the basketball court. It was the middle of the afternoon and the court had two half-court games going on at the same time, while a few people sat in the bleachers.

Georgie was braiding the girl's hair when a Jeep stopped at the light, blasting "Keep On" by D-Train.

"Every time my mother hears this joint she makes me dance like I'm a monkey or something," he chuckled.

She giggled.

"Aww that's cute, lil' monkey…Ouch!" she gasped as Georgie pulled her hair playfully.

"I got your monkey swinging."

She jacked her elbow into his thigh.

"Boy! Hey, Georgie, can I ask you something?"

"You just did."

"Why do you like doing hair? I ain't never known no boy that like to do hair…unless he's funny," she remarked.

Georgie shrugged as he finished one braid and began another.

"I just like for females to look good. A chick could be

4

broke as fuck, but ain't no need for her ever to look like it."

"I know that's right," she remarked.

"Yo Gee! What's good, Fam?"

Georgie looked up to see his man K.B. stepping up the bleachers. He gave Georgie some dap then sat down beside him, letting his book bag dangle between his legs.

"Oh, that's all you see K.B.? With your ugly self," the girl teased.

K.B. smiled, revealing his deep-set dimples. "What up, Veronica, I was just about to speak."

"Mm-hmmm, whateva."

K.B. looked at Georgie, smiling from ear to ear. "Yo, you ain't heard?"

"What, you finally got some pussy?" Georgie joked. Veronica cracked up and K.B. gave her the middle finger.

"Fuck you. I got the letter."

"You got the letter?" Georgie stopped braiding and looked at him. K.B. nodded, barely able to contain himself. "I'm going to muhfuckin' Duke! Full scholarship!"

Georgie gave him hard dap and a bump hug. Veronica reached out and gave him a pound.

"Congratulations K! Now we can get paid! I'm your manager!" Veronica laughed.

"Yo, that's what's up! You did your muhfuckin' thing!" Georgie exclaimed.

"Indeed I did," K.B. playfully patted himself on the back. "So what do you say we celebrate by makin' some quick money?"

"No," Georgie said following K.B.'s eyes across the court.

"Come on, Georgie! Look at them two niggas over there," he pointed to a couple of scrawny-looking guys rebounding each other's missed rim shots. "They can't ball worth a buck *and* they from South Philly! This shit's right up our alley!"

"I don't feel like ballin', yo."

"We ain't *ballin*, we makin' money. I'ma put up a G and we split fifty-fifty."

"Seventy-thirty," Georgie countered.

"Goddam, you a Jew! Fifty-five-forty five."

"Sixty-forty."

"That's bullshit. Fuck it, sixty-forty," K.B. surrendered.

K.B. got up and marched down the bleachers as the two dudes wrapped up their game and headed towards him off the court.

"Yo, I see ya'll got game. Ya'll tryin' to ball for money?" he challenged.

Another pair of dudes came walking onto the court, and the taller of the two spoke up. "We got next!"

K.B. took out a wad of money and slammed it on the ground.

"My thousand got next! Ya'll tryin' to match it?"

The pair shook their heads and walked off. K.B. turned his attention back to his two targets.

"So what up? Ya'll pushin' that fly ass Lexus, I know ya'll got a G to play," he smirked.

One of the dudes, his bald slender face resembling Kevin Garnett, looked at his partner, who could've been his younger brother.

"You hear this clown?"

"Man, I ain't tryin' to hear that short ass shit. I got shit to do."

K.B. reached into his other pocked and pulled out more money.

"Oh nigga, shit get longer. You ain't sayin' shit!"

The two brothers looked at each other then back at K.B., sizing him up. They were both at least 6'5" and K.B. was 6'2". Kevin chuckled.

"Man, who you playin' with?"

"For ya'll? I'll play with anybody. Matter of fact…" He

stopped and looked around as if he were randomly choosing though he and Georgie had run this scam a thousand times. "Him! That sissy in the bleachers doin' hair."

The younger brother's eyes got big.

"You gonna play with a faggot?! Oh fuck yeah, we bettin'!' he exclaimed, then jogged past the bleachers towards a black Lexus with tinted windows and chrome rims. "Yo! Ay yo, Sweetheart! C'mere for a minute!" K.B. yelled.

Veronica stifled a giggle.

"He callin' you, Sweetheart."

"I'ma kill that muhfucka," Georgie grumbled, as he went into his act. He came down the bleachers limp-wristed and loose walking, his pelvis jutting out in a feminine manner. The brothers fell out laughing as Georgie approached them, stopping just below their chin.

"Yo, can you bounce a ball?" K.B. asked Georgie.

"Hmm, I can do a *lot* of things with balls," Georgie replied sassily.

K.B. had to hold back his laughter. "Well, all I need you to do is bounce and pass. You got that? Bounce and pass."

"What's in it for me?"

"Three hundred dollars."

"Shit, I'm down."

K.B. turned to the brothers. "Shoot for takeout."

The brothers won the takeout, but after that, it was all K.B. and Georgie. The brothers dwarfed them, but they already had their routine down pat. They weren't aware that K.B. was an all-city point guard that was known for being virtually unstoppable on a real court, let alone the black top.

"What you gonna do, huh? You can hang? You can hang?" K.B. clowned, as he dribbled from hand to hand at half court.

"Kevin" stayed low in his textbook defensive stance, but

K.B. shuffled his dribble, faked right and went left with a devastating cross over, blowing "Kevin" by like the wind only to come around his back to the very same spot with a laugh.

"Damn yo, I'ma give you another chance, aight? Can you hang? Am I going right? Left? Right?" K.B. teased then double faked. As soon as "Kevin" stepped back he went up for a three-pointer that hit nothing but the chain-linked net.

"Oh my god, it's raining men," Georgie teased, with an effeminate giggle.

The brothers were vexed. The score was 6-0, going to 10 before they scored a point. "Kevin" threw his brother an alley-oop that he slammed. Georgie had to back away so his nuts wouldn't be in his face as he hung from the rim.

"You like that, honey?" the brother leered. Georgie walked away, flexing his jaw muscles as he tried calming his nerves.

The brothers, seeing themselves down 8-3, started punishing Georgie and K.B. and set bruising picks as they went hard to the rim, busting Georgie's lip as they came down.

Georgie spat the blood and growled, "play ball," the feminine act no longer in his tone.

K.B. slid Georgie a pass at the top of the key. He faked like he was going to shoot a jumper, causing the brother to jump in an attempt to block it, and side-stepped them for an easy lay up. 9-3.

Georgie took the ball out with the younger brother all over him. K.B. took "Kevin" to the top of the key and Georgie passed him the ball. When he couldn't get around "Kevin," he passed it back to Georgie with a wink. Georgie knew what to do. As soon as K.B. made a break for the basket, Georgie lobbed the ball in a high arch for the perfect alley-oop. K.B. caught it in midair then slammed the ball tomahawk style. The few people watching the game went wild. K.B. hung from the basket with one hand, his other on his nuts.

"Game, muhfuckas!" K.B. barked.

"Naw, fuck that yo, fuck that!" ranted "Kevin." "That was a fuckin' set up! Fuck that!"

K.B. dropped to the ground and stepped up to him.

"Fuck you mean, fuck that?! Nigga we *won*!"

"Nigga, just what the fuck I *said*! I ain't paying shit!" Kevin hissed.

No one noticed as Georgie picked up the basketball.

"Ay yo, just run it back, aight? Yo bruh, take out," Georgie suggested to the younger brother.

Just as the brother turned to scream on Georgie, Georgie slammed the basketball into his face. He wobbled on his feet, dazed and blood gushing from his nose, as Georgie moved in to finish the job. He caught him with a sweet 1-2 combination that leaned the bigger dude like a fallen tree. As soon as he hit the ground, Georgie was all over him. He started stomping and kicking his limp body. The brother could hardly take cover as the kicks came harder and faster.

"You like *that*, Honey?" Georgie huffed between kicks, reminding him of his earlier words.

While Georgie was taking off a piece of work on the brother, K.B. was getting it in with Kevin. As soon as Georgie had hit the brother with the basketball, K.B. caught Kevin with a stiff upper cut that rocked him, but didn't drop him. Kevin threw a sloppy jab that K.B. easily weaved, then came back with a crushing kidney shot and a hook that dropped Kevin to the blacktop. The crowd went crazy seeing the two South Philly dudes being stomped into the pavement. K.B. and Georgie, both breathing heavily, slowed their kicks to a stop, leaving the two brothers bleeding and moaning on the ground.

K.B. snatched off the brother's shoe, took the money out then tossed the shoe aside.

"West Side muhfucka!" K.B. barked, kicking him once more in the face.

The crowd went wild, hooting and hollering as K.B. and Georgie dapped each other and then walked off, splitting the money.

"Naw nigga, this fifty-five-forty-five," Georgie protested.

"I thought it was fifty-five-forty-five," K.B. played dumb.

"Quit playin," Georgie warned, throwing a playful punch.

K.B. chuckled and gave him another fifty as they mounted the bleachers.

Georgie started to sit behind Veronica, but she got up.

"You don't want me to finish?" he questioned.

"Not with those nasty ass hands, all bloody and sweaty and shit," Veronica wrinkled her nose. "And y'all need to bounce before those dudes come back trippin'."

K.B. waved her off. "Please, girl! Look at 'em limping off. They ain't goin' nowhere but back to the South Side!" he laughed.

Veronica walked down the bleachers, tossing a look back over her shoulder that said "Okay, gangsta."

Georgie followed the roll of her ass with his eyes, but as she disappeared across the court, his vision fell on the Lexus. The two brothers were sitting in the car looking at them.

"Yo, fam, she might be right. Them niggas still ain't left."

"Man, if you scared get in my pocket," K.B. chuckled, fixing his money so every bill faced the same way.

The two brothers were indeed looking at them, and Kevin in the passenger seat had a chrome 9mm in his hand. He grabbed the door handle to get out, but his brother held his wrist.

"Naw, naw yo, not here. Half these muhfuckas is strapped. Fuck that, we'll get they ass when they leave," his brother suggested, wearing a crooked, bloody smirk.

Kevin nodded, eyes swollen and seething. "Goddamn right

we will, Goddamn right."

When K.B. saw them pulling out and leaving, he turned to Georgie with his lips twisted up.

"What I tell you? Straight pussies!"

Georgie heard his words but his gut was telling him something else. He brushed it off and instead stayed at the park with K.B., kicking it with chicks and shooting ball until the sun went down.

"Yo fam, I'm out," Georgie finally stated, checking his watch.

"Let me find out Mom Dukes still got you comin' in with the street lights," K.B. cracked.

Georgie gave him the finger as he walked off.

"Hold up yo, I'm comin," K.B. yelled, grabbing his book bag.

As they walked off the court, several people congratulated K.B. on his scholarship.

"Yo, I still can't believe you 'bout to go to Duke," Georgie remarked.

"What you mean, can't believe? I'm the best point guard in the fuckin' country!" K.B. boasted, faking like he was dribbling a ball then shooting.

"Naw, I know that. It's just " Georgie shook his head, "...it's crazy, yo."

"Yeah, I know, right? One step closer to the NBA and I'll be ballin' for the Sixers!"

Georgie laughed. "I hope you get drafted by the Knicks."

K.B. shot him a mock ice grill. "Yo, don't play with me like that."

They walked towards the corner, oblivious to the Lexus that passed through the intersection behind them, a light gleaming off the chrome on the nine in the passenger's lap as they passed through the streetlights.

K.B. laughed as they turned the corner and crossed the

street. "Yo, you buggin! But on the real, what you gonna do? I know you ain't gonna fuckin' braid hair all you life," K.B. taunted.

"Man, you just don't understand, yo. You ain't the only one who gonna be a star. I'm tellin' you, when I open my chain of salons, chicks gonna be comin' from all over talkin' 'bout 'Georgie, do my hair! Georgie, play in my hair!'" Georgie imitated in a whiny girls voice. "And you know, playin' in their hair is the first step to playin' in that ass!"

He and K.B. laughed and K.B. gave him dap.

"Yo, yo, yo! Slow down," Kevin urged. They had circled the block in attempt to get in front of the hustlers. The motor hummed as they sat idle at the opposite corner. They watched as Georgie and K.B. crossed the dimly lit side street that was lined with rows of houses on both sides.

Clack – Clack!

"Kevin" slid the chamber back with a hard but smooth motion, locking a round in the chamber.

"You ready?" The brother questioned.

Kevin leered. "As ever."

Georgie saw it first—the glint of an approaching car in his peripheral vision. His street sense screamed, *Turn around!* and he did, just as the Lexus was pulling up and the passenger window rolled down.

"Yo K, look out!" Georgie barked.

"Southside muhfuckas!" Kevin based.

K.B. was caught in the open between two parked cars, totally exposed to the street.

Boom! Boom!

The shots shattered his hip, ripping right through him with agonizing accuracy. "Aaarrgggh!" K.B. bellowed.

"K.B.!" Georgie cried.

With only a split second to react he didn't hesitate. Had he wanted to, he could've fell to the ground behind a parked car, but his heart wouldn't let him. Instead, he dove out into the open, tackling K.B. at the waist, pushing him to the safety of the ground.

Boom! Boom! Boom! Boom!

The sounds of gunfire echoed loudly on the tightly parked street and bounced through the neighborhood, setting off car alarms as pain exploded through Georgie's flesh.

He felt the first bullet slice into his shoulder, and then the blood gush from his head as the second bullet jerked his neck forward. He fell on top of K.B.

The Lexus pitched to a halt and Kevin started to jump out and finish the job, but stopped short him when he saw lights turn on in the windows of the surrounding houses, and the appearance of curious expressions as heads peaked out of the doors and windows.

Witnesses.

"Yo, fuck that, get in! Let's go!" his brother urged.

Kevin was stuck for a moment, wanting to inflict the ultimate punishment for the humiliation that he had suffered earlier, but not wanting to end up like his father who was rotting away on death row in a Pennsylvania penitentiary. He allowed his brother to tug him back into the car and they screeched off.

Blood gushed from Georgie's head and shoulder. The pain had him almost praying for death.

"Georgie!" K.B. called out, tears streaming down his cheeks.

The first time the sound of K.B.'s voice was clear and comforting; the second a little more distant. By the third time, all he could perceive was K.B.'s lips moving, but no sound came out. And then, blackness.

Georgie woke up with a dry mouth and a booming headache. The first thing he heard was the beep…beep… beep of the heart monitor.

"Oh thank God!" Georgie heard his mother exclaim.

Stephanie jumped up from her seat by the window and ran over to him. He turned his head just in time to see her body envelope him in a smothering hug.

"Thank God, oh thank God! My baby is alive!" she cried, tears of joy flowing from cheeks to chin.

"Yo, Mama!" Georgie called, his voice muffled by her weight. "I can't breathe!"

She bolted up, wide eyed.

"Oh, I'm so sorry, Baby. I was just so happy! When they told me you got shot, I was so scared that I would lose you. Then the doctor said the bullet just grazed your skull, but an inch more—" she remarked in rapid fire fashion, then stopped, choked up and put a hand to her chest.

"Now you can't breathe," Georgie chuckled. "Relax Ma, I'm good."

Stephanie smiled down on him like he was a newborn infant.

"I know, it's just …"

"What's good, my dude," K.B. said, coming into view for

the first time.

Stephanie had him blocked, so he wheeled around to the other side of the bed. When Georgie saw him in the wheel chair, he got sick to his stomach. K.B. read his expression.

"Yo chill, it's only temporary," K.B. assured him, but only telling him half the story. "They say the bullet shattered my hip, but with therapy, I'll be walking in no time."

"You can't *walk?*" Georgie stressed, the realization feeling like a third bullet to the heart.

That's when he saw K.B.'s eyes. It was only for a moment, a flicker, but it had been there and it was unmistakable. Despair.

Then K.B. winked, cracked a dimpled smile and it was gone.

"Come on yo, you think *one* bullet gonna stop the kid? I'm who Jordan wish he was when he sleep at night."

Stephanie laughed, but Georgie didn't. He just looked at his man thinking, *shit ain't gonna never be the same.*

K.B. dropped his head because he couldn't take the gaze anymore.

"K.B. told me what happened," Stephanie shook her head. "Next time, if they try and rob you Georgie, just give it up, you hear me?! Nothing they want is worth your life!"

Georgie closed his eyes and swallowed. He hated lying to his mother, but he knew that if he told her the truth, she would flip.

"Yes ma'am," was all that he could reply.

His mother looked at him, but didn't say anything. A few seconds later her beeper went off.

"Shit! I forgot that Shantelle had an appointment. Baby, let me go find a pay phone and tell her she gonna have to reschedule," she said, then kissed him on the cheek and sashayed out the room.

As soon as the door swooshed shut, Georgie looked at

K.B. and said, "You told her they tried to rob us?"

K.B. wheeled up to the bed.

"She kept asking what happened. I had to tell her something!"

Georgie pushed his head into the pillow, rubbed the heels of his hands in his eyes then replied, "This shit crazy! You can't walk? For a thousand dollars?!"

K.B. brushed him off like he didn't understand the meaning of his comment and leaned towards him.

"My cousin Malik says he know who them niggas was."

Their eyes met, the look that passed between them loaded like the gun K.B.'s words implied.

"Yo K, what're you talking about? You about to go to fuckin' Duke University, and you talkin' about a fuckin' drive by?" Georgie stressed.

K.B. snorted. "Duke?! Nigga, look at me! Do I look like I'm goin' to Duke?!"

"A minute ago, you said all you need is therapy!" Georgie shot back.

"That's what they *say*. What if they wrong, huh? Then what? Then I'm fucked up, therefore somebody gonna be fucked up wit' me!" K.B. huffed, emphasizing his every word with hand gestures. "And anyway, whether I go or not, I ain't forgetting shit; that's real! Duke or no Duke, I wouldn't give a fuck if I just signed for the Sixers for a billion dollars. If a nigga disrespect me, he gettin' it right where he stand!"

Georgie shook his head, but he couldn't argue with the words because it was the same code he lived by. He felt like you couldn't survive in the hood without it, even though— deep down—it felt like you couldn't survive *with* it either.

"So what you sayin'?" Georgie questioned.

"I'm sayin', as soon as you get out of here, we goin' to pay them muhfuckas a visit. Me, you, Malik and them," K.B. answered.

"Yeah, yo."

"So you wit' it?"

"I just said yeah, yo."

"Yeah, well you don't sound like you wit' it."

Georgie glared at him.

"How the fuck I'm 'posed to sound like?"

K.B. smirked.

"Nigga, you know what I'm talkin' about."

Georgie got impatient.

"Goddamn nigga, I'm wit' it, aight, I'm wit' it!"

"With what?" Stephanie questioned as she entered with a nurse.

"Nothin' Ma, a party," Georgie mumbled.

"Boy, you ain't in no shape for a party, but look who I found," Stephanie smiled. "Denise."

Georgie looked at the nurse and a smile spread across his face.

"How you doin', Ms. Tucker?" Georgie greeted.

"Hey Georgie, how you feelin'?"

"Better now," he winked.

Denise laughed.

"The doctor said it'll only be a day or two more, but Denise promised me she'd keep an eye on you. I have to go do Shantelle's hair for a wedding tomorrow, so if you're okay…." Stephanie let her voice trail off to give Georgie a chance to comment.

"G'head Ma, I'm good."

"I'll be back tomorrow. Keon, you ready?"

"Yes Ma'am. Stay up yo, I'ma see you," K.B. said, giving Georgie dap.

Stephanie rushed K.B. out while Denise held the door for them. As soon as they were gone and Denise let the door close, Georgie remarked, "Damn Ma, if I woulda known you worked here, I woulda been got just to see you in that skirt."

Denise giggled and blushed, waving him off.

"Boy, you been known I was a nurse."

"Yeah but still," he replied, looking at Denise's ass as she bent over to pour him some water. Just looking at that ass had his dick flexing muscle. She was an average looking, middle-aged, cinnamon complexion woman with a wide smile and little titties, but her ass and thighs made her look like a stallion, especially in her short nurse's skirt.

She brought him the cup of water, but instead of grabbing the cup, he grabbed her ass.

"Boy!" she squealed, giggling.

"Shut up. You know you love it," he remarked, slowly sliding his hand under her skirt. She got the familiar quiver in her bottom lip, letting him know that her pussy was getting wet.

"No, Georgie, your mother just left," she whined.

"So?"

"She'll kill me if she knew I was fuckin' you," she added, but her voice was getting husky as he ran his hand over the crotch of her panty hose and panties.

He laughed.

"Ma, if she ain't caught us in two years, she damn sure ain't gonna catch us now. Lock the door."

She saw his dick start to tent the covers. She pulled the sheet back and gripped his dick, licking her lips with anticipation.

"You're gonna make me lose my job," she cooed, hot and heavy, bending to give his dick a kiss.

"And this skirt 'bout to make me lose my mind. Now *lock it*," he demanded.

Denise ran to the door and locked it with a quick click. Then she came back, pulling up her skirt over her shapely hips. Georgie grabbed her by the back of the neck and brought her face to his, devouring her tongue with a passionate moan. She always loved the way he kissed her as if he was always so hungry, making her feel wanted and wetter.

He pulled her up on the bed to straddle him. As she mounted him, she broke the kiss to say, "Wait, I have to take off my…"

Riiiiip!

He grabbed the seam of her panty hose and ripped it apart, lustfully reaching inside and pulling her panties to the side. Denise reached underneath and gripped his long, thick dick, giving it a rough squeeze before guiding the head inside her tight, wet pussy. They both cried out, her with a gasp, him with a grunt as if the connection was electric, causing their bodies to clap and grind.

"Ohh yesss, oh fuck, I can't get enough of this young dick," she cried, throwing her hips into his every thrust.

"Tell me you like it," Georgie growled, bouncing her on his dick in a long, steady motion.

"You know I do. Oh God you know I do!"

"Tell me!"

"I – I, oh shit Georgie, alreaddyyyy!" she squalled, her pussy exploding with a creamy orgasm.

She collapsed on his chest, but he cocked his knees up and kept fucking her.

"Baby, give me a minute," she gasped, totally out of breath.

"Naw, you gonna take *all* this dick," he demanded, dragging his dick in a grinding motion, making the base rub up against her clit, while he slid his thumb in her asshole.

"Sssssss," she sucked in her breath, dragging her fingernails across his chest. "You know that shit drive me crazy."

Georgie thumb-fucked her ass and pushed her to sit up on his dick. Denise threw her head back and rode him like a wave. He ran his hand up her nurse's outfit, up to her neck then ran his fingers along her lips before she took them in her mouth.

"Tell me."

"I – I love youuuuu," she sang, lost in the rhythm of his stroke.

He stoked her harder, firmly gripping her neck.

"Again."

"Oh it's yours, Baby. I love you!"

He saw her bottom lip begin to quiver and he knew she was close. He arched his back for better leverage and started long-dicking her furiously.

"Oh Georgie, I can't, I – I – not again!"

Her second orgasm was so intense that she saw stars. Georgie let himself go and came deep inside of her.

"I love you too," he remarked, caressing her cheeks.

"Don't play with my emotions boy. You know you just want to fuck," she answered, maintaining her womanly wall.

He looked her dead in the eyes and said, "I never just fuck you, Ma… Look at you. You're beautiful. You glow, you know that? I love the way your lip quivers when you're about to cum, the way you scream my name," he said then kissed her lips gently.

Denise's heart danced in her chest. Men rarely told her that she was beautiful. They said she had a fat ass and pretty lips, but never that she was beautiful or that she glowed. And no one had ever noticed her quivering lip. Despite her wall, her eyes misted over.

"You're something else, Georgie Mills."

Kiss the girls and made them cry…

"Boy, you want to stay here?!" Stephanie called out.

Georgie smiled at himself in the mirror as he pulled his hair back into his trademark ponytail, then put on his shades and stepped out of the hospital bathroom.

"Chill Ma, you know I have to look good for my fans," he smirked, striking a GQ pose.

Stephanie laughed, waving him off.

"Fans? Boy, bye! Only fans you got is the ol' cockeyed girls in the yellow bus, wit' your ugly self."

"You know you wrong for that," he laughed.

"Just come on, you know I hate hospitals. I ain't tryin' to spend no more time here than I have to."

Georgie grabbed his leather coat off the bed and started for the door, but Stephanie stopped him and just looked at him.

"What? I thought you were ready to go? Why you lookin' at me like that?" he quizzed.

"'Cause you mine, and I can look at you any way I want," she sassed, but she had tears welling up in her eyes. "Now come here and give me a hug."

She pulled him close and held him extra tight. Georgie could tell something was wrong when she pulled back and he looked in her eyes.

"Ma, what's up?"

"Nothing," she answered, avoiding his gaze, "I'm just glad you're okay."

"I had to be. Somebody gotta keep an eye on you," he quipped.

Stephanie mustered a smile then pushed him out of the door.

They drove along Market Street listening to Power 99, the local radio station. Georgie seemed to turn up the volume with every song.

"Georgie, turn it down."

"Come on Ma, this Craig Mack!," Georgie protested, bobbing his head and rapping along to *Flava In Ya Ear*.

"I don't give a damn, turn it down," she growled.

He sighed hard but turned the knob to the left. He could tell that his mother was tense because she loved loud music as much as he did. He reached over and gave her shoulder a squeeze.

"Ma, I'm good. It's all over."

"I know."

"Then what's up?"

"Nothing."

Georgie let it go. They came to 17th Street, which was the one they usually took to get to their house, but Stephanie kept straight.

"We ain't goin' home?"

"No."

Georgie shrugged it off and didn't pay it any mind. That is, until they pulled up in front of the bus station. Georgie looked around with a slight frown.

"What we at the bus station for? Who we pickin' up?" he asked.

"Nobody. We droppin' somebody off," she said. Then turned to him with tears streaming down her cheeks.

The look on her face said it all. Georgie started shaking his head.

"Naw Ma, what you talkin' about?! I ain't going anywhere!"

Georgie, don't *tell* me what you're not doing! You *are*!" Stephanie blazed right back.

"For what?! 'Cause I got *shot*?!"

"You think I'm stupid, boy?! Do you? You forget I was runnin' these damn streets way before I even *thought* of you! I know everybody and everybody know Steph! You got robbed? That was the best you could come up with, with your chain around your neck and money in your pocket?" She spat, flipping the thick herringbone around his neck with her finger. "You think I don't know you and Keon be in the park hustling people on them courts?! Shooting dice? Huh? Well, joke's on you muhfucka, you gettin' on that damn bus today!"

Georgie pinched his nose and squeezed his eyes as if he were trying to press himself into another reality.

"And where am I supposed to go?"

"To stay with your Uncle Michael in New York."

"Wow, New York? Good choice Ma, I'll never get shot there," he quipped with bitter sarcasm.

Without hesitation, Stephanie slapped his face—not hard, but hard enough to let him know that she was serious.

"Don't play with me, boy. This ain't about you gettin' shot, it's about what happens *next*. I know what you and Keon was talking about. I know how the game is played. Well, not with me it won't be. Keon is a good boy, but he's about to make a bad decision. That I can't help, but I can help the decision you make, and that decision better be gettin' your ass on that bus!" Stephanie fumed.

The sting of the slap awoke his pride and made him think about what K.B. had said.

"Yo ... I'm not runnin' from them niggas. We mighta took 'em fast, but *they* took it to another level. Now it's *our* turn," he spat coldly, his grey eyes looking like sheets of ice.

Stephanie took a deep breath, exhaled slowly, and then replied, "Well, Georgie ... either way you're gettin' out of this car. Either to get on the bus or get the hell out of my house."

"Pssst, whateva," he shrugged and opened the door. He put one foot on the pavement with every intention of following with the other, but he didn't. He sat there. He teetered on the edge of being a victim of fate or a captain of destiny, contemplating the leap. As soon as he opened the door, Stephanie wanted to reach out and grab him to stop him from getting out, but she knew that she had to let him make the decision on his own. For her, it felt like the moment that being a mother all those years came down to. If he got out, she would see it as her failure as much as his.

She saw the bus turn the corner in her rearview mirror; it drove past and came to a stop four car lengths from where they were parked. Georgie glanced up and saw the people standing around. Some began to hug and pick up luggage as others gave off a different set of hugs.

Deep down, beyond the pride that continued to throb in his chest, his mother was doing what he couldn't do. She was saving him from himself.

"So I'm just supposed to leave with the clothes on my back?" he asked, without turning around.

It wasn't until he spoke that Stephanie realized she was holding her breath. She exhaled, but fought to keep her reply even and relief free.

"Your bags are in the trunk."

He briefly paused.

"So you're just puttin' me out like Oran 'Juice' Jones, huh?"

Stephanie had to laugh, in spite of herself.

"Boy, get out my car," she responded, pushing him out.

They both walked around to the trunk. Stephanie unlocked it. Inside was a suitcase, a large duffle bag and a portable cassette player. He loosened the tie on the duffle bag and saw a cornucopia of sneakers.

"Ma, you pack my blue Jordans?"

"Yes, Georgie, I packed all them ugly things. And when you gonna get some real shoes?"

"Ma, I'ma miss graduation!"

"You *graduated*, that's the important thing. They can mail you the piece of paper," she replied.

He nodded pensively. She saw the apprehension and gave him a long, tight hug.

"Don't worry, baby, you're doing the right thing," Stephanie assured him.

He took a deep breath and looked around.

"Philly just ain't gonna be the same without me."

"We'll try to manage."

"Bye, Ma."

"Oh, the ticket!" She ran around to the driver's side and got the ticket and a greasy paper bag, then handed him both.

"Cheesesteaks," he chuckled.

"So you don't forget where you come from," she winked.

He kissed and hugged her again.

"I love you."

"I love you more."

He gathered up his stuff and started to walk off.

"Ma."

"Yeah, baby?"

"Why we ain't got no relatives in Bel Air?" he smiled, alluding to the popular TV show *The Fresh Prince of Bel Air.*

Stephanie exploded with laughter.

"You are so crazy! Go! I love you!" she sang, blowing him kisses.

As the bus pulled off, Georgie sat back and watched the city peel away, fading like the credits at the end of the movie. He felt a great burden lifting from his shoulders realizing that sometimes when it seems that our hand is forced, it's because we're forcing our hand. But like the song says, you've got to know when to fold them. Georgie snuggled back in the seat and fell asleep.

As soon as he stepped off the bus at New York's Port Authority bus terminal, he was greeted by the sounds of popular Brooklyn rapper Notorious B.I.G.'s debut album *Ready To Die* being played from every storefront and stoop, spilling from apartments and car windows. All different tracks from the album played simultaneously in a cacophonous symphony.

"Only in New York," he mumbled to himself as he waded into the sea of people ebbing and flowing around him. He kept his bags tight to himself, because the old man on the bus had said repeatedly, "Pickpockets! Beware of pickpockets!"

The sun was just going down, making it more difficult to see faces in the shifting waves moving around him. He started to look for a pay phone, when he heard, "Georgie! Georgie, over here!"

The voice sounded...odd. Like a woman, but not quite. He followed the timbre and his eyes landed on his uncle... aunt?

"Michael?" Georgie said, astonishment invading his tone.

"Michelle!" Michael replied, holding out his arms so that Georgie could get a good look at him.

Michael looked like his older sister, Stephanie—especially with the long, flowing wig, form-fitting mini-skirt, fishnets and spiked heels. Georgie couldn't believe his eyes.

"Surprise!" Michael tittered nervously.

"No doubt," Georgie chuckled.

"Come on, let me help you with that. I'm double parked," Michael urged, grabbing the portable radio and the paper bag.

"It was two cheesesteaks in the bag. Mama sent 'em; I only ate one."

"I can't eat that, I'm watching my figure," Michael replied demurely.

Georgie didn't know what else to say but "oh."

As they approached Michael's Honda, he noticed a gorgeous dark-skinned chick in the passenger seat.

"Damn Unk, I mean…who that in the car?"

Michael smiled knowingly.

"Easy Shug, I don't think she's your type."

It took Georgie half a beat to realize what he was trying to say. Then it hit him and he got mad at himself for being fooled. When he got in the car, his suspicions were confirmed.

"You must be Georgie," the person said in a feminized male voice, then turned around and offered a limp-wristed hand expecting Georgie to kiss it. Instead, Georgie yanked on one finger like it was a cow udder.

"Yeah."

"I'm Yvette."

"You sure?" Georgie thought as he rested his head on the glass and wondered what strange planet he had landed on.

Michelle lived in a small apartment on West 16th Street, near Greenwich Village. As soon as Georgie walked in, he was startled by two mannequins—one female and one male —clothesless and right in front of the door.

"What the fuck?!" he snapped, jumping back.

Michelle giggled with a playful flair. "They don't bite, Georgie. They're Yvette's. She's an aspiring designer."

"Yvette live here, too?" Georgie asked with concern, looking around. The apartment really wasn't large enough for three people.

"Long story, but no. She's moving to LA to open a boutique, but her lease ran out and the dates don't match up," he waved it off. "Anyway, you get the picture."

Michelle took a pack of Newport 100's out of her purse and lit one with a pink lighter, her eyes following Georgie's movements while he sat his things down.

"So what do you think?" she inquired, trying to keep the edge of anxiety out of her voice.

Georgie shrugged and glanced around at the cramped, but stylish place.

"I mean, as long as you ain't got no roaches, we good."

"No, I mean about me."

Georgie looked up and at Michelle. She was holding the cigarette like his mother did, wrist splayed, palm up, cigarette smoke curling over fingers, the crossed arm propping up the elbow. In fact, she was a spitting image of his mother, except that she was about three inches shorter. The resemblance made Georgie smile warmly.

"I've got an uncle that looks good in heels. No big deal."

Michelle blurted out in laughter, but Georgie could see that it was more from relief than humor. She inhaled then let out a steady steam of smoke, as she propped on the arm of the couch.

"Thanks Georgie, I needed to hear that."

"Why?"

"I just didn't know what to expect. I was afraid you might freak out or something. Haul ass back to Philly and tell the family."

"What? Nobody knows?"

Michelle shook her head slowly, looking at Georgie pleadingly.

"And I don't want them to. Not yet. Please Georgie, I know how close you are to Steph, but..."

Georgie help up his hand.

"Breathe, yo. I won't tell her."

Inhale. Sizzle. Exhale. Vapor.

"Thanks Georgie, again."

"But I think you're wrong."

"Wrong?"

"Momma loves you. The family loves you. But now, it's like they don't *know* you, you know? You're lettin' them love who they *think* you are, and that's not fair to them," Georgie explained.

Michelle looked pensively at Georgie.

"I never looked at it like that."

"What did they say at work when you exploded from the closet," Georgie joked.

Michelle snickered then leaned over and flicked the ashes into the ashtray on the coffee table.

"I work at the Village Voice. I'm cliché."

"Huh?"

"Tongue in cheek."

"And why do you wear that wig? Did you cut your hair?"

She reached up subconsciously and ran her fingers through it.

"No, but you know how our hair is, so it's hard to find somebody to do anything with it."

Georgie winked. "You found somebody."

She started to say it again, but hated to be so redundant.

As soon as her circle of friends saw what Georgie had done with Michelle's hair, he was bum-rushed with a flood of requests.

"I want it too!"

"Can I be next?"

"Do me!"

Some of them were even talking about hair, too. However, it wasn't only Michelle's gay friends. Several hookers lived and worked around Michelle's neighborhood, so it wasn't long before Georgie had the nickname "the Hooker Hook-her Upper."

Michelle threw Georgie a coming-out party, tongue firmly in cheek. "He even styles wigs, too!"

Michelle's apartment was packed, as Usher's song, "Think Of You" provided rhythm for love and laughter. Georgie was in his element, streaking and tinting, perming and weaving, doing what he did best: make women beautiful.

"Oh my Georgie, you must have and extra chromosome or something!" Yvette gasped playfully, admiring in the mirror what Georgie had done to her wig.

Georgie chuckled. "So I take that to mean you like it, huh?"

"Like it? I love it! I love you," Yvette cooed, winking and blowing a kiss to the mirror.

He took it in stride as he glanced around, taking in his work as the women paraded around the room.

"Am I next?"

Three words…three little words. But in those three little words, thick country molasses dripped and lightening flashed through the Southern sky in his mind. Her country cadence —slow, deliberate, sensual and assured—had him stuck even before he turned his head and saw her face.

She was the color of Camay soap, if Camay had been born. Her hazel eyes had a cat-like slant that made her look mischievous and bold. Her gaze never wavered as she looked into his eyes, almost as if she were hypnotizing him, long enough to steal his heart. Georgie let his eyes travel <u>further</u>

south, taking in her pert, luscious breasts and petite, curvaceous figure squeezed into a leopard print mini dress that had her popping out everywhere.

Georgie licked his lips then replied, "Shit, from where I'm standin', you can be *always*."

She giggled demurely.

"Humph!" Yvette grunted, then rolled out of the seat, her eyes along with it.

Georgie took her hand and helped her sit down, then stood behind her as they looked at each other in the mirror. It was then that he finally noticed that she had a short page-boy cut.

"I've never said this before but uh, I don't know what to do. You're perfect just the way you are," Georgie remarked.

Her smile blossomed into a blush.

"I'm sure you'll think of something."

Their gaze danced with one another in the mirror.

"What do you have in mind?"

The teasing tip of her tongue appeared between her teeth, giving her expression a naughty little girl quality.

"We're talking about hair, right?"

They both laughed.

"I want you to do your magic. I'm gonna close my eyes, and when I open them, I want to be transformed," she requested.

Georgie took it as the challenge that it was, but he was definitely up to it.

"No problem."

She held his gaze, licked her lips, and then closed her eyes.

"Have your way with me," she smirked.

Georgie studied her features in the mirror: her button doll nose, sensually rounded chin and kissable cheekbones. He admired her cut, knowing that he could've done better, but acknowledging the good job that was done.

"Okay, well to do this right I'm gonna need to ask you a few things."

"Like?"

"Like for starters, your name."

"Anya."

"That's a beautiful name."

"Thank you. It's African. It means 'waters of life.'"

Pause.

"Did you say something wet?" Georgie smirked.

Anya giggled.

"Stop. You're gonna make me open my eyes."

"Where are you from?"

"Georgia," she said so sweetly that Georgie swore he could smell peaches.

"Georgia? Ain't that where they make peaches? You one of them peaches?"

"You don't *make* peaches, you grow them," she replied, her tongue caressing the "t" in "them."

"Oh, my bad, so you grown a peach, huh?"

They shared a laugh.

"Georgie," someone called out.

"How old are you?" he asked Anya.

"Twenty-two."

"Georgie!"

"Somebody's calling you."

"Baby, whoever it is, they can't be as fine as you," he charmed.

Anya blushed and bit her bottom lip, subtly playing with a brother's emotions.

As he worked, they talked, learning the things each other were eager to share.

"How old are you," she asked.

"Twenty-one."

"No you're not," she laughed.

"How you figure?" he smirked.

"Michelle," she replied as her proof of age.

"Yeah, well Michelle just ain't seen me in three years."

The crowd thinned, the music played on and Georgie did his thing, until he finally said, "Okay...you can open your eyes."

Anya did, and once they focused on her new look, her mouth fell open in awe.

"What's the matter? You don't like it?" he questioned, with just a hint of uncertainty in his voice.

"No, it's not that. It's...wow. I didn't expect *this*." She gasped.

The people, still there, gathered to gawk.

"Oh my God, this is so hot!"

"Damn, why you ain't do my hair like that?"

"Orange?!"

But it wasn't quite orange. It was peach—an almost sherbet peach—simultaneously soft and subtle but bold and daring. He had captured her spirit perfectly, even down to the flicks of frosted white in her bangs and sideburns.

"Peaches and cream," he whispered close to her ear as he gazed into her eyes in the mirror. "That's what a grown peach looks like." Anya tried not to squirm in her seat as she felt the bass of his voice strumming her spine.

"Now tell me you like it?"

"I like it," she replied.

He smiled then let his lips brush her cheek as he stood up. Anya stood on wobbly legs, but hid it well. She placed a $50 bill in his hand then balled his hand over it.

"Thank you. I'll call you when I need, um...a touch-up," she remarked, but her eyes said much more.

Georgie watched her walk away, that ass—juicy and jiggling under that leopard dress—stunned him until she headed out the door. Michelle and Yvette approached.

"I see you met Anya, our Southern-Belle-in-Residence," Michelle snickered.

"You know she a prostitute, right?" Yvette huffed, arms folded across her chest.

Georgie turned and looked at her with a cold gaze that only softened around the edges as he snickered and remarked, "Aren't we all?"

Despite her jealousy, Yvette couldn't help but laugh at the statement.

"I know that's right!" Michelle hooped, giving Yvette a high five. After the laughter subsided, Michelle added, "Yvette has some good news for you. Tell him, girl."

Yvette turned to him, excitedly.

"Well! I have a friend, his name is Christophe, and he owns one of the hottest salons in Manhattan. I'm talking about rich Fifth Avenue bitches, you hear me?! And he is going to absolutely *love* you!"

Georgie nodded, taking his good fortune in stride because he perceived success as inevitable.

"No doubt."

CAPTAIN SAVE A HOE

iiKane | 04
CHAPTER

The salon was on Central Park West and was nearly 5,000 square feet, with at least fifteen chairs. The whole place was done up in glass, fish tanks, marble floors and royal blue accents. It looked like the lobby of an expensive hotel that happened to have salon chairs in it.

As soon as Georgie walked in with Yvette, he knew this was where he was destined to be. Or so he thought.

Looking around, he could just smell the money. Most, if not all, of the customers and stylists were White. Even though he didn't have a lot of experience doing White folks' hair, he had no doubt that he would master it in no time.

As they walked by the stylists, the hungry gazes of the women followed his confident swagger. He could just hear the people calling his name, the stage name that he had thought up for himself when he was twelve: *Giorgio*.

An impossibly tall Scandinavian blonde woman on even more impossibly arched heels approached them, carrying a large, gilded appointment book. She and Yvette exchanged pleasantries and air kisses.

"And please tell me this is *not* Georgie," the blonde remarked wistfully.

"But of course," Yvette replied, wrapping her arm around Georgie.

Georgie looked at her but didn't say anything.

The big blonde melted into a sigh.

"And here I was hoping that you had brought me lunch."

The two of them shared a naughty giggle, then she escorted Yvette and Georgie to Christophe's office. Inside, the office seemed to be just as spacious in its own right. It faced the street so that its entire front was floor-to-ceiling windows that sported vertical blinds, which were opened to let the sunshine in. Christophe's desk was more of a minimalist work area than a desk with a high-back leather chair towering above it.

Christophe himself, an Andy Warhol-ish looking waif of a man, was dressed in what amounted to an all-black cat suit. His starkly pale, bare white feet provided the only contrast. He was laid back on a black leather recliner as a shirtless Italian rock of a man massaged his feet. He purred, eyes closed, until the big blonde cleared her throat. Christophe's eyes popped open with a scowl until they fell on Georgie.

"And you are?"

Georgie dimpled him.

"Georgie Mills."

Christophe's eyes brightened, and he began to clap his hands and flap his feet.

"Shoo! Shoo! Shoo!"

The Italian stallion rose with a bow then disappeared through a door discretely recessed in the wall behind the chair. Christophe sat up and curled his feet under him, then patted the space his legs were just occupying.

"Sit, sit, sit, let me take a good look at you," Christophe gushed, and when Georgie sat, extended his hand to him daintily and limp-wristed.

"I'm Christophe."

Humoring him, Georgie took his hand and kissed it. Christophe giggled and shook as if an electric current had run up his spine.

"Nice to meet you."

"Oh my! You are a god! Why aren't you a model?"

"Because I'm the real thing," Georgie replied, with a sexy grin that took the snap out of his quip.

"Yes you are...so tell me, why do *you* want to work for Christophe?" he asked.

Georgie shrugged. "Because I love to do hair. I've been doing it since I was six years old. My mother has her own shop back in—"

Disregarding Georgie's answer with an air of impatience, Christophe remarked, "I've never known a man that *likes* to do hair, unless of course he's gay. Are you gay, Georgie, bi, curious? Hmmm?"

Georgie chuckled to bite back the irritation that was beginning to build. "No, why? Is it a requirement?"

Christophe saw the hard flash in Georgie's eyes.

"Easy tiger, roar." Christophe remarked, making a cattish sound and displaying a cattish claw at the same time, both to mask a nervous twitter. "It's not a requirement; it's a prayer!"

The big blonde and Yvette laughed, whereas Georgie conceded a crooked grin.

"I'm kidding...No, I'm not. Anyway," Christophe said, brushing a stray bang from his line of vision. "Yvette tells me you are simply divine and judging from her *fab* new look, I'm inclined to believer her. But, and there's always a 'but' in there isn't it, how do you feel about New Jersey?"

"Jersey?" Georgie echoed.

Christophe nodded prissily, lips pursed.

"Wayne, specifically. I have a satellite salon there. Very posh, very upscale, well … as upscaled as you actually can be in Jersey. I'm kidding. No I'm not, anyway...so, what do you think?"

Georgie glanced back at Yvette with a look that said, "That easy?" She nodded vigorously with excitement. He turned back to Christophe.

"Jersey's cool," he answered, nonchalantly.

"Then Jersey it is," Christophe concluded, getting up and heading toward his desk with a gait that showed he admired Grace Kelly. "Just give your license information to Svetlana, and all should be in order."

Georgie frowned slightly.

"License? What do I need a license for?"

Christophe stopped, turned and looked at him.

"Surely, you have a cosmetology license."

"I don't need one. I told you, I've been doin' hair since I was— "

"Yes, yes, but be that as it may, I cannot allow you to work in my salons unlicensed. Now, while you get one, I could maybe let you do washes, inventory, things like—"

"Naw yo, I didn't come all the way to New York to be a fashion busboy! I'm nice! The *best*! Put me up against any licensed muhfucka."

Christophe came and sat down beside him, wearing an indulgent smile.

"Georgie really, there's no need for such language. It's simply the way things are. Now, years from now, I would love to say I gave you your first break in New York, but you must give *me* a break now, okay?" he said, patting Georgie's hand. "Come back when you have your license."

With that, Christophe headed to his desk, saying over his shoulder, "Svetlana, hold my calls. I'm famished."

"Yes, Christophe," Svetlana replied then looked at Georgie with a polite smile. "If you would come with me please."

"What's the big deal with getting a license, Georgie?" Michelle asked as she stood at the stove sautéing vegetables.

"Exactly!" Georgie concurred, munching on a carrot.

"No, I mean *not* having one. *Having* one is the law!"

"Fuck the law."

"Michelle shook her head, chuckling.

"Boy, I *swear* you just like your mother. That's why she opened the shop in her house, because she felt like nobody could tell her nothing either."

Georgie never knew that was why his mother never got her cosmetology license, so the information only strengthened his resolve.

"Then that's what I'ma do—open my own shop."

"Well, if you had your license, or at least got in school, you could really make some contacts at the hair expo next month," Michelle remarked, pouring a little red wine in the skillet.

"What hair expo?"

"At the Jacob Javits Center. They have it every year. Some of the biggest names in the industry will be there. It's a helluva networking opportunity. Pass me the prosciutto out of the fridge."

Georgie opened the refrigerator and looked around. "Ain't no more."

"You sure?" Michelle checked then glanced around at him. "Baby, do me a fave."

"Yeah, I got you."

Georgie grabbed his keys and headed for the door.

The neighborhood store was bigger than a bodega, but much smaller than a supermarket. They specialized in gourmet foods, fresh fruits and vegetables, and weed. The latter was on the hush hush and very discrete.

Georgie spotted Anya as he grabbed the prosciutto. He came around the aisle and encountered her in the fruit section. Before she glanced up and saw him, he drank her in. She was dressed in an oversized Howard University sweatshirt and biker shorts. It made Georgie wish the sweatshirt didn't cover her ass. He glanced at her flip flops and saw that her toes were painted the same color as her hair. It made him smile to know that was because of him.

"So this is where they keep the fresh peaches, huh?"

At the sound of his voice, a smile spread over her face even before she looked up.

"Hello, Georgie."

"How you, Ma? You think you can fit on this scale? I wanna see how much your peach weigh." He flirted, reaching for her waist.

She bashfully brushed his hand away, laughing.

"Boy, you are so stupid."

"I ain't seen you in a few days. You tryin' to make me miss you?"

"I was out of town. I had to work."

"Out of town?"

"A convention."

Their eyes met. He knew what she did. She knew that he knew what she did. Her glance said, *You asked*. His said, *It's cool*.

They began walking toward the register. She was rung up first.

"So, did you miss me?" Georgie dimpled.

"No," she replied, with sass in her tone.

"Did you think about me?" he probed as he paid for his purchase.

"No," she answered, walking backward towards the door so she could maintain eye contact.

"Yes you did. Every time you looked in the mirror, you saw my smile, 'cause I left it in your hair," he charmed, leaning in to muzzle her neck as they spilled out the door.

Anya hunched her shoulders and leaned away.

"Stop," she whined sweetly, enticingly, hypocritically.

"Only when you stop lyin'…I thought about you," he admitted, taking her plastic bag and carrying it for her.

"Really?" she returned, skeptically.

"Why you say it like that? Yes, *really*, wit' your ugly self," he smirked. Anya didn't expect that. Her mouth dropped open and she laughed, hitting Georgie on the arm.

"You ugly."

"Least I ain't cockeyed," he joked, crossing his eyes and walking in a clumsy, pigeon-toed manner.

Anya threw her head back, laughing.

"I ain't *hardly* cockeyed!"

"Yeah…you gonna be," he replied, looking her dead in the eyes with a provocative challenge.

She sucked her teeth.

"Please, little boy."

Georgie howled. "Oh, I'm a little boy now, huh?"

"I don't know." She looked him up and down and came back to his eyes. "Are you?"

They had reached their apartment building, so Anya punctuated her statement by looking over her shoulder before going inside. Georgie smiled to himself then followed her in.

When they reached the third floor landing where Michelle lived, Anya reached for the bag.

"Naw, I'ma carry it for you," Georgie told her.

"You don't have to,"

"I want to."

When they reached her apartment and entered, the first thing he asked was, "Where you want me to put this?"

"Just put it in the kit--," she started to say, but Georgie pulled her body to his.

"Naw, I meant *this*," he said, kissing her gently on the lips.

"Here?" he kissed her on the neck.

"Here?" he kissed her on the collarbone. "Or here. Where

you need it most?"

A soft whimper escaped her lips. "Show me that you know."

Georgie lifted her sweatshirt over her head in one smooth motion. Underneath, she wasn't wearing a bra; she didn't need one. Her breasts sat up, full and firm. Her chocolate nipples were so hard, they throbbed. Georgie took one in his mouth and sucked it until she grabbed the back of his head, then bit it just hard enough to make Anya suck in her breath.

"Fuck," she breathed.

"I've been wanting to do this since I laid eyes on you. I wanted to pull up that little skirt and make you take every inch of this dick," he growled, while he continued to kiss her from head to toe.

"You talk too much," she stuttered, but her body betrayed her, letting him know that every word was going right down her spine and exploding between her legs.

He pulled her biker shorts down over her soft, juicy ass to find her panty-less underneath. As soon as he did, the bouquet of her sweet aroma tantalized his nostrils.

"It even look like a peach," he remarked, eyeing her clean-shaven pussy, sitting fat and plump between her legs.

Georgie pulled one of Anya's legs over his shoulder and took her clit in his mouth hungrily while he gripped her ass firmly with both hands. Anya threw her head back to scream but nothing came out. She looked like the picture of ecstasy, frozen in time. Her nails dug into his shoulders and her leg stiffened on his back. Georgie cupped the bottom of her ass cheeks, spreading them so he could penetrate her with his middle finger from the back.

"Oh Georgie," she gasped, hoarsely.

The sensation felt like too much, but at the same time, not enough. She wanted him deeper, harder, faster. The sounds of his lips feasting on her wet pussy turned her on, and she felt the throbbing building in her belly, until it exploded into hot flames that shot through her thighs and left her gasping for air and trying to push him away.

"I...I can't, wait," she whispered as he gently laid her on the cold, hard floor.

The cool surface felt good on her hot skin, as Georgie continued to kiss along her thighs, trailing his tongue along the wet tracks that her juices had left, lapping it up as he went.

Anya ground the heels of her hands into her eyes, squirming, her head thrashing from side to side.

"Georgie, put it in please. I want to feel you."

"Shhhh," he said, his soft whisper leaving goose bumps in its wake. "You talk too much."

She could feel his smile between her thighs. He kissed along her thighs until he came across sensitive areas that made her jump.

Fresh cigarette burns.

Just thinking how she got them made him burn with a murderous rage, a rage that he channeled into passion, kissing each one, all six—the last one on her calf—as he said, "Never again, never again, never again."

Tears bubbled from her eyes and ran down her temples, making puddles on both sides of her head. By the time he started sucking her toes, she was done. She felt like she would lose her mind if he didn't fuck her.

"Georgie now, I'm about to explode," she cried out.

He wasted no time pushing inside her, making her cry out again and again with each punishing thrust.

"Just like that. I want to hear you," he groaned in her ear. "Tell me what I'm doing to you."

"It feels so good, oh, so fuckin' good," she screamed.

"Tell me what you want."

"Harder," she gasped.

The sounds of their clapping bodies punctuated every grunt, every groan, every scream, every moan.

"Cum, baby. Please cum with me," Anya begged.

Georgie got in push-up position and Anya held herself behind the knees so she could cock her legs back to her chest and he could go deep enough to cum in her stomach.

"Say my name!"

"Georgie!"

"Say it!"

"Geooooo—" was all she got out before her body convulsed and spasmed, releasing her juices with a hard, satisfying squirt.

Georgie only lasted a few more seconds, then he came— hard and long— body jerking and toes curled.

"Damn," he gasped, as he collapsed on top of her.

Anya giggled.

"What you talkin' about, damn? You did it."

They laughed, and then he dropped his head. When he looked back up, his eyes were crossed.

"Wait a minute, Georgie. Let me get it together," he jokingly imitated.

She laughed so hard that she pooted, then playfully hit him.

"You make me sick! I am not lookin' cross eyed!"

He twisted up his lips with unbelief.

"Much," she admitted. Then they laughed again.

When the laughter subsided, Georgie's expression changed. He started to speak, but Anya put her finger to his lips, and smiled softly.

"Don't spoil it."

He hesitated then nodded understandingly.

"Come on."

"Where we going?" Anya inquired, eyebrows arched.

"To the bedroom," he smiled wickedly.

He helped her up, then right before she started to walk down the hall, he slapped her on the ass.

"Oy, boy!"

"Now walk like you on the goddamn catwalk," he joked.

Anya smirked then strutted so hard, Georgie couldn't do anything but shake his head and holler, "Goddamn, I love New York."

When he walked in, Michelle was curled up on the couch, watching *Casablanca* and sipping zinfandel. She took one look at the smile plastered on Georgie's face and shook her head.

"I don't even want to know. Did you at least buy the prosciutto?"

Georgie held up the bag. Michelle pointed to the kitchen.

"Refrigerator. And try not to get lost this time."

While Georgie went into the kitchen, Michelle took a sip of wine and then remembered to add, "Oh, and Steph called. She said to call her."

Georgie was coming back into the room drinking a Goya juice, something he had fallen in love with since he moved to New York. He picked up the cordless phone and dialed the number as he walked down the hall to the back bedroom. He sipped and sat on the windowsill that had a view of the street below. Overhead, a large, full moon seemed to shine like a spotlight on New York.

Stephanie picked up, and the first thing he heard was Teddy Pendergrass' "Turn Off the Lights" in the background.

"Hey baby, 'bout time you call your Mama," she huffed playfully.

"And every time I do, you either got on Luther or Teddy, which means you either got somebody over or *about* to have somebody over," Georgie surmised. "Let me find out you put me out just so you could have the house to yourself."

"Oh you ain't know? I'm about to get my woo woo woo on with some burning hot oils, baby!" she sang, the voice strong and on key.

Georgie rubbed his forehead.

"Ma, I ain't need to know all that. That's nasty."

"That's what you get for talkin' stupid. Now, how is my baby?"

"I'm good."

"Michael told me about the license thing. Believe me, you know if anybody understand, *I* understand, but you have to get one. That's probably my biggest mistake. I could've had mega salons, but my hardhead got in the way. That's my daddy in me." Stephanie shrugged, like c'est la vie, and puffed on her Newport long.

Georgie sucked his teeth.

"Ma, I *told* Michelle—"

"Who is Michelle?"

Alarms went off in Georgie's head. He had inadvertently let the cat out of the bag, so he hurriedly tried to stuff it back in, tail and all.

"Just this chick down the hall; I meant Michael. I told *Michael* that I didn't need one. I'ma do this my way," Georgie huffed, watching a police car cruise silently by.

"Okay, Frank Sinatra, Mr. 'My Way.'" she snickered.

"And speaking of chicks, do you know how many calls I've been getting from these drama ass heffas around here? Like my phone is a suicide hotline. Talkin 'bout, 'Why did Georgie leave? He said he loved me; we were getting married!'" His mother whining imitated a crying female. "Even Denise called me. She all crying, talking about, she so sorry, but she love you and she need to see you, *finally* admitting that y'all doing the nasty. I ain't say nothin,' I just acted like I ain't known *this whole time!*" Stephanie cracked.

Georgie burst out laughing.

"You knew?!"

"Boy, what I tell you?! *No-thing*! You can't get nothing past your Mama. If you think you slick, remember I'ma can of grease!"

They shared a laugh.

"Seriously Georgie, you can't be lying to these females like that, telling them you love them."

"But I'm not lying when I say it," he reasoned.

"And when is this?" she asked, her tone sounding like it had its hands on its hips. "When you naked? When you lying down? Because you know, you men gotta be standing up to think straight."

"No Ma, it's not like that, forreal. I really do love 'em; I just love 'em all differently," Georgie explained, trying to find words.

"Well, that doesn't make it any easier when you wake up by yourself," she replied, and her tone sounded like the voice of experience.

"I'm not tryin' to hurt anybody, Ma."

"I know you not, Baby... Well, let me go because I am being rude. I got this whole man downstairs simmering; now it's time to put him on the plate!" she exclaimed.

Georgie took ear from the phone.

"Bye, Ma!"

"Bye, Baby! Don't be mad 'cause I still got it! I love you."

Her voice filled the room with her Philly accent and motherly love, making him smile. "I love you, too."

Georgie laid the phone on the windowsill and let the smile linger on his lips.

It didn't linger long. A flash of color caught the corner of his eye. He looked down onto the street and saw Anya crossing, wearing a sequined miniskirt, a pair of see-through "fuck me" pumps, a halter top, and a long, blond wig. Her ass bounced with every step, igniting his passionate rage. All he could think of were the cigarette burns.

He gritted his teeth, grabbed his boom box off the floor and headed out the door. When he reached the living room, Bergman's plane was leaving in *Casablanca* and Michelle was sniffling.

"Umm, if Momma say something about a girl named Michelle, just tell her it's a chick that lives down the hall," Georgie suggested.

It took Michelle a moment to realize what Georgie was trying to get at, as she dabbed her tears; but when she did, her eyes swelled.

"Georgie! Tell me you didn't!"

"It was a mistake! She said Michael but I said Michelle, and she was like, who's Michelle? I said, a chick down the hall. Don't worry, if you stick to the script, we're good," he assured her.

Michelle jumped off the couch, pacing the floor nervously, hands clenched for emphasis.

"Georgie, how could you?!" she whined. "You *know* your mother, she's like a bloodhound. She can smell it, and once she's on the track, she can't be stopped! She's like the Terminator or something!"

Georgie cracked up at the drama queen scene that Michelle was acting out.

"Just relax, aight? Tell her what I said," Georgie reiterated, as he opened the door. "Or you can tell her the truth."

He walked out, leaving Michelle with something to think about.

Hey, you're like a Hip Hop song, you know.
Bonita Applebum, you gotta put me on.

Georgie walked the streets while A Tribe Called Quest played on his radio player. The crisp night air was good for his state of mind. A constellation of thoughts about the license everybody kept urging him to get pervaded his mind. He resisted because from his perspective, a cosmetology license was like a validation of his skill but not of his competence. His arrogance wouldn't permit his skill to be an assessment of him. To him, the proof was in the pudding and the ultimate proof were the smiles that adorned women's faces and the cream between their legs—which often *came* together. Just the thought of why he should get a license made him determined not to get one. He would do it his way.

His thoughts turned to the upcoming hair expo. He knew that it would be his big chance to make a major splash on the scene. All the industry movers and shakers would be gathered in one place. He had to make a big impression, or toil in obscurity in a city that swallows the obscure, never to be seen again, until being found floating face down in the Hudson. He had no intention of seeing his dreams as fish bait, so he knew he had to do something. But what?

Anya.

The name pulsated through his mind like a hip hop song stuck in his head…stuck in his head…stuck in his head, a song with a haunting melody, one that you felt more than you heard.

He spotted her as he rounded the corner, working the busy back streets with several other women. But her presence was unmistakable, and if there was ever any doubt in what she did for a living, it quickly disappeared.

She was a prostitute. She sold pussy for money. Sold it to any man and let them do what they wanted to do to her, just because they had green pieces of paper, just because they had a *license.*

Cigarette burns…

A car pulled up to her, a grey BMW. The shadowy figure

inside was just a blur behind the wheel. She approached the car, and as she opened the car door, she saw Georgie on the corner diagonal from her. She paused long enough for their eyes to converse silently. What she saw was concern, longing maybe? What he saw was…

Nothing.

Her eyes were blank, opaque. Dead. He knew then that wasn't Anya getting in the car, and it brought him a strange sense of relief, but also brought on a strong impulse of urgency. He had to do something. As she got in and the car pulled off, he turned and walked away.

Back at the building, he sat on the stoop, resting the boom box across his knees. He turned off the tape and flipped on the radio. The bold voice of Wendy Williams boomed through his speakers. She easily became his favorite person to listen to on the radio since he landed in New York. Georgie found himself, arms crossed, lying on his radio. The last thing he heard was Boyz II Men:

> *I'll make love to you….*
> *Like you want me to…*

He awoke to the touch of Anya's hand on his shoulder. He looked up. She was standing over him, the purplish-orange hue of the burgeoning dawn framing her figure like an aura. She smiled, an unsure, uneasy smile.

"What you doing out here, Georgie?"

"Sleeping," he quipped, then added more sincerely, "and waiting for you."

"Why?" she asked before she realized that she didn't want to know the answer.

But Georgie sidestepped the question, not wanting to indebt her to the answer.

"Why not?" he simply replied.

As he got up from the stoop, yawning, Anya fumbled for her keys.

"Georgie, I – I don't want to…"

"It's not that, Ma. Come on, let's go upstairs."

Humans have existed for thousands of years without the ability to speak, but never—not even for a day—without the ability to communicate. So for the oldest, deepest emotions, words are not only unnecessary; often, they are obstacles.

For the rest of the night, no words passed between them. They entered the apartment, shedding everything that wasn't them and stepped into the shower. His hands were like the water cascading over her body, touching her everywhere in a manner too intimate to be sexual—almost motherly. He communicated emotions through his finger tips, until her back racked with sobs and tears cleansed her face. They dried each other, her towel-his back, his thumb-her tears. Then they laid down as the sun came up creeping through the window pane. Anya rested her head on his chest as they both fell fast asleep.

Hours later, Georgie woke up to find Anya sitting naked, Indian style, looking at him as she watched him sleep.

"Why are you looking at me like that?" he asked.

"Like what" she returned.

"Like, damn, where's a butcher knife when you need one." Anya cracked a smile.

"Scared?"

"Should I be?"

She demurred, without a reply.

"Can I ask you a favor?" Georgie questioned.

"Depends on what it is."

"It's just that, I really gotta piss, right, but I'm too lazy. Hold it for me?"

Anya laughed and began pushing him out of the bed.

"Go pee. I'm the only one that can piss in this bed!"

"You don't…really, do you? EWWW!" he remarked playfully, jumping up like her bed had the cooties.

He went into the bathroom, pushed up the toilet seat, then whipped out his morning hard on. All of a sudden, he felt Anya wrap her arms around him and grab his dick.

"You ready?"

"You aim, I'll fire."

His dick swelled subtly and a burst of piss shot out of the

head. The surge threw Anya off a bit.

"Ewww, I can feel it," she giggled.

"Look out."

Being shorter, she had to look around him, and the angle made her miscalculate. Her aim made him piss on the ceramic edge.

"Spock, she's losing control!" Georgie joked.

His crack made her laugh, her laugh made her jerk, and the jerk made her aim the stream and it sprayed across the toiled paper in a downward slant.

"Oh my God, you just shot an innocent bystander!" he yelled, in a voice that made her fall out laughing

Piss went everywhere. Georgie grabbed his dick and Anya fell against the wall, laughing hysterically.

"Damnit Jim, this is a weapon, not a toy!" Georgie barked.

Anya was in tears, holding her stomach.

"Stop, I can't—" She tried to catch her breath. "You are so crazy!"

Georgie smiled, shook, and then flushed. He cleaned up the piss then washed his hands. He turned to her and she noticed that his dick was still out. Anya grabb'ed it, using it to pull him to her, squeezing and stroking it to its full length.

"I bet I know where to aim this time." She cooed, her voice soft and seductive.

She threw her arms around his neck and devoured his tongue, grinding her body against his so that his dick stimulated her clit. He grabbed her ass and lifted her up; she wrapped her legs around his waist and positioned herself so his dick slid straight up into her sloppy wet pussy.

"Oh fuck! Why am...I...so...wet?" she gasped, feasting on his tongue and lips.

"Because it's right," he gruffed, sliding his index finger into her asshole.

She cried out, body bucking up and down on his length

while he fuck-walked her back to the bedroom.

He bumped down the hall like a staggering drunk, knocking a picture off the wall in the process, the smashing glass muffled by the sounds of her screams and his growls.

Anya covered his face with kisses as Georgie laid back on the bed so that she could ride him.

"What are you doing to me? You're not supposed to be here," she moaned, the words so deep in her throat. To him it sounded like tongues.

He ran his hands up her stomach, palming and massaging her breasts, kneading her nipples.

"Your heart is *pounding*. Tell me how good it feels," he urged.

"Don't...talk. Stop talking," she replied through clenched teeth, head thrown back.

Her voice was so low, so deep when they fucked, it seemed to come out of his dick, up her spine and explode in her brain like the sledge hammer carnival game.

"You love when I talk to you with this dick all in you, don't you? Make you wanna cum all over this dick, don't it?" He growled and bit his bottom lip, giving every stroke more emphasis.

"Yesssss!" she squealed.

"Tell me you love it!"

"I love it!"

She groaned so deeply that her body shook.

"Look at me," he barked, grabbing her by the throat, his grip tight enough to make her pussy twitch. "Tell me you love me."

Her hazel eyes looked deep into his grays, making the connection electrify them both.

"I love you," she cried, and her words sent her falling... falling...falling...

Her thick, milky juices coating his hard, thick shaft and

making him cream her tight, pulsating walls.

"Goddamn, you beautiful, Ma."

Anya, sweat glistening on her skin like sprinkled diamond dust, looked at him for a long time, before asking him, "Why...did you want me to say that?"

Georgie traced around her nipple with his thumb.

"Don't you believe in love at first sight?"

"Yeah, but sometimes it pays to take a closer look," she shot back.

"What if I told you I loved you on first sight?"

Anya giggled.

"I'd say it's just the fuckin' talkin.'"

Georgie looked her in the eyes and replied, "I never just fuck, Anya."

"Oh no?" She grinned, leaning over him so that her breasts swung in his face like ripe melons, ready to be picked. "What do you do, make *love?*"

"You say it like it's a bad thing," Georgie remarked.

Anya shook her head, her eyes saying, "If you only knew..." as she dismounted him, laying flat on her back beside him.

"You're young, Georgie. You'll learn."

He sat up on his elbow, chuckling.

"Ma, you ain't but four years older than me."

She looked at him and said, "You can do *a lot* in four years." Her eyes said, *Remember who I am, what I am. Challenge my experience if you want to.*

Her gaze riled Georgie's bravado.

"I *know,* 'cause watch what *I* do in four years. Matter of fact, *one.* I'ma take this itty bitty world by storm and I'm *just* getting warm!" he rapped. Anya's back arched with laughter.

"Okay, LL Cool J, I'm glad you have such faith in yourself, but what you think? New York's supposed to throw you a parade 'cause you came? 'Cause you do *hair*? You're good, baby, but it's a million people in New York, all different languages, yellin', 'I'm here!' How you expect to be heard?"

The look on Georgie's face got distant, and Anya misread it as hurt.

"Look Georgie, I didn't mean…"

He jumped up from the bed and began pacing.

"Naw, naw, I'm good…just say that again."

"What?"

"About the language."

She scowled, bemused.

"What? A million languages, yellin', 'I'm here.'"

"That's just what I'ma do! That's *it*!" he exclaimed, punching his palm for emphasis.

Anya sat up. She didn't understand, but she could feel the energy bubbling and it created a sense of anticipation in her.

"What are you talkin' about, Georgie?"

He stopped pacing and looked at her.

"Remember, I told you about the hair show?"

"Yeah, at the Jacob Javits Center."

"No doubt. I'ma do like twenty heads, fifty—fuck it—a hundred and we all goin' down there. All they gotta do is walk around talkin' about, 'oh Giorgio' this and 'oh Giorgio' that and--"

"Wait, Giorgio?"

He smiled.

"That's me on my fly shit," he explained, striking a GQ pose—hand to chin—then squatting like he was taking a hood flick.

Anya laughed.

"Stupid self."

"Now, at the same time they gonna be dropping cards everywhere saying, *Hair Designs by Giorgio* while all I'ma do is walk around with my assistant," His tone suggested Anya would be the assistant. "People gonna come up and try and talk to me, but you be like, 'No, he doesn't speak English. No, he doesn't speak Spanish, French, Italian.'"

"Well, what do you speak?" Anya asked, caught up in his energy.

He smirked, helped up his hands and wiggled his fingers, "With my *hands*. You say, 'Giorgio only speaks with his hands!' Muhfuckas gonna eat it up, because people love that mysterious, aloof shit," he reasoned, adding—in his mind— *and nobody can ask about my license if the think I don't speak their language.*

Anya's eyes blinked.

"Wow...okay. Yeah, that could work...it really could."

"Could? It *will*! I'm tellin' you, they gonna eat it up! I'ma be *heard* without making a sound!"

"You just thought of that?" she asked, her tone saying that she was impressed.

"And I'm just gettin' warm!" he rapped, repeating his earlier point.

She laughed.

"With your country self," he chuckled.

Anya leveled her eyes at him, leaned back and spread her legs. "I see you like my molasses."

"Goddamn right; now where the biscuits!" he cracked, then dove in headfirst.

Georgie couldn't wait to talk to Michelle. The fact that she had a column in one of New York's top papers was a major part of Georgie's plan. As soon as he walked in, he called out, "Yo Michelle, where you at? I gotta holla at you!"

Michelle came out of the kitchen, but before Georgie could begin, Denise came walking out from behind Michelle.

"Hey, Baby! Surprise!" she sang, wrapping him up in a

tight, full-body hug. Georgie could hear his mother's laughter all the way from Philly, but he transitioned smoothly from surprise to affection, lifting Denise off her feet and sucking her neck, making her giggle.

Michelle grabbed her purse and keys.

"Yo 'chelle, I need to holla at you," Georgie told her.

"I'll be back soon. I have a very important meeting with my editor," she replied, then paused after opening the door, adding, "and y'all make sure y'all spray somethin'. Some Lysol."

As soon as the door shut, Denise looked at Georgie and commented, "Michael's...changed."

"Yeah, I know right. Just don't tell my mother," Georgie replied, knowing that telling Denise not to gossip was tantamount to telling her not to breathe.

Any more talking was smothered as they devoured each other's tongues and tore off each other's clothes as Georgie backed her down the hall. They left a trail of discarded garments—her shoe, his shirt, her bra, his sneakers—so that by the time they reached the bed, they were only wearing their pants.

Georgie dumped her on the bed, greedily sucking and squeezing her breasts.

"Ohh, I missed you, baby," she cooed, her pussy on fire.

"I missed you," Georgie replied, sitting up and pulling her jeans down.

She lifted her ass so that he could pull her pants off. As soon as they were off, he dropped his. Denise cocked open her cinnamon thighs, grabbed Georgie's dick with both hands and guided it into her throbbing pussy.

"Ohhhh yessssss," she screamed as soon as he was inside of her.

With her head thrown back and her mouth wide open, she looked like a fiend getting her fix, as if the drug pumping through her veins was from the pleasure pumping in and out of her pussy.

"Give me more, Baby, deeper, go deeper," she urged frantically.

Georgie slung her legs over his shoulders and began fucking her like his dick was a pile driver, trying to drive her into the mattress.

Denise grabbed the headboard, just to have something to grip, as Georgie pounded her mercilessly. Since he had just finished sexing Anya for the second time, his round three could be the fast, furious punishment that Denise was loving —every stroke of it.

"Oh baby, this dick is so good! I love youuuu!" she cooed, as her pussy spasmed then flooded the covers.

Georgie kept pounding, urging himself until he came deep inside of her.

"Whew!" Denise breathed, with a languished, "freshly-fucked" smile on her face. "Let me find out you really did miss me."

"You too sexy to forget," Georgie responded, caressing her face as he gazed into her eyes.

Denise draped her arms over his shoulders and arched her legs high up on his hips, rubbing them back and forth.

"So…tell me who she is," Denise requested, a curiously neutral expression on her face.

He looked at her.

"Who?"

A knowing smile crept across Denise's face.

"The woman you smell like."

Georgie was never about lying to women; he just hated hurting them.

"Anya."

Even though deep down Denise wanted to cry, she was old enough to expect it.

"That's a pretty name."

Georgie knew better than to comment. Denise caressed his cheek, studying his face.

"Georgie Porgie…you have a beautiful heart, but no one woman will ever be enough, and you don't have enough respect for a woman's feelings to lie," Denise surmised.

Georgie's brow furled with confusion.

"How is a lie respect?"

"Nothing says 'I love you' like a lie," she chuckled, and he could feel her pussy contract with the gesture. "It's never the lie…it's the reason for it."

Georgie's expression said that he still didn't understand. Denise pulled his face down and kissed him gently.

"Don't worry, you'll understand when it matters. As for me…I'm not about to let your young ass drive me crazy," she laughed and he smiled. "But I do want to thank you for making me beautiful again."

"You never stopped."

"Well, let's just say you got my juices flowing again…Now, come here and give me something to remember you by."

"I like it…It could definitely work," Michelle nodded, thinking about what Georgie had just told her.

They were sitting on the couch when Georgie broke it all down.

"There's more."

"Well?"

"I need to use your column," Georgie answered.

"Meaning?" Michelle questioned, one eyebrow raised.

"I just want you to talk about the expo in the next day's paper. Nothing major: who was there, what they were doing and who is Giorgio, you know?" Georgie explained.

"You mean, create the mystique."

"Yeah, that,"

Michelle nodded.

"I can do that, *but--* "

"Everything after but is bullshit," Georgie quipped.

Michelle snickered.

"Okay, *however*…I need you to do something for me."

Georgie shook his head, knowing what was coming.

"Yeah, 'chelle."

"In the event this brilliant plan doesn't work, you have to go and get your cosmetologist's license."

Georgie stuck out his hand without hesitation.

"Deal."

On the day of the expo, Georgie rented a limo. He knew that first impressions were everything. He stood in the full-length mirror, admiring his reflection. He was exhausted. He had done a marathon styling session, head after head until all twenty blurred together. He just hoped that his hard work paid off.

"Hey sexy, what's your name?" Anya flirted, sliding beside him and looking into his eyes in the reflection.

He had touched her frosted sherbet look up, giving her a sharper edge up with side burns that ice picked at her jaw line.

"Georgie."

"I thought you didn't speak English?" Anya quipped, playfully.

They laughed.

"How do I look?"

"Delicious," she winked.

But she didn't need to tell him that. He already knew it. He had to admit, Yvette was definitely a talented designer. She had made him a black-on-black silk suit, the only contrast being the blood red accents and his red gator slip- ons. She topped off the ensemble with a red silk cape, with holes for his arms to slip through. He wore his long hair loose, which—along with the shades—hid his eyes from view.

When Michelle saw him, she called Yvette over and asked, "Why you got my nephew looking like Dracula?"

Georgie couldn't help but laugh.

"Now see, only a bitch with no sense of style would say something so crass as that. Trust me Georgie, this look will totally work with this crowd. Michelle, run along and do your little type writing thing you do elsewhere," Yvette huffed, then strutted off.

* * *

Everyone who could fit rode in the limo. The unlucky rest rode in cabs. When they got there, all the women spread out, all armed with a fresh 'do' and fifty business cards to leave lying around. The females, mostly prostitutes and transvestites, all came through for Georgie, and it was a gesture that he would never forget.

Everyone else had gotten out of the car, leaving Georgie and Anya a few minutes before they were to make their entrance. He sat back, looking out the window at the people moving to and fro, acting as if he wasn't aware of Anya looking at him intently trying to figure him out.

Finally, she spoke.

"Do you think I'm a bad person?"

Georgie smiled to himself, because he knew where the question was coming from. He returned her gaze, only his was from behind shades, and replied, "I think we're all bad people, doing the best we can. I don't believe badness deserves pity, or justification, or excuses; but I do believe everybody's badness should have a shoulder to lean on. Now, you ready to go?"

A hint of a smirk played across her lips, then her expression went neutral. When he opened the door and waited for her to get out first, she paused at the door, looked at him and said, "I should've never let you do my hair... because now I can't get you out of it."

Inside, the place was packed. The Jacob Javits Center is a cavernous building; its Lower Exhibition Hall—the smaller of two, where the expo was held—was 250,000 square feet and could easily hold 20,000 people and the exhibits dedicated to their interests. In many ways, the hair show resembled a carnival. Women walked around with elaborate, colorful hairdos, some towering enormously high in the air. There were many booths, some for hair care products, other for specific stylists giving out free makeovers, others giving touchups, and some providing nail care.

Georgie had been to the hair show in Philly many times, but it definitely paled in comparison. Everything about this place screamed, "Only in New York."

When they first walked in, nothing more than his flamboyant outfit and exotic good looks drew curious glances and lustful stares. As the day wore on, however, and his team worked the room, interest in his presence began to mount and build upon itself.

"Oh my God, your hair is beautiful!"

"Giorgio!"

"Have you heard of Giorgio? No? Oh my, where have you been?!"

Comments like these were heard throughout the expo - sprinklings, like seeds sown to be watered by curiosity.

"Is that him?

"Where?"

"He's here?!"

And then, like the echo in a vacuous valley, the name "Giorgio" began to ring out.

"Are you Giorgio?"

The more he didn't answer, the more they asked, just like he had anticipated. They would smile graciously and shake his outstretched hands as Anya strutted beside him, tortoise shell glasses perched on her nose and a small leather-bound appointment book and pen in her hand.

"Please, Giorgio, may I have a word with you?" one man asked, who owned a string of salons in Connecticut.

"I'm sorry, but Giorgio doesn't speak English," Anya answered, and they kept it moving, leaving the man befuddled in their wake.

A rail-thin Cuban woman, who had just put out a line of hair care products, approached holding out her hand.

"Hello, Giorgio, it's nice to meet you," she cooed in Spanish, with a flirtatious smile.

Georgie bent and kissed her hand.

"I'm sorry, but Giorgio doesn't speak Spanish," Anya informed her.

"But…"

They moved on.

A raven-haired woman with olive skin and beautiful, gypsy eyes approached them and spoke in a language that Anya couldn't recognize.

"I'm sorry, but whatever language that is, Giorgio doesn't speak that either."

"Well, what language *does* he speak?" someone asked, exasperatedly.

Anya smiled graciously and replied, "Giorgio…speaks with his hands."

The line reverberated through the building with feverish repetition, attracting the energy of the crowd and bestowing upon Georgie a rock-star like status, punctuating the event. He took pictures with various people, while Anya scribbled down appointments furiously in the book. All the women couldn't wait to have their hair done by the man who "spoke with his hands."

As the camera flashes went off, Georgie glanced over at Anya. She had her head down, writing in the book. The distant look of concentration on her face gave her beauty a studious air that she wore extraordinarily well. She glanced up and the smile that graced her face said that she knew he had been watching her, but it was the look of pride he received that swelled his chest.

Twok!

The bubbly surged out of the bottle and ran over Georgie's fist as he gripped the neck and filled his and Anya's flutes to the top.

"You…" she started to say, but he put his hand with the champagne on it to her mouth, and she slurped it off. "You're only supposed to fill a champagne glass half way."

He looked at the label then shrugged.

"For eight hundred dollars, I should be able to fill up a tub!"

They clinked glasses and toasted to success.

You did it," she remarked.

"Naw boo, *we* did it," he corrected and leaned towards her.

She thought he would kiss her, but he licked the corner of her mouth.

"You had some on your lip, and this cost too much to waste."

She giggled.

"So silly."

"Really though, I wanna thank you. You looked real professional with your library frames. Made me wanna fuck you on a stack of books," he cracked.

"Oh yeah?" she replied, eyebrow raised, mischievously.

Georgie sat his glass down and took her hand.

"Believe me Anya, this is just the beginning. Just give me a chance to be your dream weaver."

Anya slowly pulled her hand back and sat her glass down next to his. He could tell from her expression that she was about to object.

"Listen…" he began, but she rose up, leaned over and straddled his lap.

"Shhh," she whispered, gazing into his eyes. "I thought you only spoke with your hands."

Georgie knew she was using her seduction to silence him, but her kiss was too sweet to resist…

Who is Giorgio?

Those were the words that ended Michelle's article in the next day's *Village Voice*. The name of her column was "Cliché Corner," a play on the fact that it was a gossip column, so to "cliché" was ironically to be the talk of the town.

After the expo and the appearance of the column, Georgie was certainly the talk of the town in the hair circles. For the next two weeks, Georgie had appointments with women from all walks of life: foreign females from the U.N., old rich White women, the wives of city leaders, entertainers and top shelf gangster bitches. His name tasted like wine on their lips, and some of the talk was even about his styling prowess.

The money came in, fast and furiously, and Georgie kept up appearances by always arriving in a stretch limo to every appointment. In the midst of the madness, he even got a call from Christophe.

"I love it! I love it! Bravo, my Georgie, or should I say *Giorgio*?" Christophe remarked, saying the name in a deep and breathy voice.

Georgie was riding in the back of a limo, on the way home. He held his Nokia mobile phone to his ear, laughing.

"I told you I wasn't about to be a fashion busboy," he reminded him.

"And I never doubted you; I simply had to play by the rules. Although you've found a way to change them," Christophe remarked.

"Still wanna send me to Jersey?" Georgie quipped.

"No, but I do want to offer you a job. Wait, don't bother, I already know that the answer is no. I just had to try. Besides, I can still say that I gave you your first big break in New York, because your secret's safe with me. Kiss, kiss!"

The bed was covered with stacks of money. Georgie and Anya sat on either side counting it.

"Five, six, seven…fifty," Anya concluded, putting the last stack aside.

Georgie wrote down the total.

"So that's…eighteen thousand, four hundred. Not bad for a few weeks, huh?"

"I'm proud of you, Georgie. You deserve it."

He smiled.

"A coupla more months and we'll have enough for our own salon. But our place gonna be different; not only are we gonna do hair, but we gonna sell shoes too!"

Anya giggled.

"Shoes? At a salon?"

"Hell yeah, think about it. New 'do, new attitude, and you see a fierce pair of shoes, too? Tell me you won't buy 'em." Georgie challenged her, his mouth twisted with disbelief.

"Probably. Sounds good. I'm sure it'll be great, and I'll be your first customer," Anya winked, leaned over to give him a quick peck, and then got up.

"Customer?" he echoed, following her movements. "You my partner."

Anya shook her head as she grabbed a dress out of the closet.

"Georgie, don't start, okay?"

He got up and approached her.

"Start what? Ma, look at that. *We* made that in two weeks! Niggas go to *jail* for makin' that much in two weeks! We're on the verge of somethin' *big* here!" he exclaimed.

"No Georgie, *you're* on the verge of something big. *You*, not me. It's time I get back to *real* life, my life, okay?" she said, sending an aggravated sigh.

She walked toward the bathroom, dress and wig in hand.

"Where you goin', Anya?"

"To work," she spat over her shoulder, seconds before she slammed the bathroom door.

Georgie went to turn the knob, but it was locked. That was the worst part. He heard the shower come on and he began to pace the floor, running his hands through his hair. What was *wrong* with her? Here he had all this money on the bed and a plan to get more, and she wanted to go back to the streets and... He shook his head because he didn't even want to *think* past the "and." Couldn't she see that he was doing this for her, just as much as he was doing this for himself? Sure, it was his dream, but some dreams are big enough for two, big enough for life, big enough for love... He couldn't stomach the fact that she would rather give herself to *anybody*, instead of giving herself to *somebody*. Him. Home.

He heard the shower cut off. Ten minutes later, she walked out, transformed...disguised. She had on a fire red spandex dress that hugged her every curve—barely concealing the fact that she didn't have panties on—and a long, black straight wig that hung down to her ass. She was the first to look away as she crossed the room and stepped into her see-through, fuck-me pumps.

"You don't have to do this," Georgie said softly.

"Do what? Live my life?! What do you *want* from me?" Anya barked, eyes blazing.

"I just wanna make you happy, Anya."

She snorted with derision.

"Oh, you think you can *make* me happy? Just waltz your young ass into my life, wave your little magic wand and just *create* Anya as happy, huh?" she laughed, mockingly. "How you know I'm *not* happy? How you know *this* doesn't make me happy? Maybe I like fuckin'. Can't you tell? How you know I ain't happy, Georgie?"

"Because I see it in your eyes," he replied, simply.

She remembered the moment that they saw one another on the strip, the way he looked at her, the way he saw her and hated the fact that he did so easily.

"You think you know everything, don't you?" she blazed. "Well, you don't! You don't know shit, okay?! Just stay the fuck away from me; stay the fuck out of my life!"

Anya snatched her purse off the door knob so forcefully she damn near snatched her arm out of the socket when the strap got hung up. Finally untangling it, she stomped down the hallway, down the stairs, flung open the front door and slammed it behind her. Georgie sat on the bed, his head in his hands.

"Hey girl, how you? Where you been?" Celeste, another hooker asked, as she gave Anya a hug.

"I been…sick," Anya replied, which wasn't exactly a lie.

"I know that's right, shit I'm sick everyday," Celeste joked to herself and shielded her cigarette from the wind as she lit it. She took a long drag then added, "Mr. BM been around here lookin' for you. I think he may be ready to propose."

Anya mustered a smile. Celeste paused then—since she was almost a foot taller than Anya—squatted down so they were at eye level.

"Get your game face on, girl," she remarked and walked away.

Anya knew that she wasn't in the right state of mind to be on the strip. Out there, you had to become numb, hollow, bringing nothing but the package because any trace of a soul could be swallowed in one night. Anya never had a problem doing that until Georgie came along. Now, it was like her spirit refused to be quelled, her wings refused to stay clipped, and her heart refused to stay cold.

"Look alive girls, big money on deck!" Celeste called out.

The stretch limo bent the corner, and all the hookers started preening, prepping and strutting like they were on the goddamn catwalk. Anya took one look and knew exactly who was inside. She sucked her teeth and headed in the other direction.

The limo pulled over to the curb and Georgie stepped out.

"Lawda mercy, yousa pretty muhfucka! Choose me and I *swear* it's on the house!" Celeste creamed, damn near salivating as she eyed Georgie.

He smiled and brushed imaginary lint from his lapel. He knew that he was cleaner than the Board of Health in his black Armani suit with the gold vest, Egyptian cream-colored Italian loafers and his black gangsta derby, cocked ace-deuce. In his hand, he held a single peach rose. He held it out to Anya.

"Your magic wand, Madame," he smirked, deepening his voice for playful effect.

The inside of her lips were smiling, but the outsides were upside down. "I'm working," she spat, coldly.

"I am too! Look at me!" He stepped back and held his arms out for inspection. "You can't *tell* me I don't look like sexual chocolate! Sexual chocolate!" he yelped, stomping his feet like Eddie Murphy in *Coming to America*, knowing that it was her favorite movie.

Anya couldn't help but blurt out laughter before catching herself.

"Stop being so stupid. Now go, I told you I'm working."

"And I'm payin'," he shot right back, pulling out a wad of money from his pocket, his expression dead serious.

Anya looked him in the eyes, not knowing whether to slap him or jump into his arms. Instead, she snatched the rose out of his hand and headed for the limo.

"Fine."

Georgie tipped his hat to Celeste, who had been watching

the whole exchange, then got in behind Anya as the driver pulled off.

She laid the rose on the limo jump seat, then reached for his zipper.

"What you doin'?"

"You said you was payin', right? Ain't this what you're payin' for?"

He pushed her hand away.

"No, I'm payin' to take you to dinner, take you to a movie, to have a good time and *maybe* to the top of the world if you let me," he replied sincerely. "Now, how much is that going to cost me?"

Anya just looked at him with her arms folded across her breasts.

He took her to a small Italian restaurant in the Village that had outside seating. The night air was cool and soothing, perfect for dinner under the stars. A few doors down in a small park a man was playing "A Night In Tunisia" on the saxophone.

The waiter came. They ordered. He left. They stared at each other, each trying to figure the other out.

"So…do I at least get to see the kids on the weekend? You keep the dog; I keep the cat? What?" He quipped, but he wasn't smiling.

"What are you talking about?"

Georgie shrugged.

"I'm sayin', this feels like a divorce. You told me to stay the fuck out your life. What else am I supposed to think?"

Anya took a sip of water. She smiled at the waiter politely when he brought bread sticks, then left.

"You're complicating my life right now, Georgie, and I just don't need complications," Anya said.Georgie leaned his elbows on the table and replied, "You know what brought me to New York. A bullet. Several, actually. That kinda complicated *my* life. But yo, life is complicated. You know when it gets uncomplicated?"

"When?"

"When you're dead…then it's easy," he replied, then grabbed a bread stick and took a bite. "Excuse me for a sec." Georgie got up and walked down the street to the man playing the saxophone. The music went silent. Anya saw Georgie hand him something—she figured it was money—then walked back toward her. A few seconds later, the man began playing a melody that was hauntingly familiar. It reminded Anya of what she loved about New York. The way each note seemed to be telling the story of the night—dark and foreboding, but at the same time tender and inviting.

Seeing him approach with street swag, tempered by a suave stride, he looked like he just stepped off a runway, his cologne smelling like music and the music sounding like his cologne. Anya felt the irrepressible need to go away, to leave.

Get up, don't look back, run!

The only thing that kept her in her seat was the way he only looked into her eyes as he approached, calming her spirit like the ruffling of a bird's feathers, making her insides purr.

"'In a Sentimental Mood' by Duke Ellington and John Coltrane," Anya remarked as he sat down. "How you know about that?"

Georgie sipped his water.

"My mother. She plays it all the time; well, whenever she's thinking about my father. God bless the dead."

"I'm sorry to hear that. How did he pass?"

"Car accident. Like, a coupla months before I was born. He was a saxophone player."

The waiter brought their meals, placed them down, and then left.

"So tell me something about you. Why you bring all that

Georgia to New York?" he asked, seasoning his pasta.

She hesitated a moment then said, "School. I um, came to go to school."

"What school?"

Another pause, and imperceptible winch, a small bite of linguine.

"Julliard."

"What's that?"

"It's a school for the arts. I was a dancer."

"Was? When did the music stop?" he asked.

"Georgie, I don't want to talk about that."

He took one look at the pained expression on her face and decided not to probe.

"I understand. But, can I at least ask what kind of dance? Like, was it river dancin'? Square dancin'?"

Anya laughed, in spite of herself.

"Classical dance. Ballet."

"Oh, okay. I thought you meant dancing-dancing."

Anya looked at him with sass in her expression.

"What do you mean, dancing-dancing? That *is* dancing. I can *dance*."

Georgie leaned back in his chair.

"Why you say it like that, like I'm supposed to be scared or something?"

She smirked.

"Don't be scared, be careful."

Georgie howled, wiping his mouth.

"Hold up, 'cause I can dance, too. I might not have went to Julliard, but I went to back *yard*, front *yard*, junk *yard*. Sardines! Hey and pork and beans!" he sang, bouncing in his seat, go-go style.

"Please Georgie, you are *not* ready," she taunted, rolling her neck.

Georgie scooted his chair back.

"We can take this to the street right now!" he challenged.

She laughed.

"I've got a better idea. I know a salsa club up in Spanish Harlem..."

She didn't get it all out before Georgie hollered, "Check, please!"

The club was on Broadway, between 162nd and 163rd Streets. The area in front of the club was thronged with people. Expensive cars and limos were double parked up and down the block, so Georgie's limo blended right in, and with the ghetto Latino crowd, Georgie blended right in.

"Now, *this* is New York," he remarked, as they entered the club.

The club itself had a narrow entrance that was as clogged as cholesterol in an artery, but once they wiggled through, the room opened up into a wide dance floor, framed on all sides by booths and the bar. Georgie started to head to the bar, but Anya grabbed his hand and led him to the dance floor.

"We came to dance, remember?" she said, her tone challenging, her gaze meaningful.

"Then let's do it."

And do it, they did. The night was alive with the sounds of Tito Puente, Willie Colon, Willie BoBo and Elvis Crespo. The DJ blended the rhythms perfectly, taking them on a musical journey through Salsa, Soca, and Calypso.

Georgie had never done Salsa dancing, but just like when he was younger, it didn't take him long to catch on. Before long, he was making the dance his own.

As he danced, he admired the rhythm of Anya's movements. From the bend of her wrist, the sway of her arms, the way she slid into the pulse of every melody—like she slid into that tight ass dress—the look of abandonment faded from her face as if getting lost in the music was a way to find herself.

Waters of life, he thought, remembering what her name meant. Looking at her, he could see why. Water flows, rhythm flows, and they are one in the same, music being to the spirit, what water is to the physical life.

He saw something else: the glow of happiness in her face. She was definitely in her element.

After what seemed like hours, Anya started to head for a booth.

"I need a rest," she remarked, but Georgie grabbed her hand.

"We came to dance, remember?" he reminded her, then cupped her under the ass and lifted her off her feet.

Anya wrapped her arms around his neck and legs around his waist, as he danced with her in his embrace.

"You're beautiful, you know that?" Georgie said, looking into her eyes.

She answered with a kiss.

They danced into the wee hours of the early morning. By the time they came out, the night had turned cool. He draped his suit jacket over her shoulders as they walked to the limo. They got in and headed back to Mid-town.

"So how I do?" Georgie quizzed, massaging her feet.

"You did aight, I guess," she replied with an exaggerated comical expression.

"*Aight*?! I tore that ass up!" he exclaimed, tickling her side.

Anya squealed, jumping away from his hand.

"You did not!"

"Right now, the janitor sweepin' up, talkin' 'bout, 'What's that? Somebody left a piece of ass on the floor.'" he joked.

She laughed hard.

"Oh, believe me, it's all here," she remarked, slapping her ass, making it quiver and his heart right along with it.

"I know that's right; Georgia on my mind!"

Their laughter subsided as he continued to massage her feet.

"On the real though, I ain't had that much fun in a long time," Georgie remarked.

"Me either," Anya admitted.

"And I meant what I said before. I believe in love at first sight. I love you, Anya."

She drew a breath to speak, but Georgie silenced her by putting his fingers to her lips.

"Believe me Ma, I'm not talking about a fairy tale love, probably not even perfect love, but I'll defend it, because I believe in what God intended."

"What's God got to do with it, Georgie?"

"Because everything happens for a reason. We met for a reason," he answered.

Anya shook her head, looked away then looked back.

"People meet everyday, everywhere. You think God wanted them all to meet?"

"Only if it feels like this."

She looked at him with a look that told Georgie the wall was starting to crumble. The limo stopped. Georgie realized that they were at the apartment building. They got out. Georgie went and settled up with the driver, setting the schedule for the rest of the week. The limo pulled off. They went inside, the only sounds were the scratching of their shoes on the stairs, the echo of the thoughts in their heads. They arrived at Anya's floor. Georgie took her arm.

"Come on. I want to show you something."

"Come where?"

"The roof."

She hesitated. He smiled and extended his hand.

"You scared of heights?"

She took his hand and they ascended.

The building wasn't that tall, just twelve stories but when they came out, Georgie announced, "Welcome to the top of the world, Ma."

Anya snickered.

"This is definitely not the top of the world, Georgie."

Georgie shook his head, walking her over to the edge.

"Naw Ma, don't look down, look *out*. Wherever you are, if you can see eye to eye with the sun, you're at the top of the world," he jeweled her. He turned her body and pointed to the awakening sun, just beginning to pierce the horizon.

"Look."

She turned and watched the night sky—pale and purple—gradually spreading like an orange smile over the city.

"Here, stand on the ledge. I got you," Georgie assured her, helping her onto a block of masonry that hung like a lip over the building. He held her at the waist. From there, she was able to easily block out her surroundings—the squalor, the mean streets simmering below.

"Embrace it Ma. Never be afraid to spread your wings."

Anya took a deep breath and raised her arms, welcoming the new day. She looked like Jesus over Brazil, open-armed, christening New York. The sun, like water, bathed her with light up to her waist.

"You ready to get down?"

"No," she replied, eyes closed.

The new sun—fully arisen—immersed her in its glory, warming her face and reflecting itself in the tears that freely flowed.

"I'm ready."

Georgie lifted her down slowly, until she was back on solid ground.

When he saw her tears, he lifted his thumb to wipe them away.

Anya flinched.

"Don't...I want to feel them."

He nodded understandingly, then tipped up her chin to direct her gaze into his.

"I'm not perfect, but I'm perfect for you. All I'm asking is for a chance, Anya. Okay? Yes?"

She kissed him gently, some of her tears rubbing off on his cheeks, then replied "Yes!"

And then she was gone.

Georgie realized it when he opened his eyes...sensed it even before he opened his eyes. The room felt colder, lighter, emptier. He laid on the bed trying to process it all.

He had felt it in her kiss on the roof, he heard it in the timbre of her "yes"—the way it fluttered, like dormant octaves beginning to vibrate in the caged bird's breast—like she was saying yes to something, just not him.

He sat up and looked around the room, trying to take into account what else was missing and hoping to find that her absence was temporary, but it just took a brief glance for him to know that wasn't the case. The only comfort came from the fact that she hadn't taken any of her wigs, so he knew that she had left her mask behind. That made him smile. He spotted a piece of paper on the pillow where her head should have been. It was a ripped piece of notebook paper, scribbled on in the dark that simply read:

I'm going to chase the sun.

For the next few weeks, Georgie stayed in his room and didn't move. The phone rang constantly with inquiries about unfulfilled appointments, but the calls went unanswered. He felt like someone that had been in a car accident because it hurt all over. The difference was, this pain was emotional instead of physical. It was his first heartbreak, and he hoped it was his last. Every song that came on the radio reminded him of something about Anya—her smile, her laugh, her walk, the swell of her hips, the look on her face when she came...

I won't pretend that I intend to stop living;
I won't pretend that I'm good at forgiving.

Sade's "Stronger than Pride" played softly on the radio, when he heard a knock at the door.

"What?" he called out, with an edge in his tone.

"Don't 'what' me, boy," Stephanie replied, walking into the shadowy room.

"I ain't know it was you."

"Mm-hmm, well be nicer 'cause it could've been."

She sat on the bed and kissed him on the forehead, brushing his hair out of his face.

"Michael told me what happened. You okay?"

Georgie shrugged, resigned.

"I'm here."

"You sure? I've got my Gloria Gaynor tape out in the car if you need it now," she joked.

Georgie laughed. It felt good, like a release of children at three o'clock, bursting out of the school's doors.

"Naw, Ma, I don't need no Gloria Gaynor tape."

"Just checkin'...but Georgie, didn't I tell you about playing with these girls' emotions, huh?" Stephanie scolded him.

"Ma, it wasn't that, forreal. I mean, I don't know *what* happened, that's the crazy part. It's like everything was straight, you know, then bam! She was gone. That's the part I can't figure out," he agonized.

Stephanie nodded, knowingly.

"Yeah…well, I don't know this girl or what was going on with her, but a woman's heart can be a confusing place, even to her sometimes. But what I want to say to you is, every woman isn't *me*."

Georgie looked at her quizzically.

"What do you mean, Ma?"

"I mean, that you don't have to be her savior. Just because you know her story doesn't automatically make her your responsibility," Stephanie replied.

Georgie acknowledged the point, but replied, "I know Ma, but believe me, it was more than that. It hurts."

Stephanie smiled graciously then caressed his cheek.

"Then maybe she's the one."

"Yeah well, if she is, she's gone," he snorted bitterly.

"Naw baby, if she's the one, you'll see her again. When you let someone go, if they come back to you, then they're truly yours. I'm sure she's somewhere thinking the same thing," she surmised.

"Maybe."

"And…well, I've got some bad news for you…K.B.'s locked up for murder."

Mother and son looked at one another. A look of confirmation passed between them.

"I'ma go see him," Georgie replied.

"Yeah, he probably needs that," Stephanie seconded, then patted him on the chest. "Now, come on out of this tomb and rejoin the living!"

They went into the living room where one of Stephanie's mixtapes was playing on the stereo. There was a half empty bottle of Tanqueray on the coffee table and cigarette smoke everywhere. Michelle was curled up on the end of the couch with her legs tucked under her, cigarette aloft. Stephanie sat down in the loveseat closest to Michelle where her cigarettes, lighter and drink were waiting for her. Georgie leaned in the doorway and took in the scene.

"Ya'll look like twins."

Stephanie looked at Michelle.

"I know, right? I told him the same thing."

Michelle positively glowed at the comment, because it said that Stephanie accepted her for who she was. Stephanie lit a cigarette.

"But Michael ain't the only one with an alter ego, I hear... Giorgio."

Georgie bust out laughing.

"When he told me, I said that sound just like some shit Georgie would do!" Stephanie snickered.

"And it's working! They are going crazy for him," Michelle exclaimed.

"Of course it's working; that's *my* baby! Tell 'em, Georgie, we make it happen!"

It made Georgie feel better to be surrounded by love, laughter and music, and then...it happened.

Sky's the limit and you know that you keep on;
Just keep on pressin' on...

"Georgie, come dance with your Mama!"

Georgie smoked weed back in Philly. He hadn't smoked since he came to New York. *Until.* Then he started smoking again. Blunts, big blunts. Cigars filled with weed. To roll a blunt, you split the body of the cigar and dump the guts. Then you fill it with another substance—a substitute substance—weed.

Then you inhale.

Georgie drank. There's something masculine about drinking. Being able to take the burn in your chest, the sizzle in your throat, the ability to turn the emotions into a physical obstacle to be overcome—to be able to take it.

He continued to get appointments, in fact they even increased during the time that he didn't answer the phone. But there was something missing. He didn't have his usual flair. He made mistakes, at first only little mistakes obvious only to his meticulous eye, but little by little, the mistakes got to be more obvious.

Smack!
"Ohhh Giorgio!"
Smack! Smack!
"I'm coming again!" she squealed, her whole body trembling.

Georgie had the middle-aged White woman bent over on his bed, ass up and face in the pillow. She lived in the Upper Westside. She was the wife of an investment banker. He had come over to do her hair, and like so many other appointments, ended up doing her as well.

"You like it rough, don't you? *Don't* you?!" Georgie taunted, his teeth clenched as he pounded her relentlessly from the back.

"Oh yesssss, I love it rough; I love it rough!" she gasped, her ample titties swinging and bouncing to the rhythm of his thrusts.

He grabbed a handful of her hair and pulled her head back, leaning forward to bite her neck.

"I – I – I'm going to explode," she cried.

"Cum for me, baby; come all over this dick," he growled.

"Nooo, I can't…take…not a…oooooooh!"

When she came, Georgie didn't hold back and coated her throbbing walls before they both collapsed on the bed.

She moved her hair from her face then turned to look at him.

"You are amazing," she remarked, breathlessly.

Georgie rolled over on his back, grabbing his vodka neat off of the night stand.

"I know," he chuckled, cockily.

Her eyes suddenly got wider, like a thought had just popped into her head.

"Oh! With you being so naughty, I forgot to look at my style," she exclaimed, jumping up and running over to the vanity mirror. He winked then downed his drink.

And then she saw it.

She had told him that she wanted some pizzazz, something playful and risqué, without being over the top.

"Yes, yes," he had assured her, his voice accented to go along with the Giorgio persona.

But what she got wasn't what she expected.

"Oh my...God!" she shrieked, grabbing her hair.

She turned on her heel, eyes blazing.

"What have you done?!"

She had raven black hair with an almost gypsy quality to it, so Georgie had decided to add some platinum blond streaks. But instead of vertical streaks, he wanted to go with a bolder diagonal style, with streaks cutting asymmetrically. The only problem was, he was tipsy when he did it, so it came out looking more spotted than streaked.

"I look like a Dalmatian!" she whined, her nasal tone melting into a cry.

When she said it, the image of a Dalmatian came into his drunken mind and he exploded with laughter.

"This...is...not...*funny!*" she screamed, hysterically.

It only made Georgie laugh harder. The more livid she got, the more hilarious Georgie found it.

"Look what you've done to me! You ruined my hair! Get out! Get out! You're through, do you hear me? Through!" she raged.

Finally dressed, tears of laughter in his eyes, Georgie staggered out of the door. She slammed it behind him. In the ricocheting vibration of the slamming door, Georgie could hear the floor cracking under his dreams of owning his own salon. The door slammed with such finality that he was sure it would soon echo all over New York.

But the worst part was that he didn't even care.

Come along and ride on a fantastic voyage
Slide slide slippity-slide
With switches on the block in a '65!

The club was packed with people, jamming to Coolio and celebrating Yvette' s upcoming "Fantastic Voyage" to her new life in LA. Georgie leaned against the bar, drink in hand, taking it all in. Just as he had predicted, the slamming door echoed all over the city, slamming over and over again. Just as quickly as he had become the toast of the town, the negative force of gossip's gravity made the return trip twice as fast. Within a year, the name Giorgio became anathema in the hair circles, and he had no one to blame but himself.

"Georgie! What are you doin' hiding way back here? You runnin' from me?" Yvette quizzed, simpering.

Georgie sipped his drink and chuckled.

"Naw 'Vette, just chillin', you know? You lookin' forward to L.A.?"

"Yes and no. Excited, scared; it's almost like being bi-polar," she joked.

"Yeah well, I know you're gonna do your thing. And I wanna thank you for everything you did for me. The clothes, the connects. It might not seem like it after how that shit turned out, but I definitely appreciate it," he said.

"Awww," Yvette cooed, head cocked to the side. "Don't worry, baby. New York is a fickle town. It loves you, it hates you." She shrugged her shoulders. "It'll love you again after another Quaalude."

He laughed, remembering the line from *Scarface*.

"And umm, a friend of a friend—who I know would know—says Anya went to L.A. If I see her, I'll tie her up and send her back on the first thing smoking," Yvette smirked.

"Going to chase the sun," he thought.

"Thanks, Ma," he replied, kissing her on the cheek. "I'm gonna miss you."

They hugged warmly. Yvette leaned back in the hug to get a better angle.

"You're a good man, Georgie. You just can't keep that mess in your pants. No, you just won't keep your mess in my pants!"

They laughed.

"You too much, Ma." Georgie remarked as he headed to the bathroom. When he entered the bathroom, it was empty. Along the wall were four urinals. He chose the urinal in the corner. By the time he whipped it out and began to piss, a man walked in. Georgie hardly noticed him, but it kind of puzzled him when the man chose the urinal right next to him, even though the other two were open. But he was tipsy, bordering on drunk, and in that state of mind, subtleties seldom register.

"Niiiice…you ever do porn?"

Georgie heard the words but didn't realize that the man was talking to him until he turned his head and saw that he was looking at his dick! Georgie damn near pissed on himself as he put his dick back in his pants with one hand and shoved the man with the other. He pushed him so hard that his dress shoes skidded on the slick bathroom floor and he fell to the ground. He quickly scrambled to his feet because he saw Georgie stalking toward him, fists clenched like iron

87

blocks.

"Hey – hey – hey, take it easy man; I swear it's not how it sounds!"

Georgie yoked him up by the collar and slammed his back against the wall.

"What kind of shit you into?"

"I swear it's not like that, *I'm* not like that! I'm a porn producer! Here, look!" the man stammered.

He reached into the inside pocket of his suit jacket and pulled out a business card. "See? Sid Wiseman, Backshotz Productions."

Georgie snatched the card from his hand and glared at him hard. He looked like the comedian Billy Crystal with a big, "Welcome Back, Kotter" mustache. He looked at the card. It said exactly what Sid said it did. Still, Georgie maintained his grip.

"What the fuck that got to do with you lookin' at my dick?!"

"Listen, I know you're upset, but it's kind of hard to talk with my wanker hanging out," Sid explained.

Georgie didn't even want to look down. He let Sid go and stepped back. Sid fixed himself, straightened his tie, then explained, "I've heard a lot about you; we move in the same circles, sorta, anyways. The way I heard about you, hair's not the only thing you do well. Know what I mean? So I see you here and I see you going into the bathroom. I figure, a quick peep will let me know if you're my guy, I mean, not like… well, you get where I'm coming from?"

"You coulda come at me a different way."

"Yeah, but I figure asking you to lay your dick on the bar would've been a bit awkward," Sid replied.

Georgie looked at him for a moment with a scowl, then broke out into a chuckle.

"Only in New York," he remarked, shaking his head.

Sid breathed a sigh of relief then stuck out his hand.

"Sid Wiseman."

Georgie just looked at it.

"Oh," Sid grunted. He went to the sink then quickly washed and dried his hands. Then Sid extended his hand again. This time, Georgie shook it.

"Giorgio."

Sid stopped, looked at Georgie, who cracked a smile. Sid washed his hands again because he realized that Georgie hadn't washed his.

"So whaddya say, Giorgio? Believe me, you can make a lot of money in the porn game with a rod like that."

Georgie shrugged.

"Not my thing," he replied then handed the card back.

"Gonna stick with the hair thing, huh?"

"No doubt," Georgie replied and headed out the door.

A few moments later, Sid came out and caught up with him.

"Hey, I was thinkin'…Have you ever heard of Skye?"

"Yeah, of course," Georgie replied.

He prided himself on being up on new music. Skye was an up-and-coming house music artist that the music scene in New York was raving about. They were calling her the Black Madonna, but had failed to see the irony.

"Well, the guy who manages her—actually that's his name—Guy's a friend of mine and I happen to know Skye just fired her stylist. Again. She runs through 'em. I think you'd be *perfect*," he emphasized, saying the word "perfect" with that accent common to Brooklyn Jewry.

Georgie stopped walking and looked at him skeptically.

"You know Skye's manager?"

"I even went to his Bar Mitzvah."

"And you're gonna introduce me? Why?"

Sid shrugged.

"I like your style, kid. Besides, since you didn't kick my ass back there, I figure I owe you one."

Georgie laughed.

"Yeah, I guess you do."

"So, you game?"

"Sure. When?"

"Now."

"Now?" Georgie echoed.

"This is New York, kid. Everything happens now!"

The moment Georgie laid eyes on Skye, he knew she was destined to be larger than life. It wasn't just because she was gorgeous, like Lisa Bonet gorgeous. Not Lisa Bonet when she was on the "Cosby Show," all pale and Gothic. Lisa Bonet in *Angel Heart*, when she was as golden as the Egyptian sunrise and tangy like Cajun gumbo.

Skye stood no more than 5'4"—yet in her spiked-heeled, patent leather boots that came up to her crotch, she was four inches taller. She had a svelte but shapely figure. She was wearing a black Dominatrix outfit, complete with a long leather whip that she dragged around the stage like a tail.

No, it wasn't just her look that screamed "star;" it was her mere presence. The way she worked the stage, worked the crowd: her voice, crisp and siren like. She didn't have a great voice, but what she had she used to mesmerizing effect.

The club was vibrating from the boom of the bass. It sounded like Godzilla stomping the shit out of Tokyo. And every person in the crowd was hopping up and down, wanting to be squashed next. They knew all the words to Skye's club smash, "Rim Shots" and from the lyrics, Georgie knew she wasn't singing about drumming techniques.

The song built to a certain crescendo—like the moment before an orgasm—then exploded into the break. But just before the climax, Skye waved her arm and the music stopped on a dime. The crowd groaned in unison, like a woman on the verge of orgasm.

"Silence!" she barked, shrill voice booming through the speakers.

Crrrraaaack! The whip snapped crisply over the crowd. Whoever the sound engineer was timed the snap perfectly and reinforced it with the sound of a cracking whip.

"You...are...not...worthy," she said, her mouth extra close to the mic.

The crowd went crazy, as if seconding her statement.

"You want it?" she barked, cracking the whip.

Crrrraaaack! The speaker hissed.

"Yessss!" the crowd screamed.

"Then send me a sacrifice!" Skye demanded, eyeing the crowd.

People clamored to be the one.

"You!" she hissed, pointing to a man in the front row.

He looked like a young Yuppie. He had on a shirt and tie, but no jacket. Skye bent down as he started to climb on stage. She wrapped his tie around her hand and half dragged him onto the stage. She barely let him gain his bearing before she sat him down on a folding metal chair that two females in dominatrix outfits brought out. They handcuffed his hands behind his back and shackled his legs together. Meanwhile, Georgie watched as Skye stalked the stage with a strut that would've made Beyoncé bow down, and then turned and walked up to him, put her foot against his chest and kicked him over on his back. The crowd went crazy. She then stepped over his fallen body, sat on his face then hit a big powerful note like a woman having the ultimate orgasm. The music came back on and the crowd went from wild to hysterical, screaming so loud that a few got nose bleeds.

All that Georgie could do was smile in total awe and say to himself, "She's a goddess."

Sid overheard him and nodded.

"Amazing, right? I thought the same thing when I first saw her!" Sid yelled over the music. "Believe me, I remember Madonna when she was a stringy-haired brunette from Detroit, and she didn't have half the fire Skye's got!"

Georgie only half heard him, and it wasn't because of the blazing music. Visions of Skye had his mind going at warp speed.

Her set ended and the stage went black. Once the crowd's post-coital glow had begun to wane, Sid said, "Come on, let's go meet her."

"Great show, Skye," Guy said as she walked off the stage.

He handed her a Long Island Iced Tea, her after show drink and a Newport, freshly lit.

"Thanks, but the snaps weren't quite right. Speak to the sound man," she replied then inhaled a much-needed nicotine infusion.

One of her dancers walked up.

"Umm Skye...we've got a problem."

Skye looked at her. She hated problems.

I...*we*...someone forgot the handcuffs' keys back at the studio."

She patted the girl's cheek then caressed her hair.

"Okay...just go get it, bring it back and never let me see you again," she said, then dropped the smile and added, "You're fired."

The girl, knowing better than to mouth off at Skye sucked her teeth, then rolled her eyes as she turned and strutted off.

"Stupid bitch," Skye mumbled.

The other dancer approached with the handcuffed man. Skye gave him a smile that a blind man could feel.

"Hi! What's your name?"

His face brightened.

"Skye! I mean Bob; it's nice to meet you, Skye!"

"You too…listen Bob; we have a slight, teensy weensy problem, okay." Somebody forgot the handcuffs' keys, but they're going to get it as we speak," she explained, neglecting to mention that she had just fired her. "So we'll have you out of those things in a sec, 'kay? In the meantime, would you like a drink with me, Bill."

"Bob."

"Bobby," she replied with a Kewpie doll smile.

He nodded, like a shy fifth grader.

"Come on."

As they walked—everybody trying to keep pace with her strut— Guy remarked, "Skye, you didn't have to fire her. It was a simple mistake. You can't keep firing everybody baby."

"Then hire better people, Guy. I *despise* incompetence, so don't make excuses for it. If you can't do the job, why the fuck should you have it?"

The shackles had Bob at a significant disadvantage. He couldn't walk—he had to shuffle, shuffle, hop, shuffle, shuffle, hop.

Skye stopped and looked back, trying to keep her impatience tempered.

"Bobby, honey I know it's difficult, but you really have to keep up, 'kay?"

Shuffle, shuffle, hop, shuffle, shuffle, hop.

When Georgie saw her approach, the strobe light seemed to slow time, giving him time to savor the first impression: the leather-clad curves, the nasty walk, the whip in her hand, still dragging it like a tail. And then he saw Bob and he laughed.

"*Shorty even got slaves,*" he thought.

The flash of his smile caught her attention. She glanced at him, while still talking to Guy. The look wasn't long, but the eye contact suggested her curiosity was piqued.

"Guy, how are you?!"

"Sid, you son of a bitch! C'mere!"

The two friends hugged and chuckled, while Georgie stared directly at Skye, a cocky smirk affixed, but Skye disdained returning the attention.

After a quick rib or two, Sid said, "Listen, this is a friend of mine I'd like you to meet, Skye."

Georgie, feeling like he needed no introduction, pre-empted Sid, took Skye's hand and said, "I'm Giorgio," then tried to kiss her hand.

She quickly slid it away.

"I...no. Who even does that?" she spat, her cute little nose wrinkled with disgust.

Georgie chuckled to play it off, but his charms had never been so bluntly rebuffed. His ego got chinked.

Sid cleared his throat.

"Giorgio's a stylist, one of the best."

Skye looked him up and down dismissively.

"Never heard of him."

"You will," Georgie retorted, bravado bubbling.

Skye suppressed a smirk then finally blessed him with a direct gaze.

"You do *hair*? Hmmm… you don't look like the fruity type."

Georgie's nostrils flared as he spat, "Yeah yo, I got yo' fruit. A big fuckin' banana," then he grabbed his dick at her.

Skye's mouth dropped, but she quickly shut it, narrowing her eyes to slits.

"You disrespectful bastard!"

"*I'm* disrespectful?! You just called me a fuckin' fruit, and you don't even fuckin' *know* me!"

"I don't *want* to know you!"

They were arguing from the moment that they met.

"Hey, hey! Why don't we have a drink, huh? Come on,

let's have a drink," Guy interjected, smoothly.

The five of them moved to a circular booth. Georgie and Skye glared at each other like two boxers going to neutral corners. Sid and Guy slid in first, followed by Georgie and Skye on opposite sides. Bob sat beside Skye. The waitress came and drinks were ordered and served. Skye helped Bob with his and lit another Newport.

"Well Giorgio, I *have* heard of you," Guy remarked, and they were pretty good at first...now, not so much."

Georgie finally took his glare from Skye.

"Things happen, everybody makes mistakes. But believe me, I'm the best."

"Everybody *doesn't* make mistakes; that's just some lame ass shit people say to justify that they've fucked up," Skye remarked, blowing smoke in Georgie general direction.

"Ay yo Skye, could you watch your smoke?"

Skye didn't respond. She turned to Bob and helped him with his drink like it was a sippy cup and he was a toddler.

"How we doin', Bob?"

"Okay. I just wish they'd bring the key."

"Soon."

"So where did you go to school, Giorgio?" Guy inquired.

Georgie hedged.

"Well, I've been doing hair since I was six. My mom has a shop back in Philly..."

"He asked you where you went to school, not where you discovered that you were different than all the other little boys in the sandbox," Skye sneered.

More smoke. Georgie flexed his jaws and looked dead at her. "I just asked you...*nicely*, not to do that. I'm not gonna ask you again."

Skye returned volley.

"Umm, excuse *you*. This is *my* table, so if you don't like *my* smoke, you can..." her smile said *kiss my ass*, but she concluded with a simple, "leave."

Georgie looked like a volcano about to erupt, and Skye a ballerina pirouetting on its rumbling edge.

Feeling as if her point had been made, she turned to Guy, but twisted her lips so that the smoke went directly at Georgie. Without hesitation, Georgie picked up his drink and splashed it in her face, dousing her cigarette at the same time.

"Bitch, I told you!"

With even less hesitation, Skye lunged across the table at Georgie, her hip inadvertently knocking Bob to the floor.

"I'ma kill you!" she shrieked, clawing at his face.

"Get off me," Georgie barked.

"Help!" Bob yelled, almost getting kicked by Skye's pointed heels.

He rolled himself under the table.

"Please, someone! Anyone!" Bob screamed.

But no one could hear him from under the table or over the music as the noises emanated from Georgie and Skye. Sid and Guy tried to pry them apart. Georgie had his hands around Skye's neck and Skye had her hands around Georgie's neck. Guy finally pulled Skye away.

"Get off me!   Get off me!   I'ma kill him!" Skye yelled.

"Let her go, *please*. Let her go!" Georgie seethed.

"Fuck you!" she screamed as Guy drug her off.

"Fuck you!"

"Motherfuck you!"

"Eat a dick!"

"Grow one, you fruit!"

They were still shouting obscenities when neither could hear the other as they went their separate ways. The only one left at the table—under the table—was Bob.

"Somebody…please," he mumbled, his upper lip

quivering, then he laid his head on the carpet and sobbed.

The next morning, Georgie's phone rang.
"Hello," he answered, voice sandpapered with sleep.
"Are you asleep?"
"Yeah. Who is this?"
"Good."
The crispness of satisfaction in her voice told him exactly who it was.
"How did you get my number?"
"Does it matter?" Skye sassed.
No response.
"Sid."
Georgie nodded, remembering that he gave his card to Sid the night before.
He rolled over on his back.
"What you want?"
"*I* don't want anything." she spat. "I'm doing this as a favor to Guy, who's doing a favor for Sid. Do you know where Risqué Salon is?"
"I can find it," he yawned.
"Well, find it. Be here in twenty minutes and *don't* waste my time; I *hate* for people to waste my time. Are we clear?"
"Yeah."
"Good."
Click! She hung up.
Georgie rolled over and went back to sleep.

Twenty minutes later his phone rang again. He answered.
"Yeah."
"Where are you?" she seethed.
Georgie yawned, scratched his nose.
"In the bed."
"I told you..."

Her bossy tone roused him fully from his sleep.

"Check this out, Ma. Don't nobody tell me a goddamn thing! I don't do favors and I don't need handouts! I'll shrivel up and starve in this bitch before I march to another muhfucka's drumbeat! So fuck you and fuck a favor. Call me back when you want to do business!"

Click! He hung up.

He started to get up and go piss, but the phone rang again. He smiled to himself—his armor of ego, chinkless. He let it ring five times before he answered, but he didn't say anything.

Dead air.

"I want to do business," Skye admitted, tone slightly softened.

"I'll be there in twenty minutes."

When Georgie arrived at the salon, Skye was sitting in one of the chairs, signing an autograph for a fan. There—in broad daylight—he was hit with the full force of her beauty. She was dressed in a clingy, black wool turtleneck, black stretch pants and black leather boots that came up to her knee. When she glanced at him, her eyes danced for a second before she looked away, a demur grin playing across her lips.

When he approached, she glanced at her watch.

"You're early."

"I'm all business when it comes to my money," he replied, trying to be firm. But his grin betrayed him.

"This salon belongs to a friend of mine. He said to make yourself at home," Skye informed him.

"You ready?"

"Whenever you are."

Georgie turned the chair to face the mirror and began to play in her hair. She had long, naturally curly hair, but it was frizzy and had no rhyme or reason to it.

"Who does your hair?" he asked disparagingly.

"The wind," she deadpanned.

He grabbed a handful of her hair and pulled it from her face with subtle force.

"That hurts," she said.

"Good," he retorted.

A grin curled her lips then it spread to his as they stared at each other through the mirror. He held her hair in an upsweep, then in two halves, playing with different looks.

"So what you want me to do with it?"

"You said you're the best, right? Do your best," she replied, giving him an innocent look that only the guilty can master.

He turned the chair to face him.

"I have to ask you a few questions."

"Okay."

"Why you always wear black?"

"It's a part of my image."

Georgie chuckled.

"Your name is *Skye*. How is that your image?"

"The sky is black...at night," she answered, subtle flirtation in her tone.

"Naw...the night is when the sky hides, like the night is a mask...you know? What's behind your mask?" he charmed, leaning his hands on the arm of the chair and looking into her eyes.

Skye closed her eyes tightly, like a little girl playing hide and go seek. Georgie laughed.

"Oh word, it's like that?"

"Yes. You tryin' to see into my house," Skye smirked.

"Okay. Knock, knock?"

She didn't respond.

"Maybe you didn't hear me; I said 'Knock. Knock,'" he repeated, softly, knocking gently on her forehead.

"Who's there?" she asked.

Silence...seconds ticked by. Her eyelids jumped, twitched. Finally, she opened them. George dimpled her.

"Patience. That'll always get you in."

He mused and she sat; they did the chit and the chat, talking about this and that, simply taking a stroll through conversation. Neither was trying to acknowledge the elephant in the room: the simmering chemistry between them, until he began to wash her hair. The combination of the warm water and his big, strong hands massaging her scalp made Skye remark in an unguarded moment, "I like the way your hands feel."

"Around your neck?"

Her eyes popped open and she looked at him, as if he had walked in and caught her naked.

Exposed.

Georgie's smile said that he remembered the look in her eyes the night before, when they fought and he gripped her by the throat. She tried to mask the look behind rage, but her eyes lolled like they wanted to roll up in her head. The moment was electric and he still had the nail marks in his neck to prove it.

"I don't know what you're talking about," Skye replied, her mask being a perfect poker face.

When he finished and turned her to the mirror, her face broke up like a cloudy day transitioning into a sunny smile.

"I hate to admit, this...I like," she smiled, turning her head to view it from different angles.

He had given her naturally curly hair extra kinks and framed her face with a wet, exotic look that made Skye think about blue lagoons, Caribbean breezes and ankle bracelets made of tigers' teeth.

Georgie leaned down and whispered in her ear, "It goes with black, but it is better with purple, deep...dark purple, like the twilight, right before the night puts on its mask.

The baritone of the raspy tone in his voice would have made the average woman's icing melt all over her cake, but Skye was a big girl and big girls don't...

"I don't do purple."

"You will."

A beat.

"Are you finished? May I go?"

Georgie smiled into her ear, and she knew because she heard it. He stood up, full height and removed the smock.

"Sure."

Skye stood up, rounded the chair then stepped right to him, wrapping her arms around his neck and her leg around his calf, then pushed her tongue into his mouth with the force of a home invasion, but he embraced it at the door. Their tongues swirled like yin and yang—a little of each in the other— infinitely in the moment, and when their lips parted, a thin line of saliva ran from hers to his, as if their juices weren't ready to let go.

She stepped back.

"I still want my money," Georgie chuckled.

"You just got it; you got to kiss a real woman for once," she retorted, then turned and left with a walk so nasty that a lesser man would have had to knee-walk because his legs would have gave out.

Instead, Georgie threw his head back with laughter and spun the chair so hard it twirled like a top, but his head was whirling much faster.

"Yo, I don't give a fuck *what* you say! Ain't nobody gettin' backstage without a pass, Money!" the buff, bald headed bouncer barked.

Georgie stood there, holding a bouquet of roses, getting more irked by the second by this human wall of rejection.

"Yo, I told you, I'm Skye's hair stylist."

"Fuck out my face!"

"You! Guy! Guy! It's me, Georgie! Guy!"

The irritating repetition of his name made Guy look up with a scowl. When he saw that it was Georgie, the scowl remained, but he came over.

"Yo, tell 'em I'm wit' y'all, man," Georgie urged, holding up the roses.

Guy clapped the bouncer on the shoulder.

"It's okay, Boomer; let him in."

The bouncer kept ice-grilling Georgie, but he stepped aside to let him pass. Georgie bopped by with taunt in his swag.

"Hey, Guy, I appreciate that."

"No problem. Skye looks great. I can tell she likes it because she keeps touching it," Guy told him.

"Cool. I brought her these to say thanks for the opportunity," Georgie replied, in a light tone that hid his malicious intent.

Guy chuckled.

"Hey, a little brown nosing never hurt anyone, eh?"

The shared a laugh.

"No doubt," Georgie joked.

"I'll take you to her dressing room."

"No…no, I know you're busy; just point it out."

"Third door on the right."

"Thanks."

They went their separate ways.

Georgie counted three doors, but knocked just to be sure.

"Come in!" she called out from within.

He opened the door, walked in and closed it behind him. She was alone. The first thing he noticed was what she was wearing.

Purple. Deep, dark purple.

It was a tight cat suit, something like what Apollonia would have worn in *Purple Rain*, with Skye's trademark thigh boots, which were purple too.

"Cherry, where is my..." she started to say, as she turned around, saw Georgie and froze.

"...money," he growled, finishing her statement in his own way and tossing the decoy bouquet to the side, contemptuously.

"Fuck you," she hissed.

Her words were like a match to the abrasive surface of his raw emotions that ignited, and the room exploded. He went straight to her ass and she went straight to his. Skye leapt at him like a cat with claws bared, but he caught her and sat her back hard, on the makeup table, knocking all kinds of things over. Her back slammed against the mirror, knocking it loose from its molding. It dropped, cracked and rolled over to the other side of a small love seat beside the makeup table.

"Muhfucka, that's all you got?" she bassed, trying to kick him, slap him, *something*, while he struggled to control her.

"You got a lot of goddamn mouth," he seethed.

"Then shut..." was all Skye got out before his hand locked like a vise grip around her throat and his tongue exploded in her mouth.

She bit it. He hollered into her mouth. He pinched her naked nipple through the lace. She hollered and let his tongue go, but he didn't let her nipple go. Georgie dug his fingers into the flimsy fabric, until it ripped then he proceeded to rip it further, exposing her B-cup sized breasts and erect nipples.

"You son of a bitch," she gasped, wrapping both her legs around his waist.

Georgie responded by enlarging the tear all the way to her thong, the sight of her naked flesh driving him into a frenzy. He lifted her up and pushed away at the same time to untangle himself from her legs. He dumped her on the small love seat and bent her over the arm.

"Wa – wait!"

"Shut the fuck up!" he barked back, as his jeans hit the floor and his rock hard dick hit against her ass.

He snatched her throng aside then thrust all nine inches inside of her.

"Ohhh fuck!" she creamed, his thrusts gyrating her whole body.

"Naw bitch, don't you holla now. Goddamn. Holla *now*," he gritted, alternating between long, powerful thrusts and stirring her coffee. Skye dropped her head, burying her face in the love seat to stifle her moans. Georgie grabbed her by the hair and forced her head up to look into the cracked mirror facing them.

"I want you to see who's doing this to you, so when you're sore in the morning, you'll know who did it," Georgie growled.

But Skye couldn't look, even if she wanted to. Her eyes were rolled up in the back of her head as Georgie hit that spot that made her oblivious to everything but the fire between her legs.

"Say my name," he bassed.

"Gi – Giorgio," she whispered, barely audible.

Smack! Her ass quivered and reddened from the smack.

"Say my goddamn name!"

"Giorgio!" she squealed.

Smack! The sensation of pain brought out everything animalistic in her, and she pushed back hard, knocking him off balance. He tripped over his own pants and fell into a rack of clothes that looked like something RuPaul may have left behind. He was bedded on a rainbow of silks, satins and feathered bras.

And Skye came tumbling after. She squatted down on his

dick, keeping her feet flat on the floor and her nails dug into his chest for balance.

"Oh!" he cried out.

"Don't *you* holla," she hissed lustfully, loving the agonized expression on his face. "Don't…you…god…damn…holla!" She worked her hips, fast then slow, her pussy muscles making her pussy feel so good his toes curled in his shoes.

"Say my name," she demanded.

His pride cried out, *Nigga you better not!* But when she leaned back and put one boot on his chest, her spiked heel like a dagger aimed at his heart and then squeezed his dick with her slippery wet pussy, he blurted out, "Skye!"

"Sssssssss." She sucked in air, her whole body trembling from the sensation of hearing him call out her name.

"Say it again," she gasped.

"Skyyyye," he groaned.

The word became flesh and shot through her, making her body shake like the train was coming, but when Georgie's back arched, pushing him even deeper in her and she felt his hot cum fill her up, her pussy came so hard, she saw stars.

Her arms gave out from under her and she laid on her back, satisfied. She felt like her whole body was smiling. Neither said anything for a moment, lying on their backs in opposite directions, staring at the ceiling and trying to catch their breath.

"This…" Skye began, huffing and puffing, "is not gonna end well."

Georgie replied, "But," huff, huff, "it's damn sure gonna be worth the trip!"

And it was, especially once cocaine entered the picture.

Georgie had always had a try-anything-once mentality, because he loved to live in the moment. But with cocaine, once was too much and a million times was never enough. As soon as the rush hit him and angel harps started strumming in his head, he felt like he had been holding his breath his whole life, and had finally exhaled. He had sniffed it off of Skye's naked body, inhaling the drug and her scent, and not knowing which was more addictive.

"Look in the sky," she purred, laying back on the bed, spreading her legs. "Can you see heaven?"

He entered her pearly gates over and over. He already had sexual stamina, but cocaine made him feel sexually *invincible*, and he did to Skye's body what the Devil does to an idle mind. Totally corrupted it.

Even though their connection revolved around sex, neither wanted to admit that it had quickly morphed into something much more. He even broke his own mantra, telling her "It's nothing; we're only fuckin'" but he couldn't even convince himself of that.

But it wasn't only Skye that he was feeling; it was the whole lifestyle that came with it. She was a rising star in the greatest city in the world, which in many ways is better than being a big star in the vast celebrity universe. Everything was fresh, new and exciting: the possibilities endless.

Every show that Skye did, Georgie was right there doing what he did best—being Georgie. Besides, he had his own nascent stardom to cultivate.

"Do you really do Skye's hair," the sexy Latina in a red dress asked him as they stood at the bar of the Palladium.

He licked his lips, looked her up and down slowly, then replied, "I *do*…a lot of things and I'd love to do…your hair."

She giggled like a schoolgirl.

"Lo siento, but I don't think my boyfriend would like that."

He leaned in, close to her ear so that she could feel his voice as well as hear it when he said, "Tell me you don't want to cum all over this dick, while your man thinks you're a good girl!"

He knew that he had her when her lip trembled.

"I – I have to go."

She walked away on rubbery legs and Georgie followed her with his eyes. She looked back once to see if he was watching. He blew her a kiss; she blushed. He followed her through the crowd until she reached a Spanish dude, no more than five feet even, wearing something that John Travolta might have worn in *Saturday Night Fever:* butterfly collar, hairy chest and more gold than Mr. T. The combination of cocaine and Smirnoff made Georgie bold, but seeing the Latina's man made him feel down right disrespectful.

He stalked her like a tiger would stalk a gazelle, biding his time, making eye contact, mouthing obscenities. She finally broke when he mouthed the word, "bathroom." She glanced over at her boyfriend. He seemed to be engrossed in conversation and laughter with three Latino guys. She leaned over, whispered something in his ear then slid out of the booth, pulling her tight dress back down from the hike of being seated.

Georgie instantly got hard, anticipating the conquest. He watched the jiggle in her ass and could tell that she wasn't wearing any panties. His dick leaped in his pants.

She went into the ladies' bathroom and Georgie was right behind her, ignoring the shocked look of the two women at the mirror. He grabbed her around the waist and pulled her into an empty stall, pressing her against the wall.

"Ohhh, I'm sooo wet," she cooed, as Georgie pulled her dress up over her hips. Nothing but ass and thighs fell out.

She cocked one leg on the toilet, pulling at Georgie's zipper.

"Come on, baby, I can't be gone long or my boyfriend will be mad," she whined.

"Fuck that little muhfucka," Georgie gruffed, sliding two fingers into her pussy.

"Noooo, Papi, you don't understand," she replied, melting all over his finger play.

When he saw how fast she came on his fingers, he couldn't wait to get his dick in her! He began fumbling with his belt, zipper, then—just as he was about to pull his dick out—he felt two hands the size of large oven mitts grab him by the collar and snatch him out of the stall.

"Ai-eeee!" she squealed, her dress over her belly button, looking into the beet red face of her maniac man. "Miguel! Oh my God, baby! He wouldn't stop! I told him "no" but he wouldn't stopppp!"

He knew that she was lying. He had long peeped the interaction between the two of them, but he just wanted to see how far it would go. As soon as she went to the bathroom, and he saw Georgie fall in behind her, he and his two bodyguards got up and followed them. But since he loved her, love implied that he be blind to her treachery.

But Georgie wasn't so lucky.

When they snatched Georgie out of the stall, he threw a wild, drunken haymaker that missed, but the answer didn't. It hit his stomach like a sledgehammer, bending him double over and knocking the fight out of him.

The two bodyguards were the size of small trucks and every blow felt like he got hit by one.

Crack!

The bone in his nose audibly broke as one of the bodyguards hit him with a crushing hook.

"Take him outside!" Miguel commanded.

They drug him out the bathroom door. Seeing all the blood, women shrieked and men jumped out of the way. Georgie tried to shove off and scramble away, but a swift kick that bruised his ribs quenched the attempt. They dragged him out of the fire exit into the alley behind the club.

Skye had just finished her set when she saw everyone backstage huddled around the exit door, gawking.

"Oh my God!"

"They're gonna kill him!"

Skye was used to brawls at the clubs, so she started to pay it no mind. But when a chill passed through her and her hair stood up on the back of her neck, she knew something wasn't right. She hurried down the hall, pushed through the crowd, stepped into the cool night air and lost the ability to breathe.

She saw Georgie…mangled. One bodyguard was holding him up and the other was using him for a punching bag. She was horrified. Both of his eyes were swollen, dried blood coated his face, causing the fresher flowing blood to clump. Watching the Hulk of a man punch Georgie in his face, the scene slowed in her eyes giving her a vivid view of the punches crunching Georgie's unconscious face. Blood flew from his mouth, so thick that it hit the wall two feet away, with a slap.

She snapped.

She snatched off one of her heels and leapt on the punching bodyguard's back, beating him all over the head and neck with the spiked heel.

"What the…"

"Get off of him! Get off of him!" Skye screamed like a crazed Banshee, her arm a piston of constant punishment.

The other bodyguard let Georgie's limp body slump to the ground and tried to get Skye off his partner's back.

"Man, get this bitch," he barked, his arms too buff to reach back and get a grip on Skye. Each blow felt like an angry bee that was dotting his face with stinging red welts.

His partner snatched her off him and tossed her on the pile of garbage bags lining the alley. She scrambled over to Georgie and laid her body on his.

"Hit me, you piece of shit! Beat *me*, if you're such a bad muhfucka!" she taunted.

Without hesitation, he drew back to deliver a ham fisted blow.

"Enough!"

His hand froze mid swing. He stepped back. When he did, Skye was able to see the short man and the woman in the red dress.

He stepped forward and looked down at her, studying her terrified—but defiant—expression.

"Do you know who I am!" he asked.

She nodded. Everyone did. He was one of the biggest cocaine dealers in New York.

"Miguelito," Skye replied.

"This man disrespected me with my mujer and you intervene?" Miguelito questioned his expression hard and unyielding.

It was at that moment that she found out what Georgie had done. It was at that moment that she realized that she had to either get up, walk away and not look back or stay no matter what it cost her. It was that moment that she knew she loved him.

Skye looked at Miguelito, and a single tear that rolled down her cheek was her resolute reply.

Miguelito followed the tear on its trek and it seemed to soften him.

"I know who you are, too… I like your music," he smiled, wiping the tear from her chin with his thumb, then added, "Love is blind, who am I to judge?" he said, turning to give his *mujer* a withering look. He stopped, pondered then looked at his bodyguards.

"Let's go."

As the four of them began to walk away, Miguelito looked at Georgie's broken body like a hungry lion that had been pulled off of a dying carcass.

"Tu tienes suerte, maricon," he spat.

As soon as they had left, Skye began screaming, "Please! Somebody, help me! Get an ambulance! Please help!"

Re-emerging into consciousness felt almost aquatic for Georgie. All the sounds around him—the hum and the beeps of the monitors, the footsteps and closing doors—all sounded muffled and garbled as if he was under water. He was also so heavily medicated that it altered his reality but did almost nothing for the pain. His whole body throbbed and made him will himself back under. As he sank, a face appeared above the shimmering water.

"Anya," he said, like Citizen Kane's Rosebud, "you came back," he smiled.

And then…he faded…

A few days later, his eyes popped open and he was fully aware. The pain was still sharp and pervaded his body, but he now embraced consciousness and tried to sit up.

"Aarrggh!" he bellowed.

Bad idea.

His cry awoke Skye from her sleep. She uncurled her legs from the chair and walked over to him on bare feet. She smiled down on him sweetly, moved his hair from his face and the first thing that she said to him was, "You look like shit."

He wanted to laugh, but something told him that it would

hurt too much. He settled for a default, "Fuck you."

She smiled, cocked her head to the side like a curious bird.

"I like your nose, though. It's like...crooked, makes you look tough."

This time he did laugh, then sucked in his breath with a wince.

"So I got my ass tore out the frame and it makes me tough, huh?"

"I said *look* tough; you still a little punk," she joked, leaning over and kissing him, finally exhaling her anxiety. A tremble ran through her. She put her forehead on his.

"I didn't know if I'd ever be able to do that again," she whispered, slightly choked up.

"Ma, come here."

"I'm here."

"No. *Here*," he repeated, taking her hand and pulling her up on the bed.

Skye got up and straddled him. It was then that he noticed that she had on the same thing that she had on that night at the club.

Georgie frowned.

"How long was I out?"

"Five days."

"And you've been here ever since?"

She nodded.

He paused.

"I bet that coochie stiiiink!" he teased.

She hit him, playfully.

"Shut up, it does not. I've been washing up in the bathroom. Being serious though, Georgie, I was scared to death. I – I didn't know what to do, who to call..." she told him, her voice rising and falling with relived emotions. She shook her head. "I called the number on your card and no one answered but your voicemail and I realized I didn't know anything about you but your name. I couldn't call your family to tell them where you were and if you had…" her voice trailed off into sobs.

He pulled her to him, hugging her tightly, even though the extra weight had his cracked ribs screaming.

"Shhh, chill Ma, we good, okay? I'm not goin' anywhere," he vowed.

Skye sat up, looked him in the eyes and replied, "Promise." It was a demand, not a question.

"Promise," he affirmed.

"You're never going to leave me?"

"Never…even if your coochie stink," he replied.

They laughed. He reached up and caressed her cheek.

"I love you," he said, his smile tender, almost beatific.

The words warmed her, but the smile made her wince.

Because she had seen it before.

The night that he had come to. She saw his stirring, saw his eyes flutter open. She rushed to his side and peered down at him.

"Anya…you came back," he had said, and then he smiled the same smile, one she would never forget.

Anya.

The way he had said it, she longed to hear him say her name that way.

Anya.

Her thoughts tormented her. She half expected a woman, a wife? An *Anya* to come through the door and reclaim her place, turn, point at Skye and say, "Who is this imposter?!"

Skye had cried for the rest of the night. Who was she? What was she? What did she look like? Did she leave? Or die? Death would be better, but much too permanent. Like a stain you can't get out, and even if you could, the place where it was would remain to remind you.

Skye decided that Anya was dead, and—if she wasn't—

she would strangle the bitch herself.

Georgie felt the wince.

"What's wrong?"

She mustered a smile.

"Nothing…I know what happened at the club.

He looked at her.

"Skye, I'm…"

She put her finger to his lips.

"Georgie, I lay with you…I know you, I know who you are. So understand when I say this, I'll put up with the hoes, but not another woman.

Their eyes shared a look of understanding that would serve to be the forbidden tree in their garden.

"I understand."

Skye smiled and caressed his cheek.

"Poor Georgie, don't let this world love you to death, baby."

Georgie pulled into the parking lot of the State Correctional Institution - Smithfield, a close custody prison located in Huntingdon, Pennsylvania. His head was banging. He had been in the hospital for over three months and he constantly got headaches. He was starting to believe the doctor when he said that he would have headaches for the rest of his life. The only upside was the virtual lifetime prescription for an opioid analgesic which preceded—but had properties similar to—oxycontin. He reached into his tote bag and pulled out the bottle, took two pills then put it back. He then glanced around the parking lot and fished under the seat for his stash of coke. He took a "two on" to each nostril then returned it to the stash. He checked his nose for residue in the rearview mirror, stopping to admire his new haircut—a curly fade—at the same time. He stepped out of the car, brushing off his silk pants then chirped the alarm on his brand new, silver '96 Infiniti Q45 with peanut butter interior, sitting on twenty-inch deep dish hammers. The car hadn't even hit the market yet. Expensive, but he could afford it now that Skye had inked a deal with a major label.

Her new single, "Like a Tiger," was so hot, American Records—one of the biggest labels in the world—had bought her contract out and signed her to an album deal with a seven figure advance. Georgie was officially known as her stylist, but anybody in the know knew that he was much more.

With the cocaine accelerating the effects of the pills, he felt laid back but wired, relaxed with pep as he Philly-bopped through the prison gates.

Women who had come to see boyfriends, fiancés and husbands eyed him like a nice substitute for a cold, lonely night—*any* night actually, in many cases.

The visitors were led through a maze of sliding doors, buzzing gates, beeping metal detectors and were all but stripped-searched before they arrived at the inner sanctum of the visitation room.

"Daddy!" little children cried as they ran into open arms.

"Baby!" mothers and wives and fiancés sang as they were enveloped in loving embraces.

"My man!" Georgie chortled, as he and K.B. embraced.

"What up, my nigga!   I see you finally cut that Miami Vice-ass pony tail off your damn head," K.B. cracked.

Georgie laughed and ran his hand over his curly fade.

"I mean, your girl loved it, but since I left Philly, I ain't been hittin' that lately," Georgie cracked back.

K.B. knuckled up.

"Shit, you might as well hit it. Jody got her now!"

They both laughed.

"Don't worry, player, you'll be back in no time. What you

got, three more years?"

K.B. nodded.

"Three and a half."

After a short pause, Georgie remarked, "Why you do it, K? You had it *all*. You could be about to go pro *right now*."

K.B sighed hard and ran both his hands over his waves, then looked Georgie in his eyes and replied, "You know how fuckin' *mad* I was with you when you left, yo? I went by your house and your moms was like, 'he gone to New York.' I felt like we was in a bar fight surrounded by muhfuckas, but when I turned around, ain't no *we*, 'cause *you* was *gone*.

Georgie dropped his head, but quickly lifted it to defend his decisions.

"Ay yo K…"

"Hol' up, let me finish…let me finish. You asked why I did it. You know why? Because it was my *excuse*."

"Excuse?"

"Excuse to fail," K.B. spat, and Georgie could see the tears that he was holding back because he refused to cry in a prison visitation room.

K.B. chuckled to juggle his emotions.

"You said I had it all. You know what comes with 'all'? *Everything*. The world on my back! All of Philly! If I went to Duke, all of *Philly* was goin' to Duke! But if *I* failed…if *I* failed, I failed Philly, too! And I couldn't do it Georgie, I couldn't take that chance and go to Duke, fail and come back what? A loser? Fuck no. I'll never be a 'has been.' I'd rather be a 'could've been,'" K.B concluded then sat back, glad to have finally gotten it off his chest.

"You were scared," Georgie surmised, not with judgment or contempt, but with understanding and acceptance.

"Damn right, I was scared. Scared to fuckin' death. Crazy, right? I don't know, but here I am in the State Pen instead of Penn State," he chuckled, bitterly shaking his head at his own faulty logic.

Georgie looked at his own folded hands, then back at K.B.

"What can I do, Ock? I got a little somethin' goin' with Skye. So I ain't hurtin' for nothing."

He looked at him skeptically, like Arnold at Willis.

"Skye who? That badass singer? Get the fuck outta here! You a bad muhfucka G, but you ain't that bad!"

Georgie laughed hard, kissed his hand then held it up.

"That's my word, K. That's my lady!"

K.B. twisted up his lips.

"Send me flicks! I want lingerie back shots!"

"Nigga, fuck you; all I'm sendin' you is ass shots of a fat nigga in a thong!"

They both laughed, letting the tears flow, camouflaged.

"On the real G, I'm proud of you, yo. I'm still mad at you though."

"I know, K…"

"For not takin' me with you."

They looked at each other, smiles gone—replaced with solemn sincerity.

The visit ended and they hugged. They had last seen each other as boys, but had reunited as men.

Georgie returned to his mother's house to the sounds of raucous laughter and loud music. He walked into the kitchen to find Skye and his mother huddled over a photo album, a bottle of Tanqueray and their cigarettes smoldering in the ashtray, side by side. He was relieved to see them hit it off, which was far from guaranteed, because they were both strong-willed women. When he had left, Skye was acting timid and his mother, politely cordial.

"Skye is such a pretty name. Is it your real name?"

"Yes ma'am. My mom was a sixties hippie."

"I see."

118

"My mom's White."

Now, they were acting like road dogs from way back. When he entered the kitchen, they both looked up.

"Hey, baby!" Skye chimed, with a look that said she was two steps from tipsy.

He kissed her and sat down beside her.

"How is K.B.?" Stephanie asked.

"Good," he replied, grabbing the Tanqueray and drinking straight from the bottle.

"Georgie! Stop bein' so damn ghetto! Get a glass!" Stephanie scolded him.

He chuckled and filled Skye's glass up.

"I'm glad to see y'all getting to know one another."

"Actually, I'm getting to know you, too," Skye snickered, inhaling her Newport, then added as she exhaled, "I didn't know your first girlfriend was plastic."

"Huh?" he grunted, not catching on.

Stephanie flipped the photo album back to a page and pointed to a picture that he knew quite well. His eyes got big.

"Ma! Forreal?! I can't believe you put me out like that!" He barked indignantly, but with an edge of humor.

He looked down at the picture. It was a picture of him at seven, asleep with his doll baby wrapped up snugly with him.

"Boy, hush. Many times I caught you humpin' this thing, it should be a part of the family!" Stephanie cracked.

She and Skye laughed like schoolgirls. Georgie shook his head, trying to conceal his grin.

"Ma, you know you dead wrong for that."

Stephanie waved him off as she gulped her Tanqueray.

"And speaking of dead wrong, Skye told me what you did to her when y'all met."

"What I did to her?! She ain't tell you about blowing smoke in my face, Ma," he retorted.

The two women giggled, conspiratorially. Georgie was

lost.

"What?"

Stephanie shook her head.

"Boy, don't you know what it means when a woman blow smoke in your face?"

"She want her ass whooped?" he asked, only half jokingly.

Skye bumped her body against his.

"No."

"What then?"

"Nothing," Stephanie replied, winking at Skye.

Georgie looked at Skye with a slight scowl.

"What it mean, yo?"

"Why you lookin' at me like that, like you a bully? I'm supposed to be scared?" Skye sassed.

Skye's pager went off. She reached down and unclipped it from her purse on the floor and read it.

"Sound check," she told Georgie. "You ready?"

"Naw, not until somebody tell me what it mean!"

Neither woman paid him any mind as they moved for the door.

After the show, Georgie took his mother back home.

"I like this. This is nice. It's a Q45?" Stephanie inquired.

"Yeah," Georgie replied. "Why, you want one? I'ma get you one."

Stephanie chuckled.

"Boy, I don't need no new car. I'm fine. What I need is a vacation!"

"Then I'ma send you to the moon, Alice!"

They laughed.

"I like Skye, Georgie. She's a little quirky, but that's the white girl in her. But she's crazy about you and she got fire. You need that," she surmised.

"She definitely got that," he snickered, then added, "Now,

are you gonna tell me about the smoke?"

Stephanie laughed.

"It's voodoo."

He glanced at her to check her expression.

"No it ain't."

"Oh yes it is. Trust me. When a woman blows smoke in your face, it means she's trying to cast a spell on you," Stephanie explained, then looked at him. "And from the looks of things, it worked."

Georgie couldn't argue with her assessment, as his mind imagined Skye blowing smoke at him—then winking.

On the elevator up to their hotel room, Georgie thought about what K.B. had said about being scared of failure, so he failed on purpose. He wondered how many young Black men every day, over the years were doing—will do—the same thing. As he arrived at the room, his mind was on the unfairness of the game and the stacked deck that some people had to face, so he was totally unprepared to hear Skye say, "Look, Georgie!"

He looked as she held up an inflated fuck doll.

"Your dolly grew up!"

He fell out laughing.

Looking down from the 81st floor of the mammoth American Records skyscraper made Georgie feel like if he went to the roof, he could touch Cloud Nine. The height was almost mystical. The combination of altitude and cocaine made Georgie feel weightless. He halfway expected things to start floating.

He, Skye, and Guy were sitting on one side of a long, oval cherry oak conference table, while a music director stood by an easel that displayed the story board, and Ray Devers—the head of American Records—sat at the head of the table, hands tented, taking it all in.

"Believe me Skye, you're going to love it!" the music director—who looked almost like Richard Dreyfuss—raved. "This video is going to make 'Like a Tiger' absolutely junglistic."

He laughed, making Skye giggle at his excitement.

"We're going to have *live* tigers on the set. Imagine that: big, thick jungle leaves, the tigers roar, the sun explodes! You come out of the lagoon like Venus singing 'Like a Tiger,'" he sang.

"I love it," Skye exclaimed, caught up in the excitement of doing her first video.

"Yeah, this is gonna be *big*!" Guy chimed in.

Georgie looked skeptical.

"Why does the sun explode?" Georgie asked.

"What?" the music director asked, his expression strained, impatient with the interruption.

"The sun. I asked why does it explode? What's the point?"

"The *point* is, she *is* the *sky* and her energy explodes like the sun."

"So why does she rise up out of the water?" Georgie countered.

Cornered and frustrated, the music director looked at Ray, while Ray was looking at Georgie as if he was studying him.

"Okay, who are you anyway? Aren't you, like, the *hairdresser*?" the music director asked, attempting to sound as condescending as possible.

Georgie wanted to spazz on him, but he didn't want to mess up anything for Skye, so he flinched his jaw muscles to fight back the urge.

"No, he's not just the hairdresser; he's my creative consultant," she answered, looking at Georgie with a look that gave him wings

Georgie turned back to the music director.

"I don't like it. It sounds more like a Vegas show than a music video. This isn't just about the song; it's about exhibiting Skye as an artist. It's to be her first impression. The video shouldn't be like a tiger; *Skye* should be like a tiger!"

"Branding," Ray added in. "You're talking about branding."

"Yeah...branding," Georgie repeated, like he knew the word all along, giving Ray an appreciative nod.

Seeing the argument tilting to Georgie's favor, the music director decided to lean, too.

"So how do you propose that we do *that*?"

Georgie sat back thinking, then he got up and walked

around the table to the storyboard.

"I like the jungle theme…fuck that live tiger shit, ain't no way Skye gonna be around no goddamn tiger," he mumbled, more to himself but loud enough to make Ray chuckle.

When Georgie turned around, he was smiling mischievously.

"We're going to may *you* a tiger," he remarked, gazing at Skye. Instead of the sun exploding, the sun and the moon come together in an eclipse. Skye, in the jungle begins to turn into a tiger, transforming like the movie, *Cat People*, but sexier. She can wear those cat eye contacts, like in *Thriller* and we keep flashing back and forth between her crawling on all fours and a real tiger. Do that thing where you put her mouth on the tiger's face, so it's like the tiger's singing the song," Georgie envisioned.

"Now *that*, I really love!" Skye clapped.

The music director nodded, eyebrows raised.

"Hmph…that could work. We could CGI the tiger morphs…be a bit more expensive but…" the music director mused.

"She's worth every cent," Georgie said, winking at Skye.

"Especially since we're paying for it," Guy quipped, sarcastically.

"Scared money don't make money, Guy!" Georgie retorted, but grinned to keep it polite.

Guy subtly bristled.

Georgie looked at Ray.

"There's more."

"More?" Skye echoed.

Georgie nodded, keeping his eyes locked on Ray's.

"Change the beat."

"Do what?" Guy exploded, feeling a need to show a modicum of presence. "Are you crazy?! The record is a *smash*; it's why we got the deal in the first place! Skye baby, this is crazy."

Skye looked at Georgie.

"Baby, Guy does have a point."

"Skye, listen…the track is house music. Perfect for New York, but it's too fringe for mainstream. You think about Madonna. All her early music is house, but when she went pop is when she *became* Madonna, you see? And Baby, *believe* me, you *will* be bigger, you're gonna own the *world*, but we've got to expand the audience," Georgie explained.

No one said anything for a moment. Finally, Ray said, "It makes sense. It makes a lotta sense. When we do a remix for a record, it's to extend the life of rotation. But no one's done it with a video format, so if it fails, we'll know who to blame."

Ray gave Georgie a knowing look with a suppressed smirk, and Georgie grasped the implication immediately.

"So, can we still use Andre?" the music director asked.

"Andre?" Georgie echoed. "Who the hell is Andre?"

"I am Andre."

Skye and Georgie were standing on the stage at a small theater, with a man Georgie had to fight not to laugh at. He was dark skinned with a pompadour hairdo, wearing a leopard leotard and carrying a wooden staff as tall as he was. When Georgie first laid eyes on him, the first thing he thought about was Debbie Allen in *Fame*.

But for Skye, it was no laughing matter.

"I love you, you're my favorite choreographer; I've admired your work for years. It's an honor to work with you," she gushed, extending her hand for a shake.

Andre looked at it, like it had shit all over it.

"Yes it issssss, but I don't touch…people," he sniffed, disdainfully. "So much negative energy in the world, which I must avoid from others." He concluded, giving Georgie a subtle—but approving—once over, before turning back to Skye. "Shall we get started?"

"I'm ready!" Skye exclaimed, practically bubbling.

She kissed Georgie with a peck then followed Andre like a puppy with its tail wagging. Georgie chuckled and headed back into the seats. He sat a few rows back, one row behind Guy, who was talking incessantly on a mobile phone. Georgie watched Skye rehearse with the seven other dancers until Guy hung up and began to dial another number. Georgie leaned forward, resting his elbows on the seat back beside Guy.

"Hey Guy, I didn't mean anything at the meeting the other day," Georgie apologized because he could tell that Guy was still feeling a way about it.

Guy shrugged it off.

"No big deal kid, I'm a big boy, besides we're on the same team, right?"

The words said one thing, but Guy's tone said something else.

"Right," Georgie replied, and leaned back in his seat while Guy made another call.

Georgie had begun to nod off when he heard, "No! No! No! What are you *doing*? My *God*, you are uncoordinated!"

He looked up and saw Andre berating Skye.

"It's not bam, bam, step; it's bam bam...step," he ranted, demonstrating the move. "Now do it again!"

Georgie bristled at the way he was talking to Skye.

"Who the fuck this muhfucka think he is?? Lydia?!" Georgie gruffed.

"He's supposed to be the top choreographer. All the stars use him," Guy explained.

"He's gonna *see* stars if he don't learn how to talk to people," Georgie grumbled. Georgie stayed alert, hawkeyed and itching.

"You are *terrible*! How can you be this stupid?!" Andre shrieked.

"I – I'm sorry Andre, I'm really trying," Skye replied, almost in tears.

Georgie was out of his seat and on the stage as soon as the light was reflected by her shiny cornea. He walked up to her, taking her by the arms.

"Baby, take a breather. Let me speak to Andre, okay?"

She nodded and walked off. Georgie turned to Andre with a smile so wide, it hurt.

"Andre, can I have a word with you back stage? Please honor me with your presence, un momento," Georgie requested with a sugary tone.

Having already approved of Georgie's "energy," Andre deigned to accompany him backstage, looking like a lamb going to slaughter.

As soon as they were behind the curtain, Andre turned to Georgie, like the Queen of England and said, "What is—"

Wap!

Georgie slapped Andre in the face. He dropped his staff, his eyes got big and he took a flood of air, ready to bellow.

"Shh, shh, shh! Don't do that. I swear – I swear to God, I'll do it again! Calm down!" Georgie whispered feverishly.

Andre shut his mouth and let the air our of his nose, eyes trembling, following Georgie's every move.

"Now listen, you fuckin' faggot, that's my lady out there, okay? Now I know everyone thinks she's like Miss Invincible, but deep down, she only wants to be loved, you got me, and right now, she isn't feeling any love," Georgie growled in rapid fashion.

"But I was just—"

"No, it's not your turn yet, okay? Just listen. Now this is what we're gonna do. We're gonna go over there and be nice, right?"

Andre just nodded, remembering that it wasn't his turn to talk.

"And put on the happy face, right? Put it on; let me see it."

Andre smiled, a panicked smile, like Diana Ross in *Mahogany*, right before the crash.

"Oh beautiful, I love it. See? Positive energy," Georgie remarked, pinching Andre's cheeks. "One more thing. When I called you a fuckin' faggot, I was wrong, okay? I respect your homosexuality; that's why I'm back here, treating you like a bitch. By law, I'm supposed to be kickin' your ass, okay? Okay, now, happy face... Perfect. Pick up your staff. There you go," Georgie remarked, turned Andre around by the shoulders, slapped him on the ass. "Now, go light up the sky like a flame."

For the rest of the rehearsal, there were happy faces for everyone.

As soon as they got in the limo, Skye was all over Georgie. She hiked up her skirt and straddled his lap.

"That was wonderful! Don't you just love Andre? Where's the candy?" she questioned, darting in and out of Georgie's pockets.

He chuckled at her friskiness, until she found the bottle of coke in his hoodie pocket.

"Yeah, I love 'em to death. Damn, Ma, slow down; you gonna save some for me?"

Using the little spoon attached to the inside of the bottle lip, Skye scooped out hits of cocaine, two for her then two for Georgie.

"Ay Skye...Ma, look at me."

Skye put the coke up then focused on Georgie. He took her face in his hands.

"Ma, you can't let people get to you like that, okay? None

of this shit really matters, you know; they can kiss our ass," Georgie told her.

"Oh yeah, I almost forgot. We'll shrivel up and starve before we march to another muhfucka's drumbeat, huh?" Skye laughed, reminding Georgie of his own words.

He chuckled.

"No doubt."

"You'd starve with me?"

"Starve, shrivel, eat beans out the can, rob a bank; what you wanna do next?" he smirked.

Skye bit her bottom lip seductively then leaned close to Georgie's ear.

"Doing all those sexy dances made my pussy so fuckin' wet 'cause all I could think about was your big, juicy dick fuckin' me into a coma." She purred, then brought her finger up from her pussy and put it in his mouth. "See?"

Once he tasted her juices, his dick boned instantly. She began kissing him passionately and fumbling for his zipper.

"Ma," he tried to resist between kisses. "We in a limo. The driver can see us."

"I don't care," she hissed passionately between clenched teeth. "I want to *fuck!*"

The passion of her kiss overruled his every objection. Georgie lifted her so she could pull his pants down to his thighs, then she gripped and squeezed his dick. Georgie pushed her skirt up and tried to slide her panties to the side, but the positioning made it impossible.

"Rip 'em," she groaned.

Riiiip!

Once freed, her pussy pulsated and throbbed, begging to be filled.

"Put it in, Georgie!" she squealed.

He slid low in the seat, spreading his legs for leverage as he pushed deep inside of her.

"Ooooh!" she moaned, throwing her head back as she rode him, hard and fast. He cupped her ass and spread her pussy lips wider, changing the angle so he could bang her walls. Her whole body shuddered.

"Take this dick like a big girl," he grunted.

"I – I am; oooh fuck me Georgie, fuck meeeee! I – I feel it, I feel it," she panted and Georgie knew she was in that blissful state of closeness.

He speeded up his thrusts until their bodies were clapping together, trying to pace his release to coincide with hers.

"I'm ready, Georgie!"

Their rhythm built, powerful and strong, faster and harder until they climaxed and came like…

Boom!

For a fraction of a millisecond, Skye thought she had come so hard that the earth moved. But then she realized that it wasn't her, and he realized that it wasn't him, and they both realized that it wasn't them. It was the driver. He had run a red light and had an accident in the intersection, ultimately backing up traffic in a four block radius.

He had tried to ignore it. He had been driving limos a long time, so he had seen a lot of things. But the sight of Skye's pretty ass bouncing up and down and hearing her sultry sex song, he couldn't keep his eyes on the road or his mind on driving.

"I – I'm sorry sir, ma'am," he apologized sheepishly.

Georgie and Skye looked at each other and busted out laughing, while outside, horns blasted, cabbies cursed and a multitude of people were forced to bask in their post-coital bliss.

"Don't worry yo, just make sure when the press ask, tell 'em you were watching us fuck!" Georgie instructed him.

Georgie had an uncanny knack for using the moment to his advantage, and he proved it with the limo scenario. As soon as word got out as to why midtown traffic was backed up, the newspapers jumped all over it. The *Village Voice*, in Michelle's "Cliché Corner," a short piece in the Life section of the *Daily News*, and the *Post* gave the headline, "*Stuck* in Traffic." There was even a picture of Georgie and Skye—with that freshly-fucked look— getting into a cab leaving the scene. The incident gave her an even bigger buzz when a State Legislator in Albany introduced legislation banning all sex acts in limousines and taxis because it was both a "moral and traffic hazard." The legislators couldn't stop laughing long enough to vote on the bill.

All the publicity just made the single hotter and anticipation for her video more intense.

"Ma, you trust me?"

"Yes," she replied, without hesitation.

They were in the trailer on the set of the video shoot. She was sitting in the salon chair and he was standing behind her. They were looking at each other through the mirror.

"You know what I thought to myself when I first saw you?"

"What a bitch?" she quipped.

Georgie shook his head, keeping his gaze steady and solemn.

"No. I said, 'that's a goddess.' You owned me from jump. When you walk out of this trailer onto that screen and into the hearts of millions, that's what I want them to see, too. A goddess. Will you let me do that?"

Staring into the reflection of his grey eyes and his voice felt like warm brandy in her ears. Skye was almost mesmerized. How could she say no?

"Yes."

Georgie smiled.

"Okay... Close your eyes, and when you open them, you'll see what the world will see."

Skye's eyes fluttered closed.

Several times, she wanted to peek, especially when she felt the snip of her first fallen lock of hair.

"Georgie!" she gasped, with a start.

"Shhhh... Trust me, baby."

And she did, agonizing minute after agonizing minute, until they linked and seemingly stretched into an agonizing forever, prompting Skye to impatiently whine, "Georgieeee."

"Almost finished."

And then he was.

"Okay...you can open them now."

She did. She saw. She marveled in awe.

"I'm...beautiful," she gasped.

Georgie smiled like a proud father.

"You were already beautiful, Skye; this is just another interpretation of it."

She loved the short, pixie cut, the sharp, ice pick sideburns and razor-edged definition. But most of all, she loved the color: sky blue with frosted tips of white.

"I love it, baby; I love you," she cooed.

"I love you too," he said, and then...

He smiled.

It was the smile she'd never forget. *Anya*. But this time, she imagined that it was for her.

Georgie could do no wrong. The video was a smash. It pushed the single into double platinum status because everyone wanted the video version remix. The album became one of the most anticipated of the year. The album advertisements were everywhere, but Georgie's favorite was the gigantic billboard in Times Square. It featured the album's artwork of a gorgeous blue sky. Skye's face was superimposed, as if it was that of a goddess. She seemed to be one with the sky, and the sky blue contacts made the picture that much more vivid.

"I hate the contacts; they make me look like a white girl," Skye complained.

"You're half white. Embrace your inner Caucasian," Georgie cracked.

Everything was going Georgie's way...until the *Rolling Stone* cover.

"No, Georgie! *Hell* fuckin' no! I'm doing this cover!" Skye screamed as she and Georgie squared off in her living room.

"Georgie, you've got to be joking," Guy chuckled, shaking his head. He was just glad that he and Skye were on the same page for a change. Lately, it had been like Georgie was running the show.

"Skye, just hear me out!"

"For what?! You're talking crazy right now! It's fuckin' *Rolling Stone* magazine, Georgie! They want me on the cover, and I don't even have an album out! It's unheard of !" Skye exclaimed.

"Unprecedented," Guy seconded.

Georgie snorted a frustrated sigh.

"So...the...fuck...*what*?! Why do you think they want you on the cover?! To promote you?! Fuck no. It's to sell magazines."

"Yeah, and both hands wash the face," Guy retorted, his expression like, C'mon, man!

Georgie pointed at Guy.

"I'm not talkin' to you."

Guy bristled.

"The hell you mean, you're not talkin' to me?! I'm her manager. *I* make the decisions!"

"Ay yo Guy, who are you barkin' at?" Georgie hissed, taking a menacing step toward Guy.

Guy didn't back down. Skye stepped in between them, putting her hands on Georgie's chest.

"Baby, baby, look at me. Look at me. Calm down, okay? Just make your point."

Georgie glared at Guy and Guy glared back for an extra beat, then Georgie began to pace as he spoke.

"All I'm sayin' is, I get that it's *Rolling Stone*, but that's exactly my point! You're *supposed* to do the cover if they ask, because *everybody* does. Who the fuck would say 'no' to *Rolling Stone*? But if you do it, it's no big deal. People will forget about it in a month," Georgie surmised, then stopped pacing and approached Skye. "But if you say 'no,' then everyone will want to know *why*. MTV will want to know why, BET will want to know why, *VIBE*, *Spin*, see? We give up one cover and I guarantee you, we get three more to replace it."

Skye raised her eyebrows.

"I hadn't looked at it like that," she admitted.

"And what if it doesn't work, huh?" Guy snorted. "What if they just think she's some vain cunt that believes her own hype? Then what we got? Dick! That's what."

Georgie looked Guy in the eyes and replied, "These are the types of decisions that make life worth living. You want security, get a nine to five."

The room got quiet and Skye weighed her options.

"Skye, as *your manager*, I can't let you do this. It's too risky. Once you're established, yeah, but not now," he advised.

She looked at Georgie then back at Guy.

"Call *Rolling Stone*...tell 'em I said...no," Skye announced.

Georgie smiled and winked. Guy chuckled to himself.

"Did anyone else feel that?"

"Feel what, Guy?" Skye questioned, her tone neutral but

expecting a snide remark.

"The plates just shifted," he retorted, then walked out.

Georgie and Skye looked at each other. They knew what was coming next.

A couple of days later, Georgie invited Guy to a bar and grill around the corner from Skye's apartment. Guy arrived a few minutes after him, looked around then spotted Georgie and came over to the table. Georgie stood as he approached to shake his hand.

"How you, Guy?"

"Gettin' old in a city forever young, but other than that, I'm peachy," Guy joked.

They sat down. Georgie waved the waitress over.

"What you drinkin' Guy? It's on me."

"Bourbon, and sweetheart put the ice cubes in first, will you? I hate when they bruise the bourbon," Guy stressed.

The redheaded waitress gave him a wink.

"Southern style, I got you," she said, turning to Georgie. "Another?"

"For now," Georgie flirted, watching her as she walked away.

He looked back when he heard Guy laughing.

"What?"

"Kid, are you even old enough to drink?"

Georgie smiled.

"My I.D. says I am."

"Not even old enough to drink; how are ya gonna handle managin' a megastar?" Guy questioned.

Georgie looked at him, as if he had beat him to the punch. Guy smiled knowingly.

"That's what this is about, right? Firing me?"

Georgie finished off his first drink, as the waitress brought the other, then sashayed away, now fully aware that Georgie was watching.

"We were thinking of splitting the duty. I'd be more of the road manager," Georgie proposed.

Guy sipped his Bourbon then waved him off.

"Never work. I'd be there just to get my brain picked, while you'd have veto power, carte blanche. A clean break's better," Guy surmised, sipping his drink again, then mused, "You know, maybe I shoulda tried my hand with Skye. No offense, but it seems the only managers that last are the ones layin' the talent...like Jon Peters and Barbra Streisand. Matter of fact, he started out as a hairdresser, just like you."

"Never heard of 'em," Georgie spat, cockily.

"Yeah well, he's over at Sony Pictures now, running the whole show. You could learn a thing or two from that guy."

"Come on Guy, think about our offer. There's still a lot I don't know. I admit that. And you have my word, if we ever bump heads, I'll come to you first to straighten it," Georgie offered.

Guy sighed wistfully.

"Naw kid, I think this is for the best. Besides, you'll do fine. You're smart, quick on your feet, and the broads love you. And in this business, beauty covers a multitude of sins. Me? I guess I'm a saint," Guy cracked, making Georgie chuckle. He downed his drink and paused as if considering something. "You know Georgie, I like you. You have a zeal that can take you far in this business, but it can be your downfall, too. It's a tightrope, but if you can walk it, you've got it made.

Georgie nodded. Guy stood up.

"Stay. Have one more," Georgie urged.

"I've got a date. Now that I'm unemployed, I figure I'll need a sugar mama, too," Guy winked.

Georgie laughed and they shook hands.

"Take care, Guy."

"You do the same."

Guy walked away and the waitress came over.

"Need anything else?" she asked.

Georgie looked her up and down, licked his lips and replied, "Yeah. What time you get off?"

The waitress bit her bottom lip.

When Georgie got home, he found Skye playing the piano. He knew that she hadn't heard him come in because when she played she usually got lost in the vibrations. He leaned against the exposed brick of her apartment and watched her. She was wearing only his Philadelphia Eagles jersey and she had a blue bandana wrapped around her head. He waited for her to stop playing and mark notes on the music sheet before he spoke.

"That's a pretty melody," he remarked, approaching.

She turned to him with a beaming smile.

"Oh hey baby, I didn't hear you come in."

"I know," he chuckled.

"You like it? It's not finished. I've got a lot of tinkering to do," she said, picking up her cigarette out of the ashtray and taking a drag.

"You got the lyrics yet?"

"Yeah; well, kinda. You want to hear it?"

"Of course. You know I love to hear you sing," he replied, his smirk saying he was referring to another kind of song.

"So nasty," Skye blushed, then turned back to the piano and putt her cigarette in the ashtray. Ready?"

"Yep."

Georgie rested his elbows on the piano as she began. The

song was in A Minor, giving it a melancholy brood that complemented her husky hum. Then she opened her mouth like a bird, and the lyrics took flight:

Have you ever loved without taking off your clothes,
Have you ever been with someone who really knows,
Knows you …
Deeply …
Completely …
Like a melody of ecstasy,
I want to sing you …

Even though he was smiling, deep down she was killing him softly with her song. The words spoke of something deeper, fuller, richer and stood in secret condemnation of the fact that he had just fucked the redheaded waitress in the staircase of her tenement building. The contrast was nearly perfect. While she was singing of pure love, his mind couldn't help but reflect on the pure lust he had just committed. The pure animal heat that he felt as he grabbed the redhead on the darkened stairwell, like a stalker snatching his victim into the shadows. The way he clawed and pulled, it would look like she was resisting if played in reverse. The way she cried out when he entered her with pure abandonment, slamming her back against the wall with every thrust. The way she cursed when she came and the way he came when she cursed. He thought about it all when Skye sang:

Have you ever been with someone who knows.

He realized that he didn't even know the redhead's name. Georgie looked into Skye's face, her fluttering eyelids—now open, now closed, now in the room, now in the music— seeing all the fire and vulnerability that little girls are truly made of, and he realized how much he truly loved her, but could never love her truly because he loved too easily. Georgie loved with a spatula and not a spoon. The realization had him spaced.

"Georgie? Did you hear me? I said, do you like it?" Skye asked, the anxiety of an artist coloring her voice.

He blinked back, refocusing on her face, even though he had been staring at it the whole time.

"I mean…wow. Yeah. It's beautiful; it just…made me think," he replied.

Skye smiled radiantly.

"Is it new?" he asked.

"Truth or dare?"

He laughed, because she loved to play the game.

"Truth."

She bit her lip demurely then turned sideways on the piano bench.

"I probably shouldn't tell you this, because you already have, like a planet-sized ego…" Georgie laughed. "But…I wrote it the first night we met."

"Forreal?" he asked, amused.

He sat down on the bench with her and she draped her legs over his and faced him, nodding.

"Because I knew the minute I laid eyes on you, you were gonna get on my damn nerves," Skye stressed through clenched teeth.

Georgie laughed.

"Please. You wouldn't even let me kiss your hand."

"I couldn't," she replied, eyes bulging, "because I knew if I let you put those pretty ass lips on me *anywhere*…" she cooed, rubbing her thumb over his lips, "Umph! I would've wanted them everywhere."

He smiled knowingly then licked his lips to tease.

"Oh yeah?"

"Yeah."

"Like where?"

She looked him in the eyes, then pulled the Eagles jersey up over her head and tossed it aside. Her beautiful, bronze body was always breathtaking to him.

"Guess," she smirked.

He ran his fingers along her collarbone, to the swell of her breast and to her nipple. Then he picked up her hand and quickly kissed it. Skye sucked her teeth.

"Cold."

He leaned in and gently kissed and sucked her bottom lip.

"Cool," she conceded.

He laid her back on the piano bench, hovering over her. He kissed her neck then gently blew his breath over her nipples. Her eyelids fluttered.

"That's cheating."

"How about...here?" he questioned, kissing her belly so softly, it quivered.

"Warm," she replied, the quiver rising to her throat.

He ran his tongue in her belly button, then to her pelvis.

"Hmmmm. Hot," she purred.

He kissed, licked then sucked the inside of her thigh.

"Burning up," she groaned, spreading her legs and cocking one foot on the piano, hitting the keys.

"Here?"

"Fire," she gasped and arched her back, as Georgie sucked her clit into his mouth.

Skye gripped Georgie by the hair and began grinding his face, and he feasted on her pussy like a bowl of passion fruit. Her leg spasmed, making her heel hit the keys again and again, giving her ecstasy percussion and sounding like the laughter of voyeuristic fairies in the last key of the first octave.

Georgie slid two fingers in her pussy as he tongue-kissed

her clit. Her pussy was so wet that the sound of the smacking suction of his fingers darting in and out filled the room.

"Oh fuck Georgie, I'm…" she squealed, then arched almost double, covering his nose, lips and chin with creamy goodness.

Skye pushed him back on the floor then got down and straddled him, her wet pussy soaking his jeans.

"I love you," she breathed.

"Still think this is going to end badly?" he asked, grinning.

"No," she pecked his lips. "Now, I think it's not gonna end."

Skye's album release was like wild horses stampeding up the charts, making it a platinum seller within the first 48 hours. No one expected for the album to do so well, so quickly.

"It's like hitting the lottery!" Skye gushed to *Billboard* in an interview.

Just as Georgie predicted, she got more coverage for turning down *Rolling Stone* and turning up the heat on every other pop star on the charts – and for a few years after that, *Rolling Stone* wouldn't offer her another cover.

But she wasn't the only rising star. Every female—and some particularly flavored men—wanted the Giorgio look. Georgie's skills were in high demand. Actresses, entertainers, and wives of such all wanted Giorgio to play in their hair… among other places.

Their lives changed overnight. Skye—and by extension Georgie—couldn't go anywhere without being mobbed, so she hired a team of bodyguards, including Boomer, who instantly remembered Georgie.

"Georgie, you a cool muhfucka. I'm glad I ain't have to beat yo' ass that night!" Boomer guffawed humorously, slapping Georgie on the back with a hand that felt more like a bear paw.

"Yeah, me too," Georgie replied, knowing he definitely wasn't a punk, but goddamn.

Georgie bought his mother a house in Cherry Hill, New Jersey near Philly, while he and Skye moved into a sky rise apartment so high that Georgie kept blurting out parts of the Jefferson's theme song as they toured it with the real estate agent.

"Beans don't burn on the grill!" he sang, in a playfully strained voice.

Skye bent double laughing. The real estate agent didn't know what the hell was so funny.

The toys got bigger, the diamonds got clearer, their clothes straight Milan and their cocaine straight Peruvian. They were so high—literally and figuratively—that the altitude gave Georgie nose bleeds.

"Oh fuck! Fuck yo, call the hospital!" Georgie exclaimed in a panic. His yellow silk shirt was now bright red from all the blood.

They were in a studio in Atlanta, doing a remix for her second single, with an up-and-coming producer named Darmaine Suplee. Skye had just gone into the sound booth, while Georgie sat with Darmaine and the engineer. He had sniffed so much coke his whole face was numb. At first, he didn't even know he was bleeding. He was looking at Skye, when he saw her expression turn from a smile into pure horror. She snatched off the headphones and ran out of the sound room. Georgie didn't know what happened. Neither did Darmaine, until he turned around and saw blood gushing out of Georgie's nose.

"Ay yo man, you bleedin'!" Darmaine exclaimed, jumping out of his seat.

Georgie looked down at his shirt and it was soaked with

blood. He didn't even know where it was coming from until Skye came busting into the room.

"Oh my God baby, your nose!" she yelled.

Georgie jumped up and looked at his reflection in one of the platinum records on the wall. His nose looked like a faucet that someone had left on full blast.

That's when he said, "Oh fuck! Fuck yo, call the hospital!"

"Baby, baby calm down," Skye urged, turning to the engineer. "Get some ice!"

"Calm down?! I'm fuckin' bleedin' to death!" Georgie bassed.

"You're not going to bleed to death, baby. It's the coke, that's all, okay?"

The engineer rushed back with a champagne bucket of ice. He quickly took off his black t-shirt and handed it to Skye. She dumped the ice into the shirt.

"Georgie, I need you to lie down, okay? Just lie down on the floor," she instructed him.

The calmness in her demeanor helped Georgie to trust her judgment. He got down on the plush studio carpet. Skye laid down beside him, applying the makeshift compress to his nose.

"I can't breathe."

"That's because you're talking. Breathe out your mouth."

He did. His heart was beating hard, heavy and rapidly. Skye felt it pounding against her, so she began to sing in his ear. A few minutes later, his heart slowed down to normal and his nose stopped bleeding. Her voice in his ear was so soothing that he was almost asleep when Skye said, "Baby? You okay? It's stopped bleeding."

"Huh? Yeah, yeah I'm okay," Georgie replied, as they both got up.

Skye turned to Darmaine.

"Can we lay the vocals tomorrow?"

Darmaine looked at his Movado.

"Yeah, no problem. It is kinda late. Seven good?"

"Seven it is," Skye confirmed.

She and George walked out into the lounge area where Boomer was waiting for them. As soon as Boomer saw all the blood, he said, "Yo! I know you ain't let that lil' nigga beat yo' ass like that!"

Georgie laughed.

"Boom, shut the hell up. It was a coke bleed."

"Oh, I was 'bout to clown yo' ass forreal!"

When they got in the limo, Skye turned to Georgie.

"Baby, I think we should slow down on the coke."

"Naw Ma, I'm good. I'm good. Besides, slowin' down is too much like stopping, and if we stop, we won't have nothin' to do tomorrow," he winked, his grin saying 'wait for it.'

Skye let it go because deep down she didn't want to stop either. She looked out the window at the passing scenes.

"I like Atlanta. It's slower but it's cool. Maybe we should have a little spot down here."

"Yeah, 'cause this spot gettin' to be like a Black Mecca." Georgie remarked.

"What do you think of Darmaine's sound? He definitely has a good ear. He played me some stuff from his new groups and..." she stopped talking when she sensed that Georgie wasn't listening, and looked at him, "Georgie?"

But Georgie had slipped into his own world. As they passed through Peachtree Street, he spotted a bevy of prostitutes walking the track. He felt an irresistible urge to go back, just to see if...

"Huh? I heard you Ma, hold up," he replied, lowering the partition between them and the driver and Boomer. "Ay yo, go back. Turn around and go back to those prostitutes.

"Prostitutes?" Boomer echoed.

"Just go back," Georgie retorted, raising the petition back

into place.

Skye looked at him.

"Georgie…what are you doing?"

"I just need to handle something real fast," he answered, vaguely.

The driver did as he was told. They pulled up to the prostitutes. They began to swarm, trying to see inside.

"Looking for me, baby?"

"This is what you need, honey."

They called out and Georgie stepped out. Even bloody, he was still fine.

"Umph! Baby, I don't know what you into, but let me get into it with you!"

One blond-wigged chocolate stallion flirted.

Georgie scanned the faces, relieved and disappointed at the same time.

"Honey, you lookin' for somebody in particular?" a red bone with micro braids and a micro dress asked.

"Naw," Georgie replied, digging into his pockets, "just coming through to show love."

He began to hand out hundreds, fifties and twenties, until he had no more to hand out.

"Christmas is early!" one cackled.

Georgie stepped back into the limo and closed the door. The limo pulled off. For a moment, neither of them spoke. Georgie just looked out the window and Skye looked at him.

She had watched the whole thing. At first, she was completely baffled. But then her heart told her, pay attention. She did, and she understood. She just didn't know what she was understanding.

"Georgie, what was all that about."

"Payin' my tithes," he replied, still looking out the window.

"Paying your tithes?"

He looked at her.

"Prostitutes are the most honest people in the world, while all the rest of us pretend we're not doing the same thing," he explained, then turned back to the window.

She couldn't argue with his reasoning.

Two days later, Titanium Records had a listening party for their new artist, Shoni. The place glistened wall to wall with the luminous shine of celebrity. Everywhere Georgie looked he saw faces he knew and faces he wanted to know. He was dressed to the nines, clean and working the room like a politician. His agenda was simple: Skye's career, his career and new pussy—always in that order. He exchanged hugs and handshakes, humor and hallelujahs, as he bounced from group to group, networking like AT&T.

Skye kept one eye on conversation, the other on Georgie. She watched him being playful and making Shoni giggle, hugging up with stars for the pop-pop-pop of the paparazzi, and dance body to body with celebrity ladies while their dates watched on. But her blood pressure whistled like a tea kettle steaming when he picked up lil' Jazz.

As soon as Georgie saw lil' Jazz alone, he went straight over to her. He had been trying to get at her all night, but each time they spotted one another, one of them was preoccupied. She would wink her eye but keep walking. So when he finally had her to himself, he didn't hesitate to bop over and pick her up off her feet.

"Boy!" she gasped, taken totally by surprise. "Put me down!"

Georgie chuckled and put her down, replying, "I just wanted to see if you were 'Jazzy as a rock'" he joked, referring to her album title.

She couldn't help but laugh.

"You got some shit with you, *Giorgio*," lil' Jazz said, with that aggressive flirt that Brooklyn girls do so well.

Georgie smiled easy.

"Okay, you know me and I know you, but what I want to know is, who does your hair?"

"You like it?"

"Noooo," he stressed. "Whoever it is needs to be shot without a cigarette! Baby, you too beautiful to let just anybody up in it," he remarked, innuendo abounding. Georgie then played with one of her curls.

"So you could do better?" she smirked.

He looked her up and down, slowly as if he was pouring brown liquor.

"What? Your hair?"

They both laughed.

Skye walked up.

"Georgie, I have someone you need to meet.

"Okay, but meet lil' Jazz. Jazzy, this is—"

"Yeah, I see her. You coming or what?" Skye replied, dismissively.

Georgie could tell Skye was hot, so he let it go.

"Ma, I'ma holla at you a little later," Georgie managed to get out before Skye drug him off.

When they had made distance, he chuckled and remarked, "Don't you think that was a little rude?"

She turned to him with fire in her eyes, but with the calm of David Banner, and replied, "Would you like to see rude?"

No.

They took the last few strides in silence and Skye steered them over to a well-dressed Black man in Armani blue, holding a drink. Skye shed her fury, sparking the man with her smile.

"Here he is Stan; this is my manager, Giorgio. Baby, this is Stan Manuel," she introduced. "He's a movie producer," she added, barely able to contain her excitement.

The two men shook hands.

"Stan Manuel. I guess I should call you 'Stan the Man,' huh?" Georgie joked.

"Why not? Everybody else does," Stan chuckled. "Nice to meet you, Giorgio. I've heard all about you."

"Call me Georgie, unless you want a perm."

Stan laughed heartily and ran his hand over his receding hairline.

"No, all my fried and died has been *laid* to the side. I was just telling Skye about our newest project. Have you heard of an author named Rashad Clemens?"

Georgie shook his head.

"Nah, I'm not a real big reader."

"Well, he has a book called 'Bad Habits,' and it's beautiful. It's about a girl growing up in Philly— "

"Oh word? I'm from Philly," Georgie cut in.

"Good omen, good omen. Yeah well, I just optioned it for a film. We're working on the script as we speak. Like I said, I was telling Skye this would be a wonderful vehicle to launch her acting career," Stan explained.

"Acting," Georgie echoed, looking at Skye. Her excitement was clear in her face. "Tell me more. Is it straight to DVD or what?"

Stan smiled.

"No. We're hoping to get a studio budget green lit. A little background...I'm pretty well versed in the movie biz. I had a hand in bringing *Coming To L.A.* and many other classic films to the screen."

Georgie nodded, impressed.

"Okay, so where do we go from here?"

"Lunch," Stan chuckled, handing Georgie his card. "In L.A., say Tuesday?"

"No problem. We'll be there."

They shook hands with parting pleasantries, then Stan walked off. Georgie turned to Skye.

"So what do you think?"

"I read 'Bad Habits.' I think it'll make a great movie," she replied.

He pinched her cheek and winked.

"You already my bad habit. Come on, let's dance.

"Georgie, these shoes are killing me. I'm ready to go."

"G'head, baby. I'ma stay and work the room a little more. The guy from L'Oreal is here, and I want to talk about getting you an endorsement," Georgie explained.

"Mm-hmmm," she replied, skeptically.

Georgie wrapped her in his embrace and kissed her neck.

"Come on Ma, don't be like that. I love you."

"Whateva, Georgie."

She watched Georgie wade back into the sea of people, like a kid splashing around in the neighborhood pool. As she left, she saw who Georgie was breast stroking toward.

"Yeah, Skye."

"I beeped you ten minutes ago. Why are you just calling me back," she huffed.

Georgie sighed and rubbed his eyes.

"Skye, it's four o'clock in the morning.'"

"And you damn sure wasn't asleep! Where are you, Georgie?!"

Her voice was so loud, the female rapper naked beside Georgie had to stifle a giggle. Georgie gave her a cold look and her smile flatlined.

"Ma, calm down, okay? I'll be there in the morning.'"

"On Valentine's Day Georgie, really?! You had to fuck her on Valentine's Day?!" Skye barked, voice trembling with a combination of anger and pain.

Georgie had totally forgotten what day it was. He pinched the bridge of his nose.

"Ma, Valentine's Day is just a day. You my valentine year

'round," he tried to charm, but even he knew that it was lame.

"Georgie, you are so full of shit, I'm surprised your fuckin' head doesn't explode!" she spasmed, then slammed the phone down.

Georgie hung the phone up with a sigh.

"Sound like somebody is in trouble," the rapper quipped.

Georgie pulled her flat by the ankles and spread her sticky legs.

"Shut up and let me suck the big toe and play with the middle," he said, then punctured her with a grunt.

Four hours later, Georgie and the female rapper were on the elevator.

"You better call me when you get back to New York," she said, her raspy voice aggressively flirty.

"Come on yo, you already know."

The elevator door swished open on the lobby.

Blah!

Before either of them could move, the female rapper looked straight into a sucker punch that dazed her.

"Skye!" Georgie yelled, totally surprised.

But Skye was too busy whipping the female rapper's ass. Georgie quickly grabbed her, struggling to pull her off.

"Get off me!" the female rapper squealed.

"Let me go, Georgie!"

"Skye, let her go!"

He finally pulled Skye off and carried her out of the lobby, screaming, kicking and cursing. Everyone in the lobby was stuck on the spectacle.

As soon as he got her outside, Skye struggled loose and turned on him.

"I can't fuckin' believe you, Georgie! I fuckin' hate you so much right now! On Valentine's Day?! You do this to me or

Valentine's Day?" she huffed, pacing until the last word made her punch him in the chest. The release felt so good, she tried to hit him again. Georgie was quickly getting irritated by her rants. He grabbed her by the wrists.

"Skye! Calm the fuck *down!*" he growled, eyes leveled on hers firmly. "Now *listen* to me! This ain't about Valentine's Day and you know it! You wanna talk, then talk and say what's really on your mind!"

Skye snatched away from him.

"You're right, Georgie; you're absolutely right! It *isn't* about Valentine's day; it's about *every* day! I'm sick of your shit, of you fuckin' whoever and whenever, and I'm supposed to take it?! Look at me! Look at me, I can have any man I *want!*"

"You're right, you can. I agree. And you're sick of my shit. Now what?"

"I can't take it any more!"

"Or what? Or what, Skye?" Georgie questioned, voice low and in control. She looked him in the eyes and said, "It's either me or them."

Without hesitation, Georgie coldly replied, "Them." He then turned to walk away.

The swiftness of his response felt like a punch to her stomach. The ease of his reply seemed to make a total mockery of everything she felt.

"Just like that, Georgie?! You can walk away just like that?!" she gasped, gut wrenched.

Georgie stopped and looked at her, his grey eyes colder than steel.

"Skye, listen to me. I'm only going to say this once: I love you, with EVERY. THING. IN. ME., but don't ever give me an ultimatum! There ain't a woman *born* that can fit me in her box of expectations! I am who I am; you can either deal with it or you can't. If you can't, I respect that, so even if you walk away, I'll never stop loving you," he concluded, his glare softening to a gaze.

Tears lined Skye's cheeks.

"You don't love me, Georgie; you don't…"

Georgie stepped over to her, taking both her hands in his, and her eyes in his.

"Ma, I swear to God the love I feel for you leaves me breathless, you my heart…but you gotta love me for me. You can't change me. If we're going to grow, we grow together, but you have to let me be me. If you can't…walk away."

Looking into his eyes, Skye couldn't have walked away if she wanted to. But she didn't want to. She already made that decision in a New York alley.

"I…can't," Skye whispered, but deep down, her heart didn't know if she could.

For the next few months, Georgie and Skye ping ponged back and forth between New York and L.A., between setting up her first tour and taking meetings and schmoozing on behalf of getting "Bad Habits" turned into a movie. Georgie got a crash course in Hollywood 101, and Music Industry Rule Number 4080: Movie industry people are also shady.

At every meeting, party or power lunch, he could see all the sharks, snakes and cutthroats trying to move in, but since he was a Philly-born hustler, he didn't miss a beat joining their dance.

The project changed producers three times because Stan had to check himself into rehab. The second producer wasn't as crafty as the third producer, Benny Greene, who convinced the second producer to turn over the project, in exchange for Benny's help in green-lighting an artsy-fartsy film the producer's director wife was obsessed with.

Benny may have been a sneaky snake—and some said, a closet racist—but he was an A-list producer, so once he got involved, things began to move at breakneck speed. He invited Skye and Georgie to his mansion in West Malibu overlooking the Pacific Ocean. He literally lived in a glass house and it reminded Georgie of where the South Africans lived in the movie *Lethal Weapon*.

From the beginning Skye hated his guts. Benny's favorite subject was Benny: who he knew, who knew him, who owed him favors, who owed him their careers. He talked endlessly, as if trying to impress upon these two young people how fortunate they were that he got involved and how a meeting with him was akin to a meeting with God.

"Skye, baby, did you hear me? I asked if you were familiar with Niia Akimbe's work?" Benny asked, chewing his fish then washing it down with some red wine.

They were sitting at Benny's huge mahogany dinner table that seated twelve. He was at the head, while Georgie and Skye sat across from one another.

"Oh, I'm sorry Mr. Greene, I—"

"Benny. Call me Benny.

"Benny, I'm sorry. Jet lag. What did you say?"

"Niia Akimbe."

Skye scowled slightly, as if trying to remember something.

"Britain. By way of Africa. Cameroon, I think. She's really a talented actress. She's done a lot of theater over there. But I really think she can be a big star over here. She doesn't look African; not that there's anything wrong with looking African, it just… doesn't translate well on the screen," Benny stumbled and explained.

His maid walked in, stage right.

"Mr. Greene, Mr. Schwarzenegger is on the phone," she announced.

"Arnie? What the fuck does Arnie want. Cigars? Doesn't he know I'm eating?"

"Yes Mr. Greene, I told him that. He said it's important."

Benny sighed with feigned exasperation in an attempt to play up his importance by being irritated by it.

"Please, you kids excuse me," he said, wiping his mouth and pushing his chair back. "Have some more wine; it's

Château Latour Pauillac 1990. He followed the maid out of the room. As soon as he was gone, Skye's face grew animated.

"Baby! I'm soooo fuckin' bored! Let's sign the contract and go!" Georgie chuckled.

"Baby, be easy. He's just giving us his spiel."

"Shh, spill it already," she snickered.

"This is how they do business."

She bit her lip, seductively.

"I wanna do business with you."

"Oh yeah?" he smirked. "What kind of business?"

Before she could answer, he heard Benny in the other room say, "Arnie, relax. I'll take care of it. Go bone Maria or the maid, whoever you see first."

Benny walked back into the room, chuckling.

"That fuckin' Schwarzenegger, what a shmuck! You gotta love 'em," he said, then looked around. "Hey, where's Skye."

Georgie looked across the table and saw that she was gone. He was dumbfounded for a second until he felt his zipper go zzzzzzzzz...

"Umm..." He gulped. "She went to the bathroom."

"Oh. I could've shown her."

He felt Skye pull his dick out of his pants. Georgie coughed, almost choking on the wine.

"She, uh, couldn't wait."

Benny sat down. Skye took Georgie's dick in her soft, wet mouth, her tongue ticklish and probing. Georgie fought back a reaction.

Benny downed his wine, then leaned forward and rested his elbows on the table.

"Enough of the foreplay; let's get down to business, okay?" Benny began.

"Mm-hmmm," Georgie nodded with a flimsy grunt, because he couldn't talk. All he could feel was the back of

Skye's throat.

"I love this fuckin' book. I want to see it become a movie because I know the audience will love it."

"*Love it*," Georgie growled, trying desperately to keep his eyes from rolling into the back of his head.

"Exactly! And I'm prepared to take care of Skye on the front, a piece of the back end, and—between you and me—maybe a little under the table," Benny explained, with a wink.

Skye took Georgie's balls in her mouth, one at a time, while jerking his dick with firm strokes.

"Yeah, yeah; fuck yeah!" Georgie grunted, his hands balled tightly.

Benny was pleasantly taken aback.

"Excited? Okay, excitement is good."

Skye started working her neck, her mouth suction the perfect replica of her pussy. Georgie yelped; Benny frowned.

"Are you okay?"

"I'm – I'm, it's hard, this chair is hard," Georgie struggled to make a complete sentence.

"We have been sitting down for a while. You want to go?"

"No!" Georgie blurted out. "No, No, I'm good right there, right there; I mean *here*."

He was so close that his stomach fluttered.

"So let's get the lawyers together, cross the t's and dot the i's, and I promise Georgie, when you see the numbers, you're gonna… Georgie, are you sure you're okay?"

Keeping the ejaculation spasms from the waist down took all of Georgie's willpower, so much so that the strain squeezed a single tear drop from his eye and it trickled down his cheek.

"It's just… I'm so happy to be here," Georgie sighed, feeling like a bag of jellybeans.

Benny beamed, thinking that his schmoozing had wooed

the young Black man.

"I am too, Georgie."

"Here's my earring," Skye announced loudly, holding her diamond teardrop in her hand.

"Oh Skye, I didn't see you come back," Benny commented, surprised.

Skye waved him off with a casual wave.

"You were talking, so I didn't want to disturb you. Then I dropped my earring and—" she held it up, "here it is."

"Oh," Benny said, pausing as if trying to process the image, then added, "well, I was just saying how we're going to get you signed on as a gross player. Do you know what a gross player is? Well…"

As Benny droned on, Georgie looked at Skye, shaking his head, a "you're amazing" grin on his face.

I love you, he mouthed.

I know, she mouthed back with a smile and a wink.

The next day, Georgie was relaxing on the hotel bed in his boxers, scratching his nuts and watching the Bulls–Lakers game. They were taking a much-needed day off. Life became a cocaine blur of whirlwind activities. Georgie wanted to spend the day doing nothing, while Skye spent it shopping.

As he watched the game, Phil Jackson led Michael Jordan, Scottie Pippen, Dennis Rodman and the boys on an all-out tirade against a young Kobe Bryant and Shaq, putting on a spectacle of pure wizardry. Seeing Jordan fly through the air, tongue hanging out, ball cocked, he couldn't help but think of K.B. and what could've been.

"Georgie, I'm back" Skye called out, jolting him out of his trance.

She was carrying a gaggle of bags from various boutiques on Rodeo Drive. She kicked the door closed with her wedge sandal, put all the bags down except one, and then walked over and looked at Georgie.

"Look at you…all that's missing is the fat and lazy," she snickered.

"I'm workin' on it," Georgie deadpanned, eyes glued on the screen. "And I thought you were bringing me something to eat."

"I did," Skye grinned, reaching into the bag then pulling out a pair of red panties that looked like they were made of licorice. "See?"

He reluctantly looked away from the screen.

"What is that?"

"Edible panties."

"Who gonna eat 'em?" he chuckled, turning back to the game.

She huffed then went and stood in front of the screen, her demeanor screaming for attention.

"Skye," Georgie said, scratching his nuts, "the game."

"I've got a better game," she replied, naughty little girl written all over her face.

She slid the spaghetti straps of her yellow sundress from her shoulders, then the dress itself fell from her body. She stood sexily, hand on cocked hip, candy panties extended from a finger of the other hand. Her naked bronze body seemed to glow.

"You wanna play?" she purred.

"Ma, could you spread your legs a little? Jordan's about to slam that" Georgie joked, with a monotone delivery eyes still on the screen.

She sucked her teeth and shut off the TV.

"Fuck Jordan; fuck *me*," she growled, like a panther in full stalk.

Georgie had noticed how needy Skye had been the past few months, but he knew it was his fault, so he accepted the responsibility.

He dimpled her.

"You know I can't tell you no, baby. Put them panties on and c'mere. They better not taste like watermelon Now and Laters."

She stepped into the panties, replying, "they're cherry."

"Then let me taste your cherry," he smirked, flicking his tongue out.

"Wait, there's more. I got you…these," she announced, holding up a pair of handcuffs with pink fur all over them.

"No. No, Skye. *Fuck* no, Skye," Georgie instantly started shaking his head.

"I thought you couldn't tell me no?"

"I ain't; I'm tellin' you *hell* no."

"Please, baby," she pouted, crawling up on the bed and straddling him. "We never do what I want to do. I let you fuck me in the butt."

"That's 'cause you wanted me to."

"No, *you* wanted to."

"*No*, Skye. Remember the last muhfucka you put handcuffs on? He probably still under the table." Georgie laughed.

"Bob!" she gasped. "Or was it Bill? I wonder what happened to him."

"He probably dead," he laughed.

She hit him. "Don't say that. It'll be my fault and anyway, *I've* got the key this time."

"*No*. N–goddamn–O! You ain't puttin' no handcuffs on me! Never!"

"Ohh Georgie, right there, baby! Oh fuck, I'm about to cum!" Skye squealed, riding him reverse cowgirl style.

The edible panties she had been wearing were totally eaten away from her crouch to the seat of her ass, giving Georgie a perfect view of his dick vigorously pumping in and out. Her milky juices began gushing out, coating the base of his dick and making him explode inside of her at the same time.

Exhausted, Skye fell back, lying beside him, her right leg thrown over him.

"Damn," she gasped, trying to catch her breath. "I can feel my pussy still shaking," she arched her back, body trembling, cumming again. "Damn."

"That's the afterbirth," Georgie boasted, jokingly.

Skye giggled, cuddling up to him.

"Damn, I love you boy."

"I love you too...but Skye."

"Hmmmm," she hummed, ready to go to sleep.

"You got your way; now take the cuffs off," he said, looking at how he was cuffed to the headboard.

"Whyyy," she whined. "Don't you think they're cute?"

"No, Skye, I don't think they're cute. Now where's the key?"

She sat up, waving dismissively. "Somewhere," she snickered, picking up her cigarettes off the night stand and standing up.

She looked down at his body, spread-eagle and naked, his face fuming and red. "Besides, I kind of like the idea of you being my love slave."

She lit a cigarette, mumbling, "At least I'll know where you're at all weekend."

"Weekend?! Hol' up, hol' up, hol' up! *Fuck* that! Take these goddamn handcuffs off !" Georgie bassed, jerking uselessly against the heavy head board.

She cupped her lips to bite back a smile, walking backward.

"These panties feel sticky. I'm going to take a shower."

"Skye!"

"Yes?" She said it so sweetly you would've thought that she

was answering the phone.

Georgie saw that the bullshit wasn't working, so he changed his approach.

"I – umm – want to take this opportunity to say…if I *ever*, in any way, ever did anything that – umm – I should've apologized for, I'm apologizing now," Georgie said, tone restrained. "And I want you to know how wonderful you are."

"Awww, thank you baby; I love you, too."

"So you gonna take off the cuffs?"

"Sure, when I'm finished," she giggled, going in the bathroom. She paused and took one more look. "So sexy."

"I *knew* I shouldn't have let her put these fuckin' handcuffs…Skye!"

CAPTAIN SAVE A HOE

iiKane CHAPTER 12

The first day of spring is in March. When the air smells like love and imaginations are fertile; it's called Spring Fever.

He met her on the first spring evening. When the L.A. night threw on a silky, black dress and the stars sprayed across it like celestial diamonds. He met her at a restaurant on Sunset. He and Skye had arrived in a vintage Rolls Royce with suicide doors. Boomer opened the door for them. As soon as Georgie's ostrich and Skye's Gucci hit the carpet, the pictures started flashing like a thousand suns. Georgie was so high the champagne tasted like coke and the coke tasted like champagne. Coupled with his ever-present painkillers, his every step was smoother than Fred Astaire's.

"Georgie. I don't want to stay long. Benny just wants us to meet and get a vibe going for the set," Skye told him, feeling anxious for reasons that she couldn't explain.

"No problem," he replied.

Until it was.

The first impression he had of Niia was that he was eight-years-old again, and his doll baby had come to life. Her skin was smooth and as dark as a Hershey bar, her hair long and silky, hanging down to the small of her back, but worn over one shoulder, with the type of shine that you only see in commercials. And her figure...

She had the kind of body that should *never* be dressed, a body that could start a war or *end* one.

As first, he thought it was the cocaine, because he could've sworn someone exclaimed, "goddamn," but when he saw the look on Skye's face, he realized that *he* was that someone.

Skye rolled her eyes but kept her game face on. Niia pretended that she didn't hear it, but the subtle blush in her cheeks made a mockery of her mask.

"Niia! It's nice to meet you," Skye gushed, appropriate smile glued in place.

"Skye, it is an honor. I love your music; you have such a pretty voice," Niia replied, her accent like global gumbo—a little French and British English with an African inflection.

Air kisses and half hugs were exchanged. Seeing that Skye wasn't going to introduce him, Georgie stepped forward and said, "I'm Giorgio," taking her hand.

He started to kiss it, but there was no telling what Skye would do, so he simply shook it softly, raking his index finger across the palm as he withdrew.

"And I'm Alphonse."

Georgie turned his head, and for the first time noticed the man beside Niia. He was a good two inches taller than Georgie, broad shoulders and looked like an African Denzel Washington.

"I'm Niia's fiancé," he added, with a cocked half-smirk that said, *Yeah.*

Georgie gave him a subtle up and down then accepted his extended hand.

"Yeah, yeah, congratulations."

Skye shook his hand next.

"It's nice to meet you."

"And you Mademoiselle," Alphonse charmed, then spat something in French as he kissed Skye's hand, making her giggle.

"Let's get a table," Georgie said, a bit sharply, feeling a way about not being the smoothest dude in the room.

The maître d' showed them to their table. Orders were made and small talk ensued between Skye and Niia.

"Have you read the book?" Niia asked, as the orders were being brought out.

"I'm reading it again now. I really like it," Skye replied.

"Yeah, it is good, but I may be a little biased because I'm from Philly," Georgie chimed in, then glanced at Alphonse. "You ever been to Philly?"

Alphonse looked confused.

"Philly? I have never heard of it. I've been to many countries, but not Philly," Alphonse replied, as if he were already bored with talking before he finished his sentence.

Georgie bit back his irritation, feeling like Alphonse had gotten in a subtle dig. Alphonse said something to Niia in French. She replied, then averted her eyes from Georgie, focusing her attention on Skye.

"So Skye, are you from Philly, too?" Niia questioned.

Skye laughed lightly.

"No, I'm from here. California. Oakland, to be exact. I haven't been home in a long time. When I was 16, I ran away from home, stole a car and drove to New York." She explained, like it was the most natural thing in the world.

"Mon Dieu, you did? I could've never done that," Niia said, shaking her head.

"What? Stolen a car?" Skye asked.

"No. Ran away."

To Georgie, Niia seemed as beautiful—and as fragile—as a rose with its thorns stripped away. Her every move had feminine grace that bordered on timidity, a timidity that told Georgie something wasn't right.

Skye sipped her wine.

"Actually, I was running *to* something: my music. I knew if

I was ever going to make it, it would be in New York."

"Oui, I love the music, too. American music, especially. Prince, Michael Jackson, Nina Simone, Gwen Guthrie."

Georgie stopped, mid bite of mignon and said, "Gwen Guthrie. What you know about Gwen Guthrie?"

Niia's demeanor lit up.

"She's the best. I love…" She caught herself, shot a quick glance at a tense-eyed Alphonse, and just like that her cage shut, and she concluded, "umm, yes, she's really good."

Skye and Georgie exchanged a quick, knowing glance. Skye's held pity, whereas Georgie's held annoyance, but he forced a smile.

"Yeah, yeah, 'Padlock' was the joint, right? Lock it up," he sang with a thought—as if it hadn't already been there— then said, "You know…a friend of mine is half owner in a dance club not too far from here. Let's go!" he suggested effused, then looked at Alphonse. "What about it; you wanna dance, bruh?"

Alphonse didn't have to be from Philly to understand the subtle invitation.

"I – uh – don't think…" he started to grumble, but Georgie cut him off.

He turned to Skye.

"What up, baby? We're suppose to be getting acquainted; let's go to 'Vette's spot."

Skye's look said, *I told you…* but Georgie, dimpled her.

"Come on, Ma! You don't wanna go? Okay, we'll dance right here. Waiter! Bring my banjo!" he said, loud enough to garner a few disapproving stares from proximate patrons.

Skye stifled her laugh.

"Georgie," she whispered feverishly.

He nuzzled her neck, making her giggle.

"*Stop.*"

"Then dance with me," he charmed.

"*One* dance, Georgie," Skye conceded.

"*One* dance," he echoed, with a mischievous grin, but truthfully thinking—he wasn't picturing Skye as his partner.

Seeing his silly behavior and playful banter, Niia couldn't help but smile and snicker. Alphonse fumed.

And then it happened in a blink. Skye had looked at her watch. Only Georgie saw it.

"Waiter," Alphonse growled and threw up his hand—the one closest to Niia—in a gesture to get the waiter's attention.

There was nothing menacing about the motion, it had been occurring in restaurants since restaurants had bills, but the movement was quick...sudden...sharp...and Niia flinched.

It was subtle, yet so engrained as to be reflexive, with the strange significance of déjà vu.

That flinch became a flame in Georgie's veins with the whoosh of total consumption, as their eyes met, or rather flickered, long enough for her to register his reaction and him to see her lower her eyes in shame.

Pop!

Went the starter pistol in Georgie's mind—in his ears, he could hear his own breath—and his blood shot out of the blocks like a bullet aimed straight at Alphonse's ass.

Georgie downed his drink.

"Let's go."

The name of the club was Xandu and was co-owned by Yvette. Since coming to L.A., she had looked nowhere but up. Her boutique began to thrive, but quickly became a trend. Celebrity after celebrity came for her designs, including Skye, courtesy of Georgie's introduction.

As soon as they entered, Georgie spotted Yvette speaking to a famous choreographer. From the back, in her rainbow spandex cat suit, Yvette's feminine figure was totally convincing.

Georgie snuck up behind her and hummed into her ear, "Have I told you lately how good L.A. looks on you, and if I *ever* lose my mind, you'll be the one to help me find it?"

Yvette looked nonchalantly over her shoulder, and replied, "Hmph! Not *nearly* enough," then broke into a fit of laughter, turning to give Georgie then Skye a hug. "What's up Georgie, with your crazy self ! Skye, hello Miss Gorgeous! I hate you!"

Skye laughed.

"How you doing, Yvette?"

"'Vette, this is Niia Akimbe and uh—bruh, what's your name again?" Georgie introduced.

Alphonse sneered. "Alphonse."

Pleasantries were exchanged; drinks were offered then sent for.

"'Vette, listen. Niia thinks she knows something about music. So I need you to tell the DJ what time it is. I need him to show her ass! Take me back to sweaty Philly basements, aight?" Georgie instructed her.

"Oh, you want the Georgie?" Yvette replied, referring to the famous New York club that helped birth the house music scene.

"*Exactly.*"

"Done," she confirmed, then sashayed away.

Several minutes later, while Madonna's "Vogue" was playing, Georgie heard the cascading opening baseline of "Love Thang" by First Choice, and grabbed Skye's hand.

"Come on Ma, let me show you how we do down Richard Allen!"

Georgie took Skye to the dance floor and put her body to the test. However, in reality he was toying with Skye, doing an elaborate two step, but two steps nevertheless, being playful. He was like a tiger trying to hide his stripes to convince the gazelle that he is just a cat, because he knew she was watching. The DJ turned it up another notch, taking him through a "Love is the Message" mix that broke into "Break for Love" before da-da-daing into "Gypsy Woman."

"Georgie, my feet hurt," Skye complained.

He picked her up and wrapped her legs around his waist.

"I gotta pee."

"Pee on me," he snickered, freaking like they were fucking. Skye threw her head back, laughing.

"Boy, put me down."

He did.

"I'll be right back."

By the time the crowd swallowed her departing back, he had already started over to Niia. She couldn't look directly at him, but he could feel her eyes on him because—when he got close—she started to tremble slightly, like a tuning fork hitting true pitch.

"Alphonse, with all due respect, you don't mind if I dance with your fiancée do you? I mean, you ain't gotta hold her that tight do you, bruh?" Georgie asked, adding the last part to challenge his manhood.

Alphonse bit, his smile like a leer, then, "Not at all," he replied in measured British tones. "Be my guest."

Georgie took Niia by the hand and led her to the dance floor.

Before I let you in, there's just one thing I want to say;
There's no need to pretend that this will end another way.

Jocelyn Brown crooned the beginning of "I'm Caught Up" as they reached the spot.

"Now listen ma, I don't know how y'all do it over there, but you might want to get a seatbelt," Georgie smirked.

Niia eyed him demurely, but with a smoky gaze that said so much by saying less.

"Believe me, I can keep up. Music is one of the universal languages."

"What are the others?"

"Love and money," she replied, and then…she began to move.

When man first laid eyes on woman, and realized that she was a woman and not a rib, she was dancing because the taste of apple made her hips sway.

When Julius Caesar met Cleopatra, she had slithered out of a basket with the sensual sway of a snake, hypnotized him, and he ended up dead on the Senate stairs. And when the ancestors of Africa wanted rain, they relied on the pulse of the drum, the gyrations, grinds and sensual suggestion of the dance that *is* the Black woman to make God himself fall to his knees and soak the earth with tears of joy.

That's how Georgie felt. But Georgie was nothing if not a competitor, who was more than equal to the task. He came out of his suit jacket and let it fall to the floor.

Umm-umm, yeah, yeah, umm-umm, yeah, yeah,
Umm-umm, yeah, yeah, all I can say was ….

"Nu-Nu" banged from the speakers, as Georgie pulled Niia close, grinding her, pelvis to pelvis, looking into her eyes for reaction.

"He told you not to look at me, didn't he?" Georgie questioned.

She looked away, but not before giving the subtlest of nods.

"Look at me now," he growled.

And she did, with a gaze as naked as the way he was picturing her body.

And then Georgie began to freak her.

Likethislikethislikethislikethislikethislikethis

He ran his hands down the contour of her body as he Philly-rocked lower and lower until his face was pussy level. One by one, and without missing a beat, he freaked her out of her shoes, making her laugh at his ingenuity, but cream at the implications. By the time he rose up, he was behind her, riding that juicy ass like the world's hardest jockey. The DJ threw on "French Kiss" by Lil Louis.

"It's not over for you yet ma, rock with me," Georgie huffed, sweat pouring from his face and every fourth step screaming, "Double up!" *1.2.3.4* "Double up!" in order to get her in synch with his flex.

When you're as high as Georgie was, the record "French Kiss" sounds like a musical trance—wordless and brain numbingly repetitious—but that's the point; don't think, *feel.* The bassline feels like blood rushing through the veins, pulsating to a rhythm of its own, and the melody feels like you're flying through a black hole, until you emerge on the other side...

Like an orgasm.

A woman begins to moan, purr, gasp and squeal to the rhythm of the track, like the sound itself is long-dicking her into a melodic ecstasy. And then the music begins to slow down, BPM by BPM. At first, you think it's you, but it slows and slows and slooooooows...

By the time that it had slowed to the tempo of a slow jam, Georgie had leaned Niia so far over, she had to wrap her legs around his thighs to keep from falling. And by the time the beat slowed to a crawl, and the woman's moans echoed through the club acapella, Georgie had Niia lying down, pinned beneath him and looking into her eyes.

Their chests heaved in unison, then as the beat began to speed back up, Niia—without smiling—said, "Okay…you win."

Georgie smirked and helped her to her feet. It was then that he noticed that half of the dance floor had stopped to look at them.

Georgie picked up his jacket and Niia stepped into her shoes.

"Thank you for the dance, Giorgio," Niia remarked.

He normally corrected people, but she said it with her luscious accent and damn near made it the only word he wanted to hear for the rest of his life.

"Don't thank me yet. Tomorrow, on the set, I'ma be the one doing your hair," said the spider to the fly.

Niia smiled.

"We'll see."

As they left the dance floor, Georgie looked around just in time to see Skye's head getting smaller as she stormed out of the door.

When she had come out of the bathroom, she returned to the booth about the time of "French Kiss," so she had missed the foreplay, but she saw every moment of the climax.

It was like they were making love without taking off their clothes.

Skye froze. Bile rose in her throat that she had to swallow to keep down. Her stomach churned and she saw Georgie as he truly was and always would be. Untamable.

By the time he had laid Niia on the floor, she had seen enough. She headed straight for the door, brushing past Yvette, who could do nothing but shake her head.

Georgie Porgie.

Alphonse sat in the booth, silently seething. A murderous rage gripped him, but it wasn't aimed at Georgie, because at heart he was a coward. As soon as Georgie led Niia back to the booth, Alphonse jumped up and began berating her in French. Her timidity re-appeared, like Clark Kent after experiencing Superman, and Georgie got heated.

"Yo, yo bruh, that was on *me*— " Georgie emphasized, pressing his hand to his own chest. "You ain't gotta holla at her like that."

"Do *not* tell me how to speak to my woman!" he huffed then turned to Niia, grabbed her arm and demanded that she come with him.

He led her off and it took everything in Georgie not to go after them. But he respected the rule that is, whatever is between a man and a woman is between *that* man and *that* woman…for now.

"Skye, Ma, open the door," Georgie knocked on the hotel door.

"Fuck no! Go knock on that French bongo bitch's door!" she yelled form inside.

"Ma, we were *dancin'*! It ain't that serious!"

No response. He knocked hard.

"Georgie, go *away*!" she shouted, through clenched teeth.

"Fuck!" he barked, giving the door a kick. He hated locked doors. He paced the floor in front of the door. Stopped. Thought. Shook it off.

"Fuck that."

Paced again. Stopped. Looked around.

"Fuck it!"

He shot through the stairwell door, ascended the stairs, two at a time to the next floor up. He went to the door directly above his and knocked. It took a while before a man's voice said, "Yes?"

"Listen, I'm sorry to disturb you. But I need…" he began to dig in his pocket, pulled out his money clip and peeled off a hundred dollar bill, then held it up in front of the peephole, "just a minute of your time."

The lock clacked and retreated, then the door opened. In its place stood a tall, grey-haired White man in a robe, looking like all that he was missing was a pipe.

"Yes?"

Georgie put the hundred in his hand.

"This is going to sound crazy, I know. But I need to use your balcony," Georgie requested.

"Balcony?"

"I…uh…got locked out of my room and I can't find my key," Georgie lied.

"So why don't you just go down to the front desk?"

Georgie peeled off three more hundreds and put the in the man's hand.

"Because I'm embarrassed. Can I use your balcony?" Georgie repeated.

The man smiled slyly.

"Girlfriend locked you out, huh? I heard her yelling from up here."

"Yeah, yeah, sorry we disturbed you…again…"

The man stepped aside.

"Thanks a lot."

"No, thank you," the man chuckled, pocketing his take.

"Who was it, Jerry?" a woman with a nasal voice called out from the bathroom.

"Just some guy who wants to jump off our balcony."

"Okay."

Georgie reached the balcony and looked down. The L.A. streets squinted up at him from seventeen floors down. Jerry peeked over.

"Sure you don't want to go to the front desk?"

"You gonna give me my four hundred back?"

"Be careful."

Georgie stepped carefully over the cast iron railing then paused. He looked down. He should not have looked down.

"Man, if I ain't love this mother…" he grumbled as he slowly lowered himself, stretching his body toward the rail of his room's balcony. If he had been three inches shorter, he would have been dangling 'til this day. Once he got his footing, he carefully inched his hands down, splay palming the top of the balcony as he jumped to solid ground, breathed a sigh of relief as his asshole unclenched.

Skye was lying in the bed, looking at MTV. He opened the sliding balcony door and stepped into the room.

"You know, I could've killed myself."

"So," she spat, not taking her eyes off the screen, exhaling smoke.

"Oh, so you want me to die now? Fuck it, I'ma jump," he joked, turning back to the balcony.

Skye threw the lit cigarette at him; it hit him and sparks flew everywhere.

"Will you stop playing all the time, Georgie! It's not funny!" she screamed, jumping off of the bed, eyes red with dried tears.

Georgie sobered up quickly. He knew he had fucked up because he could usually laugh Skye out of her anger. He stepped toward her.

"Skye look, my bad okay, but I got on my Philly shit. The music, the mood and that nigga Alphonse…" he shook his head. "But forreal, I was just dancin' and I was in a zone; I remember one time in the tenth grade…but you don't want to hear about that right now. Forreal, I apologize."

Skye folded her arms, shaking her head—not at him but at herself. She looked him dead in the eyes, and with a look that melted his heart, asked, "Why can't I be enough?"

She looked so weak, so vulnerable, so unsure that he pulled her into his arms, tears stinging his own eyes, because for the life of him, he didn't have an answer.

"Skye…Skye, I swear to God, I love you so much…"

"I know," she sobbed, "I know, that's why I can't understand…"

He covered her face with kisses to give his tied tongue something else to do. Skye threw her head back, allowing him to nibble her neck, then her nipples, as he laid her on the bed. He peeled her panties from her body and ran his tongue over her pelvis.

"No," she whispered, "Just…put it in; I need to feel you inside me."

Georgie took off his clothes and laid on his back. Skye straddled him, taking the full length of his manhood.

"…don't move. I just wanna feel you," she said again, laying her head on his chest.

He wrapped her in intimate embrace, and kissed the top of her head. They laid like that, quietly. The only sound in the room were various videos on the TV, giving an acoustic sound to the silence.

Finally, Skye leaned up, looked in his eyes and said, "Georgie. One day you're gonna wake up, and I'll be gone."

The look she received told her all that's she needed to know. His pupils dilated, and – somewhere – Sunshine Anderson echoed:

Heard it all before...
Played the fool before...
But your lies ain't working now...

"No, don't say that, okay? I'm here; don't say that. I need you like sunlight; don't leave me," he begged, with an urgency that warmed her, and scared her at the same time.

That night, he held her tighter than he ever had, and Skye slept sounder than a newborn in her mother's arms.

The next day Georgie arrived at the movie studio lot after twelve. Skye had been on the set since seven, a time when he was rolling over.

"How you doin' today, Georgie?" the security guard—who struck Georgie as a dead ringer for Sammy the Bull—asked.

"Always good on this side of the grass."

"Hey Georgie, I got one for you," the guard remarked.

Georgie chuckled. Everyday, he had a joke.

"Let's hear it."

"So a guy and his wife are watching TV, one of those relationship shows; the show is about mixed emotions. So the husband says, 'This is bullshit! There's no such thing as mixed emotions. I never have mixed emotions. Do you think you can give me mixed emotions?' The wife says, 'Sure.' He says, 'Okay, shoot.' She shrugged and says, 'Of all your friends, you've got the biggest dick.'"

Georgie laughed, but replied, "Womp, womp, wooomp Don't give up your day job, Tony."

"Why do you think I *got* a day job?!"

Georgie pulled his black on black Maserati Ghibli into the lot. It was only a week old and he planned to keep it in L.A. to match the other four cars he kept in New York, Philly, Atlanta, and Miami.

He walked onto the set, greeting and joking with the crew as he headed for Skye's trailer. He noticed Benny pacing in front of Niia's trailer with his assistant furiously fielding a phone call.

Georgie walked over.

"Benny, you okay? You're as white as a sheet."

Benny shook his head.

"On a scale of one to ten, this is a five and escalating. Have you seen Niia?"

Georgie ears perked up.

"No, why? I'm supposed to do her hair. Is she here?"

"In the trailer, but…"

"But what?"

"Makeup's doing all they can. I'm sure it'll be fine."

That is all Georgie had to hear. He pushed past Benny, threw open the door and stormed inside. Niia was sitting with her back to him, facing the makeup mirror, but he couldn't see her reflection because so many people were gathered around her.

"Move. Move. Move!" Georgie barked, scattering the crowd like a flock of seagulls.

He stepped in front of Niia. He looked at her. Blood vessels exploded like a string of firecrackers, all over his body.

Her eye was black and swollen; the rest of her face—still beautiful—was flawless, and timid…and scared.

Rage shot though Georgie, transforming him like there really was such a thing as werewolves, and they howled in his razor grey eyes.

"Where…is he," he whispered, his adrenaline leaving no extra energy for a louder voice.

"Georgie please, I…"

"*Where?!*"

"He's here. Out there, somewhere…"

He was gone before she finished the sentence. He emerged

from the trailer like a heat-seeking missile and spotted Alphonse talking to the director. He saw Georgie coming, felt it like the coming rumble of a freight train. He didn't flinch; he shot straight at Georgie.

As soon as they clashed, with the force of two butting rams, Alphonse made the mistake of missing a haymaker that—if it had connected—would have ended the whole fight.

But he did miss.

He had never been in Philly, so he didn't know that cheesesteaks aren't all it's the home of. It's also the home of Bernard Hopkins, "Smokin'" Joe Frazier and the boxing gyms that peppered the city. Georgie spent a few summers in one of those gyms, so he ducked the haymaker without trying and caught Alphonse with a bladder ripping kidney shot followed by a sharp, stinging upper cut that struck Alphonse on the chin so hard that he bit his own tongue bloody. He staggered. Georgie wasn't finished. The next straight right hit Alphonse like a V-8, splashing human tomato juice everywhere.

He fell flat on his ass then Georgie went to work.

He kicked him dead in the face, shattering his jaw and splattering Georgie's Jordans with blood. The way Alphonse slumped to the ground, he *had* to be dead. One of the gaffers ran up to try and restrain Georgie, but Georgie turned and blasted him with a left cross so hard, he was asleep before he leaned, but the ground woke him up.

After that, no one else tried to intervene.

Georgie sat on Alphonse's chest, drew back like a sculptor —Alphonse's face was the clay and proceeded to rearrange it with every blow. But it wasn't enough. No matter how much blood flew, he had to do more. If he had a gun, he would have shot him; a knife, he would have stabbed him. But he didn't. He found a water fountain—the kind you might find in a park with little fishes and into which kids toss coins to make wishes. He grabbed Alphonse by the shirt, dragged him over to the edge and proceeded to drown him.

Alphonse thrashed around with the energy that he had left, but it didn't even register with Georgie. He had blacked out. He was back in Philly where the only justice for hurting someone he loved was death, pure and simple. Alphonse's struggle became more lethargic, and nothing was going to stop Georgie from killing this nigga.

Except the softness of the hand that he felt on his shoulder.

"No, Giorgio."

He let Alphonse go, staggered back and fell to his knees. Alphonse gulped and gasped for air as he slumped against the fountain wall. He looked at Georgie with the fear of God in the only good eye he could see out of and bellowed, "Police!"

But someone had already called them, though not as loudly, and two security guards ran in, one being Tony. Tony took one look at Alphonse, and he knew exactly what had happened, and agreed wholeheartedly.

"Georgie, you gotta get out of here. I'm supposed to call the police, but I can't because I left my walkie talkie in the booth," he lied. "But I'll find it if you don't leave *now*."

Georgie hardly heard him. He was looking at Alphonse as if from the opposite corner, waiting for the bell for round two.

"Giorgio, you must go. Please. I'll go with you," Niia urged.

Only her voice could reach him. He slowly stood, rubbing his head like it was buzzing, then replied, "Let's go."

When they reached the Maserati, he handed her the keys.

"You drive."

She did.

When she started the car, the sound system leaped to live.

I want you and I want you to want me too
Just like I want you.

Marvin Gaye serenaded their silence as they rode, until Niia asked, "Why did you do that?"

"Because he deserved it and you don't," Georgie answered, matter-of-factly.

She glanced over at him.

"I mean *why*? There will be police, there will be trouble."

"Niia," he chuckled, "I'm a Black man in America. I'm always in trouble."

She couldn't help but laugh, and the sound broke the tension in Georgie.

After the laughter, the question became more obvious. Neither knew what they were doing; neither knew how they got there, or why.

"Where are we going?" she questioned.

"I don't know," he answered.

They looked at each other. Both knew that he wasn't talking about direction.

"You hungry?" Georgie asked.

"Yes."

"Ever had Roscoe's?" he smirked.

"Mon dieu, this is delicious," Niia raved as she dug into the chicken and waffles.

They were sitting at one of the open air benches at the world-famous Roscoe's House of Chicken and Waffles. Georgie chuckled to himself, watching her eat her food. There was something really sexy about a beautiful woman not afraid to eat.

"Yeah, it ain't a cheesesteak, but it'll do," Georgie

quipped, sipping his tea through a straw.

Niia licked her fingers then wiped them with her napkin, all the while looking at Georgie.

"You were going to kill him, weren't you?"

"Yeah," he responded casually, but defiantly. "Does that bother you?"

Half a beat.

"No."

"It doesn't bother you that I was going to kill your fiancé? Don't you love him?"

She looked away, as if the answer was somewhere else.

"I did…once…I don't anymore."

"Then I don't understand. Why are you still with him?" Georgie questioned.

Hesitation filtered across her demeanor, but looking into his eyes and seeing deep concern, she answered, "Alphonse comes from a very powerful family in my country, very political. He has done a lot for my career. I am indebted to him."

"In *blood*?" Georgie stressed.

Niia blinked back tears and looked away.

"You're right, you don't understand."

Georgie reached across the table and held both her hands. "Then help me to."

She looked at him, looking for a reason not to tell him. She couldn't find one.

"My family depends on me. Everything I do is for them. They are very poor. This movie is my chance to be successful in America, the one place in the world that…" she chuckled lightly, but almost bitterly. "My family thinks that gold lines the streets of this country. They think it is the answer to all their prayers, so I must be the answer as well."

Georgie dropped his head, blinked back the tears, then lifted his head and said, "Niia…I've got six hundred grand in the bank, I've got five cars. I've got this watch and this ring. I'll sell it all and dump the account; we can send it all to your family."

The sincerity in his tone made her tear up.

"No Giorgio...Merci, but it's more. I have to go back to him," Niia cried, then stood up and walked away.

"Go back to him?! Are you crazy? Look at your face! I know that ain't the first time and it damn sure wont be the last," Georgie fumed.

"What else can I do?" Niia sobbed. "I am not an American citizen! Alphonse is a diplomat. He has connections. He is going to make me a U.S. citizen!" She leaned against the car, crying. Georgic just stood there, numb. He felt responsible for the situation. Regardless of the fact that Alphonse undoubtedly beat her before, *this* beating was because of the dance. His dance. His ego. His decision. It seemed unfair that she had to suffer. The thought made him feel helpless. Georgie didn't do helpless. He would rather make a big mistake than do little or nothing. He had to do something. He knew what he had to do.

He pulled her close, tipped up her chin to look into his eyes and said, "Marry me."

It took a while for his words to sink in, and when they did, her eyes got big and she gasped. "What? No, Giorgio, I don't want to marry you!"

"What's wrong with me? What do you mean, you don't want to?"

"No, no, I didn't mean it like that."

"So you want to marry me?!" he dimpled, playfully.

Niia laughed, out of exasperation.

"No, I don't mean that either, I mean... This is crazy!"

"Why?"

Because we don't..."

"Know each other?" he finished her sentence with a smirk.

He pulled her close again. "Don't you believe in love at first sight?"

The look he received told him that she did.

"This is crazy," she repeated, in the tone women use when they really mean *this is right.*

"You know what I thought to myself when I first saw you?"

"No," she replied, looking at him shyly.

"I thought, *she looks like my doll baby.* I had a doll baby when I was little, and I loved that doll. I used to wish and wish that God would make her a real little girl, if only for one day. Looking at you now, I feel like my prayer has been answered," he told her then kissed her gently to seal the deal.

"Do you know what I thought when I saw you?" Niia asked, with the inflection of a little girl with her first crush.

"What?"

She started to say, but then shook her head.

"Tell me," he urged.

"I thought...we could make pretty babies," she replied, looking at him from under hooded eyes.

He smiled.

"No doubt, and even prettier puppies. That's an inside joke," he winked. "So...will you marry me?"

She looked into his eyes for what seemed an eternity, then asked, "What about Skye?"

Giorgio sighed but his gaze didn't waver.

"Ma, I've never been the type of dude to lie to a woman. I love Skye very much and she loves me. But I fell in love with you hard and fast. Believe me, I'm not marrying you to keep you *here*; I'm marrying you to keep you with *me*. When I'm with you, I just wanna dance until my feet come off. Do you understand what I'm saying?"

She nodded.

"I feel the same way. It's never happened to me so quickly;

I feel...*full*. Besides, in my country, it is not uncommon for a man to have several wives," Niia responded.

"Well shit, we might be doing this all wrong. Maybe I need to move to Cameroooooon!" he laughed, howling the word like a wolf.

Niia laughed.

"Giorgio, you are so crazy!"

"Ma, I'm a bad boy and I sometimes get lost on my way home, but I *always* make it home, and I swear I'm gonna make you happy, okay?"

She nodded, smiling.

"Okay?" he asked.

"Yes?" he reiterated.

"Oui."

"Oui, oui, oui, we gettin' married!" he exclaimed, lifting her off her feet and spinning her around.

"Georgie, where are you? I've been beeping you like crazy! I heard what happened on the set. Do you know that man wants to press charges? But he doesn't knowyournameyoualmostkilledhim!"

"Skye, Skye hit the space bar, goddamn," he chuckled.

She exhaled.

"I'm just worried about you; where are you?"

The question echoed in his head as he glanced around the lobby of the MGM Grand in Las Vegas. He wasn't about to lie, but he knew this was no way to break the truth.

"I'm good Ma, believe me. But listen, I'll be home tomorrow, okay? Then I'll explain everything."

She paused. "Is Niia with you?"

"Skye please, I promise—tomorrow I'll explain. I love you."

"You better," she replied, then hung up.

Georgie sighed and did the same. He spotted a gift shop in

the lobby and went inside. The blond girl behind the counter reminded him of Vanna White. She cocked her head to the side, the way blondes do.

"Don't I know your face from somewhere?"

"Look down and try to imagine it. If you can't, then no," he joked, but she was a blonde; she didn't get it.

"No…you're somebody famous aren't you?"

"My mother likes to think so. How much is the ring right there?" he asked, pointing to the biggest and brightest ring on display.

She pulled it out and handed it to him.

"This is by Graziella. It has three-and-a-half carats of G4 color diamonds, set in white, rose and yellow gold," she explained, with perfect saleswoman diction.

Giorgio eyed the way the ring swirled and crisscrossed in a style that resembled the wrap-twirl of a turban, except that it was covered in diamonds.

"How much?"

"Fourteen thousand, four hundred.

"I'll take it," he replied, handing the woman his credit card. "I need a band for me. How much is that one?"

"The white gold? Thirty five hundred."

He tried it on. It fit.

"This, too."

"Don't you want a sizing for this one? What if it doesn't fit?"

"Then I'll definitely be back. No, no boxes. Just gimme the rings. I'm in a hurry," he urged.

She shook her head.

When he left the gift shop, he was just stuffing the rings in his pocket when Niia approached. She kissed him gently and handed him the key. "The Presidential Suite," she remarked.

He took her by the hand and twirled her around as if they were dancing and replied, "That's for the honeymoon; first let me put these papers on you before a man prettier than me steals you away. Oh, I forgot, shiiiit, we can walk slow then," he chuckled cockily, making her giggle.

The Chapel of Love—or Love's Chapel—was a small room, squeezed in between a tattoo parlor and a sawdust casino. It seemed to be a family-owned business because the officiator —a tall, grey-haired Wayne Newton lookalike—kept referring to the organist, who looked like Edith Bunker as 'honey'. The rice-thrower resembled them both, but was a midget. Giorgio laughed to himself, imagining that they were probably from West Virginia.

The officiator cleared his throat.

"We are gathered here today to wed this man—" he looked at his notes, "Georgie Mills and—" he squinted, waiting for some help.

"Nigh – e – ya," Georgie pronounced, giving Niia a reassuring wink to assuage her nervous expression.

"Nigh – e – ya," the officiator articulated slowly, then having gotten the hang of it, continued. "And this woman, Niia Akimbe...As you know, marriage is a wonderful insti—"

Georgie cut him off.

"Ay yo, Rev? Yeah, we're kinda in a hurry, so you wanna cut to the chase?"

"Fine, fine. Do you have the rings?"

"Oh, we don't have any..." Niia started to say, until the sparkle accompanying the rings that Georgie pulled from his pockets caught the chapel's light and took her breath away.

He smiled and shrugged.

"I just happened to have a lil' sumptin' sumptin' in my pocket, just in case I ran into a pretty girl I wanted to spend the rest of my life with."

The tear in the corner of her eye looked like a diamond

about to fall. Georgie wiped it away with his thumb, tasted it, and then turned to Wayne.

"We're gonna say our vows."

Wayne nodded. Georgie handed her his band and she slid it on his finger. Niia took a deep breath, looked in his eyes and began, "I have *never* done anything like *zees* in my life, but it just feels right, no, Georgie?"

"Keep saying Giorgio. I love the way you make it sound." She smiled.

"Giorgio, you have a beautiful, but complicated heart. I want to thank you for letting me in."

Georgie slid the ring on her finger, looked in her eyes and said, "You're all the proof I need that fairy tales do come true. Standing here, looking at you, my heart is beating a mile a minute, letting me know this...this condition I got is crucial. You can say that I'm a terminal case. Do what you want with me baby. Burn up my clothes, smash up my ride..."

"Well maybe not my ride," they both then said in unison, breaking up a fit of giggles.

The officiator looked at his wife. She shrugged. Georgie continued.

"But I've got to have your face all up in the place; I like to think that I'm a man of exquisite taste. Hundred percent Italian silk, imported Egyptian lace, but nothing, baby, nothing can compare to your lovely face. Do you know what I'm tryin' to say? I'm just tryin' to say that, until the end of time, I'll be there for you."

He didn't sing it, but she knew it was a song. She knew it was Prince. But hearing those words drip from his lips had her dripping from hers.

"I love you," she breathed, breathlessly.

His answer was a kiss...a kiss that lasted off and on through the last of the ceremony, in the limo on the way to the hotel, in the elevator on the way to the room, and in the hallway as they reached for the key. Their lips didn't stop touching, teasing, tasting and tantalizingly torturing one another until they stood in the middle of the luxuriously decorated suite. But it may as well have simply been a big old empty room, because all that mattered was them, naked staring each other down.

Georgie eyed her from her tiny doll feet with delectable, perfectly pedicured toes to her long, shapely legs that blossomed into curves so deep, there should've been danger signs on her thighs. Her breasts, heaving with nervous anticipation, stood out, full and firm. Her chocolate chip nipples stuck out like elevator buttons. Her whole body quivered because his gaze felt like a tongue giving her a full body massage.

"You are so beautiful," Georgie whispered.

"I'm...not," she answered, eyes downcast, speaking barely audibly.

Life had been so ugly for so long, it had seeped into her pores.

Georgie turned her to the mirror, stood behind her, and caressed her shoulders.

"No...you *are*," he corrected her.

Instead of looking at the reflection in the mirror, she slipped into the reflection of the reflection in his mirror-colored eyes, and in them would rediscover her beauty. His reflections slowly disappeared from the mirror, like the sun setting over her shoulder, sinking lower and lower...and lower, with his tongue leaving a trail of wet kisses. She looked at herself as passion, and lust enflamed her. She took a sharp breath as she felt his tongue licking along the crack of her ass, never stopping until he was under her soft, juicy pussy.

Niia couldn't take her eyes off herself, watching, riding his tongue like it was a dick, gripping handfuls of his curly hair, sucking in her breath, sizzling, ready to explode, her whole body trembling.

"Oh my…" was all she go out, before she came so hard, she used both hands to try and push him away, but he lifted her hips, sucking her dry. She fell over and curled up on her side.

Georgie scooped her up and laid her on the bed, on her side, lifting her legs and sliding into her hot, tight pussy. The length of his dick seemed to rise right up her spine. The way she clawed the sheets, if her nails had been much longer, she would have ripped them to shreds.

"You feel so fuckin' good, baby; don't hold back. Give me all of you," Georgie urged, long-dicking her steadily.

Whatever she said, he didn't understand, because it was tongues mixed with French, but her body language was easy to read. She started bucking, biting her bottom lip, throwing that pussy like her body had a mind of its own. He maneuvered her body, turning her on her stomach, then pulling her up on her knees. The sight of her soft, voluptuous ass brought the animal out of Georgie and he began to pound her stroke for stroke. Their bodies were exploding in ecstasies unreal; she was as soft as a pillow and he was hard as steel.

"You…are sooooo deep," she cooed.

"So fuckin' good," he grunted in broken sentences.

When they came, her squeal sounded like the squeal of tires right before a crash, and then they did, all over his dick, and her all over her walls, until they both fell on the bed, breathless.

"I can't stop my legs from shaking," Niia said, running her hand through her hair.

Georgie pulled her on top of him, massaging her ass.

"Goddamn, Niia, what are you *made* of ? Your ass is so soft; what is this, velvet?!" he joked.

She laughed hard.

"You are so silly, Giorgio. I feel like I could sleep for days."

"But you can't," he replied, thinking of Skye. He kissed the top of her head. "We've got a return flight in an hour."

She groaned and pouted, like a little girl who didn't want to get up for school.

"Okayyyy," she whined, rolling off of him, "I'm going to take a shower."

Niia got up and walked to the bathroom with that languid sensuality that women display when they have been fucked royally. Her ass was bouncing, jiggling. Not a lot, but enough to make Georgie's dick jump with every jiggle.

Man, we can't miss that fight, the sane side of him stressed, but he said, "God...*damn* Ma, hol' up; I'm comin,'" he announced, as he jumped off the bed.

The second round made him miss the first flight.

"Okay, take the car and go to Yvette's boutique. It's on Grand Avenue; you can't miss it. She's gonna help us find an apartment. Until then, get a room at the L'Ermitage Beverly Hills, okay?" Georgie explained, handing Niia the keys to the Maserati.

They were in the long-term parking lot at LAX.

"Yes. But what about all my clothes? They are at Alphonse's apartment," Niia told him.

"What clothes? All your clothes are on Rodeo Drive, waiting for you to pick 'em out," Georgie smirked, holding out his credit card.

Her eyes swelled with wonder and excitement. She reached. He pulled it back.

"Remember, you're French. Less is more," he quipped, only half jokingly. He handed her the card, knowing the words went in one ear and out the other. She was a woman; she was going to burn up that card and bring it back warped.

She gave him a kiss, jumped into the car, then pulled off. Georgie headed to the nearest payphone to beep Skye. He purposely avoided his phones while he and Niia were on the trip. He paced as he waited for her to call back. He knew this was big. Even though—in his mind—the marriage wasn't about love, it was about support, he knew it wouldn't go over well. That's why he gave Niia the car, so that Skye would have to pick him up. He figured that the best way to tell her was as she was driving a car at 80 mph. Even Skye would have to be calm under those conditions.

The phone rang. He picked it up.

"Hey, baby, how you?" He smiled hard, trying to make his dimples show through the phone.

Skye was having none of it.

"Where are you?"

"LAX. I need you to pick me up."

Pause.

"I was beginning to think that tomorrow would never come," she retorted, saucily.

"It didn't. It's today, so I'm early, smart ass. Come get me."

"Mm-hmmm," she replied, but he could hear the smirk in her tone. He hung up and proceeded to pace.

"Okay, I can do this…Skye, I married Niia…no, too direct." He chuckled. "Damn, I missed you. If I wasn't already married, I'd marry you. No, hell no! She might cut me." Georgie surmised.

People looked at him strangely as he paced and mumbled to himself, half expecting him to blurt out, "The end of the world is near!"

A Black stewardess came up, rolling her wheeled suitcase behind her. She had flicks of grey in her hair that complemented her attractive face. eorgie took the grey as wisdom.

"Excuse me miss, can I speak with you a moment."

She stopped and smiled graciously.

"Yes."

"Listen, I know you're probably in a hurry but I need your advice," Georgie remarked.

"Okay," she replied, her body language saying, *I'm listening.*

"See, a friend of mine was in a tight spot. She's from another country, but she needed to stay here, so I flew her to Vegas and married her. But my girlfriend doesn't know and she's on the way to pick me up. How should I tell her?"

She took a breath, considered it, then asked, "Is your girlfriend Black?"

"Mostly."

She nodded.

"Very carefully and from outer space," she replied with a straight face, then turned and walked inside the terminal.

"Take me with you," Georgie called after her.

Skye arrived about a half an hour later. She pulled up in a red Corvette, top down and sporting temporary plates. She slid over because he went around to the driver's side. He got behind the wheel, then leaned over and gave her an '*I miss you*' kiss. She matched it with one of her own. He pulled off.

"Who's car?" he asked. One of Skye's tracks was playing on the radio.

"Who do you think?" she grinned.

He looked at her and read her expression. He smiled.

"Ma, I just bought a car," he chuckled.

"So."

"I was thinking about you," she shrugged. "Now where were you?"

"Vegas."

"Did you win?"

If she only knew…

Georgie glanced at her. "Yeah."

Skye rolled her eyes, and propped her elbow up on the

door. The wind slightly tussled her short cut.

"You know…as soon as I saw her eye, I *knew*, I just *knew* you were going to do something. I just *knew* it! It's just like your mother told me, you think you're fuckin' Captain-Save-A-Hoe, flying to every woman's rescue…" she shook her head.

"You say it like it's a bad thing. I mean, forreal, the muhfucka ain't have no business beating on her!" Georgie fumed.

"If she doesn't want her ass whooped, then she should leave!" Skye shot back.

"You know why she was with him?"

Skye shot him a look.

"Was?"

Like a boxer, he lowered his shoulder and dipped that one.

"Her whole family Ma, her whole family is countin' on her. The movie is a chance to get them out of poverty, but if she ain't a U.S. citizen, she can't keep workin.' He was gonna help her become a citizen."

"Why you keep saying *was*, Georgie?" Skye asked calmly…too calmly.

Richter scales can only measure so much, but maturity can pick up on the subtlest shifts. Birds from miles around felt it and took flight to higher ground.

He glanced over at her. It was now or never. He pushed the speedometer to 83.

"Because…she don't need him no more.

Skye didn't blink.

"Why?"

"Because…I married her."

Before volcanoes erupt, the ground usually rumbles. The ground rumbled. But it was California, so he hoped it was only an earthquake.

"What did you say?" she hissed, her voice barely audible

above the whistling wind.

"I did it for her family Ma, not for her. If she's a…"

"Did *what?* Did what, Georgie? Say it. Say it again."

He looked at her.

"I married…"

She punched him in the face so hard that he saw stars.

"Skye!"

It wasn't his words so much that pushed her over the edge; it was the fact that—when he turned the steering wheel to switch lanes—the slight shift made the sun strike the surface of his ring and gleam blindingly in her face. It was as if God himself was flaunting the ring in her grill, and she totally lashed out. She was on him with her cat-like agility, grabbing at his hand—the one he was steering with—causing him to swerve in the lane.

"Take it off! Take it off! No! No! No!" she barked, clawing and punching, crying and screaming. "Can't you see she using you, you stupid muhfucka!"

Her body was between him and the windshield. He just barely missed hitting a truck.

"Ma, I'm drivin'"

"I don't give a *fuck*! Take…it…*offfff!*" she gritted, digging her nails into his neck.

"Aaarrggh!" Georgie grunted then shoved her hard against the door.

Skye gasped.

"You gonna hit me behind that bitch's ring!? Huh?! I… will…kill… you!" she spat, kicking him in the side with her sharp stiletto heel. It felt as if she was stabbing him in the ribs. He snatched her shoe off and threw it out of the window, but by the time he did she had the other in his neck.

"Skye, you gonna kill us both!"

"At least *you'll* be dead, muthafucka!"

At that moment, Georgie had never been so grateful to

hear police sirens as he was then. The cops witnessed them struggling and assumed that it was Georgie attacking her. They quickly gave chase. Before that, Georgie couldn't get over to the lane next to the shoulder. He was too busy trying to keep them from having an accident. But with the police behind them, people slowed up or switched lanes, giving Georgie a clear path to the shoulder of the road. Both officers—both black—jumped out, guns aimed.

"Let the woman go *now*! Hands in the air!" the driver bellowed.

"I ain't got her, she got *me*!" Georgie yelled, adding, "Skye! Skye! My nuts, my nuts! Fuck! Officer!"

The two police looked at each other with confused scowls. They carefully approached the car. What they found was Skye, with a spiked heel on Georgie's neck and her bare heel trying to crush his crotch, with him gripping her ankle.

"Ma'am, are you okay?"

"No! I'm trying to *kill* this muhfucka!" she growled, kicking him for emphasis.

Her skirt had slid all the way up and—since she almost never wore panties—the officer couldn't help but get an eyeful of her shaved pussy. It was so pretty, he got struck. Skye turned on him.

"What the fuck you staring at, you perverted bastard?! You ain't never seen no pussy before, you piece of shit? Here, get a good look!" she spazzed, cocking her leg up.

The officer looked at his partner, he looked at Georgie, then said, "Just drive safe, man."

"Don't you want to see my license and registration?" Georgie asked, his tone practically pleading, *please don't lever me her with this crazy bitch*.

"Naw, naw. Just…go," he replied, then he and his partner returned to their vehicle.

The people in the lobby all paused when they walked in. All conversation stopped. It almost seemed as if all breathing stopped as they watched Georgie and Skye walk by. Georgie held his hand over his crotch and was limping, nose bloody, scratched up face, shirt ripped and untucked, neck looking like he had been attacked by angry birds. Skye—with one spiked heel and one bare foot—stumbled along like a drunken sailor with a peg leg and an attitude, her dress wrinkled and ripped so far up the side that one could see her ass with every other step she took, her mascara running and lip busted. They looked like the last two survivors from the Titanic, and after 80 plus years, had finally made it to shore. The only sound was that of their footsteps—one for Skye then the ding of the elevator as the door swooped closed.

When they got to the room, Skye went straight to the bathroom and locked the door.

Georgie knew that he had fucked up.

The explosive Skye he understood, he could handle, if barely. But the quiet storm threw him off. The rest of the trip had been in silence. No matter what he said, she wouldn't respond. Now, standing in the hotel room, he had to try once more because the whole room felt fed up.

"Skye," he knocked.

No response. All that he heard was a buzz.

"Ma, I know it seems like a big deal, but it's not. It's a fuckin' piece of paper! I did it to make her a citizen; that's it! That's me... Super Georgie, right?"

Still no response. Just the drone of the buzz. He knocked again.

"Skye! Say something, Ma, please. I love you. Talk to me. What's that noise?"

He heard the door unlock, and when she stepped out, he knew what the buzz was. It had come from his clippers. She had shaved all her hair off.

"Now you don't have any power over me," she said quietly, then turned and walked out of the door, barefoot.

Georgie was so shocked that he couldn't do anything but watch her walk out. He went into the bathroom and saw all her blue hair in the sink and sprinkled on the counter, looking like the cold of a warm summer day left behind. He put his hand in it and felt its softness then sighed, shaking his head as he looked at himself in the mirror.

For the next few weeks, Skye took a hiatus from the film to do some tour dates. The director shot around her. During that time, Georgie didn't talk to Skye, but he heard from her often. It seemed like she was everywhere, on the radio, on TV, in the newspapers, and all she wanted to talk about was her new love, her bodyguard, Boomer.

"It just happened," Skye exclaimed, with a girlish giggle as she was interviewed on MTV, snuggled up in Boomer's lap. "I mean, he's always been here for me and drew me like metal to a magnet."

Boomer looked like a Black man who not only hit the lottery, but was guaranteed all the fried chicken that he could eat for life. His smile was that wide.

"What about Giorgio? So much has been said..."

"Who, my *hairdresser*? As you can see, I don't need him anymore," she replied, with a cold, arrogant façade, her baldhead gleaming.

Georgie had to admit that it looked good on her as he stared at the screen, shoveling coke like the city in a snowstorm, scarfing it with both nostrils.

Everywhere that he looked, he saw Skye and Boomer, and he knew that was what she wanted, because in every picture, her eyes stared into the camera—through the camera, through the pixels, space and time—and looked dead into his eyes saying, *I dare you to let go.*

Georgie's reaction was a mixture of cold humor and sizzling rage.

"I'ma *kill* this mother," he chuckled, on fire.

And in moments like that, he took it out on Niia's body. He ravaged her whenever the combination of her breathtaking beauty, the euphoria of cocaine and his heart-stopping lust for Skye exploded within. In the elevator leading to the apartment, in her trailer on the set, the dressing room of the House of Bijan on Rodeo Drive, on the hood of the little red Corvette, he beat her pussy until his dick was raw and he had changed the sway in her stride. Now, she couldn't help but walk nasty, and he couldn't help becoming addicted to her.

Sniff...sniff...sniff. "Ahh!" he grunted, shaking off the sting of the freeze as the Bolivian fish scale painted him the color of high. In the background—that is, on the other side of the harp playing in his head—he heard the sizzle of the shower, which always reminded him of frying bacon. Then a few minutes later, Niia emerged from the bathroom with a towel wrapped around her. Georgie stopped mid-sniff and looked at her as if she had two heads.

"What are you doing?"

She stopped, confused.

"What?"

"What you wearin' that for?"

Niia giggled.

"Georgie, I cannot be naked all the time."

"Why not? That's why we live in an apartment, not the park. Réduire," he said, using the only French she had taught him that he had a use for.

Niia seductively let it fall to the floor. Her cocoa complexion glistened, screaming to Georgie that it wanted to be licked. Their bed was big, round and only eight inches off the floor. She got down and crawled across it like a panther, coming up behind him as she sat and wrapped her arms around his neck. He continued to sniff. She looked down at the fluffy white powder.

"It sparkles like diamonds. How does it make you feel?"

"Like God," he replied.

Georgie knew that she had the curiosity of a precocious little girl. Everything about America was new and she asked endless questions. Therefore, he didn't sense anything different about this one.

He put the tray down and laid on the bed. She leaned on his chest, her hand on his heart.

"Your heart beats different," she noticed.

"Huh?"

"Regular people's heart beats like boom – boom – boom – boom. Your heart beats like – like a drum."

Georgie smiled.

"That's 'cause I'm made of music."

Niia laughed.

"I'm serious Giorgio, is it that stuff? Maybe you shouldn't do so much. It may, how you say, burn you out?" Niia remarked, her tone ending in a turned up inflection.

He caressed her cheek and replied, "It's better to burn out than to fade away baby."

She smiled and kissed his fingers.

"What do you want for dinner?"

He raised an eyebrow, mischievously snickered.

"I mean *food*," she replied exasperatedly, as if she wasn't loving every moment of his attention.

"Whatever you put in my bowl, I'll eat; sit in it and see."

She got up to go to the kitchen. Georgie grabbed the coke tray and fell in behind her. He was sniffing and watching, sniffing and watching, sniffing and watching her ass jiggle like it was giggling.

"Ma…can you *have* a more perfect ass? Is it even possible," he marveled.

"Giorgio stop, you're embarrassing me," she blushed as they entered the kitchen.

"Listen, check this out," he began, sitting the tray on the table, "I'm not saying I would, but if like we get a divorce, can I still come over and just look at your ass?" he cracked.

Niia opened the refrigerator, bent at the waist and looked over her shoulder, just enticing a brother.

"You divorce me? No."

"No visitation rights?"

"No!"

"No Christmas card with a picture of your ass on the front?"

She threw her head back, laughing.

"How you say, hell to the no!"

"Fuck it, I guess you stuck with me then, huh?" he smirked.

She put the steak that she had just removed from the refrigerator down and wrapped her arms around his neck.

"I better be, because I'm falling in love with you, very, very fast and very, very much."

Georgie looked into her eyes and caressed her cheek.

"In I is all you'll ever need."

Her breath caught lightly in her throat, because she got it instantly. He had used each letter in her name to make his point.

"No one has ever said my name like that."

"And no one ever will."

She kissed him passionately then replied, "I love being your wife."

"Your wife?!" Stephanie exclaimed loud enough to draw a few looks. But she was in her backyard, so she didn't care.

She was having a cookout for Memorial Day, so Georgie decided to use that time to introduce her to Niia.

Stephanie turned to Niia.

"Baby, it's not you, it's just so -" She was thinking so *Georgie* but she said "so sudden, *and* I wasn't invited."

"Ma, it was a spur of the moment thing," Georgie explained.

Stephanie glared at Georgie.

"Niia, I love you honey, but let me talk to this nigga... Georgie for a second."

"Oui."

Stephanie all but grabbed Georgie and led him through the throngs of people, the music, laughter and smell of the grill. On the way, they ran into Denise and a man who looked like he might be a deacon in the church.

"Georgie, heyyy! It's so good to see you," Denise sang, giving him a church hug. She stepped back. "I want you to meet my new husband, Harold. I'se married now!" she snickered, showing off her ring.

Flashing a wedding ring in front of Georgie was like flashing red in front of a bull.

What? You think you safe?

"Nice to meet you," Georgie remarked, shaking Harold's hand.

Pleasantries over, Stephanie cut in.

"Denise, I need to speak to Georgie," and without waiting for a reply, led him inside.

More hellos and hugs ensued. But they finally made it upstairs into Stephanie's bedroom. She slammed the door, turned to him and said, "Nigga, have you *lost* your mind? *Married*, Georgie?!"

"Ma, listen..."

"I *knew* something was funny when Skye called me and told me to tell you the IRS sent you a letter to the apartment in New York."

"The IRS?" he echoed.

"Yes, Georgie, the *government.* You are paying taxes, aren't you?"

Georgie waved it off, dismissively.

"I'll get my lawyer on it."

"You better... I asked her, why you can't tell him. She said, 'I'll let him tell you.' So I know you fucked up, but I didn't know you tore your whole ass!" she ranted.

Georgie leaned against the desk and sighed hard.

"You gonna let me talk or what?"

Stephanie sat on the bed and folded her arms.

"Talk, Georgie. Talk."

"Niia is from Africa. She just came over to do this movie. Her whole family is counting on her, but to *keep* working she has to be a U.S. citizen. The dude she was with was beating on her, so I like, kinda beat him up, so I knew he wouldn't— so we flew to Vegas and got married. That's *it,*" he explained.

"That's it? That's *enough!*"

"Ma, I did it for her family...mostly. It's just a piece of *paper*; it's no big deal!" he shot back.

"Well obviously it's a big deal to Skye that you have a *whole* wife. And this...Niia, why do you think she married you?"

He shrugged.

"Of course, citizenship is a part of it, but it's not the only reason. I mean, it ain't like she playin' me or nothin'."

"And I bet you didn't even tell Skye before you did it, did you?" Stephanie surmised, knowing her son. When he didn't answer, she shook her head adding, "You're so selfish."

"*I'm* selfish? Yo, I'm so *tired* of hearing that!" he bassed.

"Because the truth hurts."

"It *ain't* the truth. If I'm selfish for having the capacity to love more than one woman, how is that *not* selfish for wanting to be the only *one*?! Gimme, gimme, gimme *all* your love; mine, mine, mine! That ain't selfish?!"

Stephanie stood up.

"No, that's *love* Georgie, *true* love, which you obviously know nothing about!"

"Not *my* love. And what makes theirs any truer than mine? When I'm with a woman, I'm with *her*, I'm loving *her*. I'm loving her smile, her laugh, her walk, her conversation, her smell…" he explained, but let his voice trail off. "I swear to God, I want that moment to last forever, but it can't and life goes on."

"What if a woman told you that? When I'm with you, I'm with you, but I'm with him, too?" Stephanie questioned.

Georgie shrugged with a chuckle.

"That's why I love the married ones."

Stephanie sat back down, shaking her head.

"I hear you, player."

"Player? You of all people should know I'm not a player, Ma. I'm not out here lying to these women. Those dudes, *they* ain't even players! It ain't game when you gotta lie to keep a woman. Drop one off at eight, pick another one up at nine…or maybe fifteen minutes apart. *That's* game! But I don't ever run game, this is just *me*! I tell 'em exactly what it is; hang if you can hang!" Georgie ranted, pacing the room furiously, his arrogance on full display.

"So you think it makes it right because you're honest about your bullshit?" Stephanie asked with an incredulous chuckle.

He stopped, looked her in the eyes and replied, "I'm not interested in being right! I'm interested in being *me*."

Stephanie held up her hands in mock surrender.

"Then that's all I got to say. Just be careful you don't love everybody…and end up loving nobody."

She stood up, came over and took him by the shoulders.

"Well, you know your Mama love you regardless, unless you got another mama somewhere that carried your nappy headed ass for nine months and changed your shitty diapers," she smirked.

Georgie laughed and kissed her on the cheek.

"Naw, you my only girl."

"Just checking. Well, let me go down here and meet my new daughter-in-law while I have a chance," she signified with a chuckle, then added "and Georgie, see about that letter. The IRS does not play."

"I will, Ma."

She nodded and walked out. Georgie went to the bathroom then headed downstairs. He was just in time to see Denise coming through the patio door carrying two plates of food, one of which was for Harold who was in the living room playing bid whist.

"Denise," he whispered furiously, hidden from view by the hallway. She looked and saw him. He jerked his head in a gesture saying, *come here.*

"Denise," he stressed in a whisper, "bring your ass here!"

She bit her bottom lip and looked at Harold, who had his back turned to her, unaware of the decision being contemplated behind his back.

"Denise."

She sashayed quickly in Georgie's direction. He opened the door, which led into the laundry room.

This will do.

He ushered her inside, then closed and locked the door.

"Georgie, I can't…"

"Shhh, you come to talk?" he dimpled, sliding the plates from her hands, her tongue from her mouth, her pants from her hips and the objection from her mind.

"Ohh, I've missed you so much," she cooed as Georgie

picked her up and sat her on the washing machine.

The mischievous little boy in him turned it on, so it would jump and vibrate underneath her. He rammed his rock hardness into her throbbing pussy.

"Sssssssooooo," she gasped, wrapping her legs around his waist and spurring him deeper.

Her pussy was so wet that each stroke sounded like the smacking of hungry lips.

"Oh Georgie, fuck meeee," Denise squealed, the vibration of the washing machine adding a whole other tingle to her spine.

"Tell me you love me!"

"Oh I do, you know I do; *goddamn* I doooo," she growled, through clenched teeth because she was so close.

"Cum for Daddy."

"I'm cummin' for Daddyyyyy," she sang, spasmed, shook and slumped.

Georgie let the spasm past then helped her down.

"Lawd Georgie, I'm glad you don't live here anymore," she giggled.

"Shit, I'll be back Christmas."

"I'll be waiting."

"Now remember, go put the plates in the microwave for sixty seconds, okay?" he winked.

She nodded, started to walk out.

"Hey," he said.

She looked back.

"Lookin' good," he chuckled, slapping her on the ass.

She sashayed up the hall.

When Stephanie saw Denise come into the living room, wig slightly ajar, walk somewhat unsteady, then Georgie turn the corner grinning like a Cheshire cat, all that she could do was to shake her head, thinking, *Lawd have mercy, my baby goin' straight to hell.*

"Okay Skye, this is the scene where you find out the new girl in school is trying to take your boyfriend," the director explained.

He was about Skye's height, but shorter than Niia, and bore a striking resemblance to Spike Lee. *And* his name was Spike. He told Skye without a trace of irony, because he did know about the Bermuda Triangle of love that he was currently standing on Ground Zero in. Art imitates life.

He turned to Niia.

"Now Niia, Skye's the most popular girl in school, and you're trying to fit in. The boyfriend thing just…happened," Spike explained, thinking that he was giving them their scene motivation.

He walked away, putting his headphones on.

"Okay, let's get it. No mistakes, I wanna wrap this by lunchtime."

Everyone took their places.

"And action."

Niia closed her locker. Skye was standing right there. The script called for Niia to be startled.

"Oh, I didn't see you standing there."

"Why? Did you blink? I bet you didn't even blink, did you?"

Skye's words threw Niia off, because they weren't in the script. Niia tried to stay in character.

"I didn't get a chance to talk to you before the party," Skye started, leaning on the locker to square her stance.

"What would you have said, what *could* you have said, huh? Tell me."

No longer able to stick to the script, Niia replied, "I – I never meant…"

Skye breathed a chuckle.

"Of course you didn't…they never do. The wind blows in Kansas and Dorothy ends up in Oz, right? Problem is, those baby shoes don't fit your foot Shug. So when he gets tired of you clop – clop – clopping around, 'cause even I know you can't strut in 'em, then he'll say, who is this imposter?! And then he's coming home…believe me, he's coming home," Skye spat, with sass as sharp as the heel of a stiletto.

The ironic part was that when Skye spoke of home, Niia assumed Skye was referring to herself. Her eyes bordered on tears.

"I – I love him."

"Love him?" Skye echoed, looking her up and down like she was covered in slime. "You don't even know him. What's his favorite color?"

Niia bristled.

"I will not play your game," she replied, turning to walk away.

Skye laughed.

"Why, because you don't *know*? Run along, little girl."

Skye's laughter crawled up Niia's spine like a swarm of fire ants, sparking the fight that even the most timid survivors possess. She spun back around and replied, "Rainbows."

The laughter ceased, Skye's eyes narrowed.

"Favorite time of day?"

"Golden."

"If he were an instrument,"

"Saxophone," Niia replied before she finished.

Skye flexed her jaw muscle, vexed that Niia returned every serve.

"Favorite song?"

"Then…or now," Niia replied with the slightest of smirks, but it might as well have been the loudness of a last laugh.

As Skye took a menacing step toward her, Niia stepped back, almost recoiled. Now it was Skye's turn to chuckle.

"You've been preparing that step all your life, huh? I'm surprised every man in here didn't fly to your rescue."

"If you had lived my life, you would have too," Niia replied, without regret. "Your weakness is your strength."

"Then that would make your strength your weakness. No?"

The two women eyed each other down, immovable and irresistibly.

"Cut! I loved it. I *loved* it!" Spike exclaimed as he stepped back onto the set. "The energy, the imagery…Skye, I loved the Dorothy thing. Go with that. But this time, can we maybe use the script? Same energy though, loved the *energy*."

Neither woman heard a word that he said; they were too busy finishing their conversation with their eyes. Last look being spoken, they both walked off.

"Skye? Niia? Where are you going? Hey!" Spike questioned then threw his head back like Charlie Brown. "We're supposed to be making a movie, people."

Georgie stood off camera, watching the whole thing. When Skye left the set, she walked straight for him, looking seemingly right at him. But she wasn't looking at him, she was looking *through* him. And when she passed, walked through him like the ghost of Christmas to come, leaving nothing but attitude and the smell of Chanel in her wake.

Georgie went right to her trailer. When he arrived, she had already taken off her wig and was putting on a pair of large golden hoop earrings that complemented her minimalist aesthetic. He slammed the door.

"What do you want from me?" he asked, as if picking up where they left off.

"Nothing. Believe me, I've got *all* I need," she retorted, neck swiveling.

"Is that right?"

"*Damn* right," she spat back, chin aloft.

He laughed at her false bravado, stepping toward her.

"Fuck you laughing at? And his dick bigger!"

He snatched her into his arms, hard.

"But is it better?" he quipped, with a knowing smirk, one that she wanted to slap off of his face.

"Fuck yeah."

He kissed her gently.

"You lyin' to me."

She pushed away.

"*Much* better."

He ran his tongue over the ticklish crest of her upper lip. Skye gripped the ribs of his shirt into little wrinkled silk balls. He sucked her bottom lip and her upper lip trembled with jealousy.

"Does he kiss you like this?"

"All," eyes fluttering, "all the time."

He ran his tongue along her neck to her collar bone.

"Here?"

"Huh?"

He bit her neck, right on her hot spot.

"Sssss!"

"Say it!"

"No, no, he don't, he don't," she blurted out, wrapping

her legs around his back, like only Skye could.

He took her straight to the floor, pulling off her robe, as she snatched away his pants.

"What you want me to say, baby? That her lips ain't as soft as yours?" he huffed, kissing her with the urgency of a madman. "That her sweat ain't as sweet as yours?" He licked behind her ear for a drop. "Her nipples don't taste like yours?" He bit and sucked her hard nipples, making her arch into him.

"Yessssss," she hissed, sensually

She was so wet, he slid inside of her effortlessly. Her pussy gripped him like a glove.

"You want me to say her pussy ain't as good? That she can't take all this, fuck this dick, cream this dick?" he growled in her ear, pounding her like a jackhammer on high.

"Georgie, stop talking please!" she begged, because the sound of his voice was driving her crazy.

He was in pushup position, her legs cocked back, his arms like two pillars on either side of her head, her nails digging into his wrists like she was trying to slit them. The air was heavy with raw, urgent sexuality, pure lust. Coated contempt that was hard and fast.

"Aaarrgggghh!" she growled like a lioness as his thrusts ripped a powerful orgasm right out of her.

He hadn't cum but he stopped, kissed her trembling eyelids, nose and lips, the whispered, "But if I did I'd be lyin'…slut."

Control of her body was just beginning to return, as he got up, pulled up his pants and headed for the door. Tears ran backward to the floor and her cream drenched her thighs.

"I hate you," she sobbed. "I hate you! I hate youuuu!"

When he got to their apartment, Niia was sitting in their

picture window, clad only in his Eagles jersey, her knee drawn to her chest watching the rainfall. On the stereo a melody played in French, but the voice felt familiar to Georgie.

"You were with her, weren't you?" she asked, looking at her own reflection in the window.

He didn't answer. He didn't need to. He went and sat beside her, straightening her legs and putting them on his lap.

"Who is that? She sounds familiar," he asked.

"Sade. She has albums in French, too."

"I never knew that. Why you never played it before?'

"Saving it for a rainy day," she said, mustering a smile.

He began to massage her feet. She watched him for a comfortable moment then asked, "Georgie...why did you marry me?"

He shrugged, stopped massaging her feet and looked at her.

"Why did you marry me?"

She lowered her eyes, eluding his gaze. He slipped her chin back up and stared into her eyes.

"Don't do that. Listen...do I make you happy?"

Her smile lit up her face.

"Like a little girl on Christmas day."

He smiled.

"Then that's all that matters. People get together under false pretenses every day. They meet, lie, fuck, lie some more then one day, one week, one *lifetime* later, wake up like, what the fuck am I doin' here?!" he chuckled, but her expression soured.

"Like an imposter," she confirmed, pulling her legs off his lap.

He pulled them back.

"Ma, you're *not* an imposter. Don't listen to that bullshit.

What makes Skye who she is, is she's so fuckin' cold blooded," he explained, the admiration evident in his voice, "but you just gotta know how to handle her. She get cold, you get *colder*, and if that don't work, then slap the shit out of her," he joked.

"I'm not that kind of person, Giorgio."

"Niia, sometimes you have to *be* that kind of person," he stressed. "Ma, your heart is so pure, the world doesn't deserve you, but understand that pure beauty like yours... invites abuse."

Her face took on a horrified expression, as if he had slapped her.

"Are you saying I deserved to be beaten?!"

She jumped up to run off and Georgie jumped up to stop her.

"No Niia, *fuck* no! I'd throw myself out the window if I even *thought* that. But *listen*," he stressed, putting his hands together as if he were praying. "Listen...it's like a rose. A rose is beautiful, it's delicate, it's vulnerable. And that's why God gave it thorns. *Never* lose your thorns, because if you do, the world will eat you *alive*.

"I'm *not* Skye, Giorgio," she hissed through clenched teeth.

"I'm not talking about Skye, Niia! I'm talking about *you*!"

"Yes you are. You want me to be tough and mean like her! What next? You want me to cut off all my hair, too?!"

She started to storm away, but Georgie jumped in front of her and pulled her into his embrace.

"Shhh, shhhhh...we're not going to do this. Not over that, okay? Let's dance, hmm? You want to dance with me, sweetness?"

She wrapped her arms around his neck.

"I don't want to call you Giorgio anymore. It's not your name. I want to call you Georgie...like everybody else."

He knew what that *everybody else* consisted of, but he joked it off.

"Ma, you can call me anything you want, just don't call a cab and lock the door!"

She giggled into his neck.

"Never."

"Okay, I don't know this French shit, so I'ma sing *my* song...*if this world were mine, I would place at your feet, all that I own, you've been so good to me*," he sang, slightly off key.

She leaned back in his embrace to look at him.

"Would you really, Georgie? Would you really give me anything?" Niia asked.

Give a woman everything, but never anything. Georgie knew the rule, but Niia looked so sweet, so innocent, so very vulnerable, like a rose without thorns, so he broke it.

"Anything! Name it."

"Your heart."

He smiled, caressed her cheek, then replied, "I love you, baby, but—" As they kissed – they both knew what his words really meant.

In retrospect, it's inevitable.

One of the things you just *knew* would happen. Like seeing a fragile glass vase in a room and a precocious, sticky-handed toddler motoring toward it, or a drunk teenage boy staggering to the car in an ice storm with a "Bridge Is Out" sign a mile up the road.

It was bound to happen.

It began with the hair cut.

"I want you to cut my hair, Georgie," Niia told him, sitting in the stylist chair in their apartment.

Bad Habits had just wrapped and she had a reading for a new film. Hollywood was just beginning to fall in love with her.

"Ma, stop playing. I'd rather cut my wrist than cut your

hair." Georgie shot back, brushing her long, silky mane.

"I'm serious," she pouted, like a spoiled little girl.

"Niia," he said, looking at her in the mirror. "What are you talking about? Your hair is beautiful. I can maybe pin it up, sweep it, leave bangs to frame your face..." he mused, playing with the look.

She snatched the scissors off the counter.

"I'll do it myself," she huffed.

"Noooo!" Georgie bellowed, breaking down as if she were scratching her nails across a chalkboard. "Okay, okay, I'll... cut it; just put the scissors down."

She slowly put them down, as if still not convinced to release the hostages.

With much trepidation, he cut it. He gave her a Halle Berry in *Boomerang* look that fit her slightly oval face like a glove. She loved it, he loved her, so it worked out fine.

Then, it was her appetite.

Not for food, for Georgie. Niia had always been sensual, but its expression was more like the shy boldness of a virgin on her wedding night. She became amorous and adventurous, with the aggression of a vixen. It was like she was trying to drain him. If he wasn't at least limping, he wasn't leaving. All she had to do was whisper French in his ear and half of him would turn to putty, the other half would turn to steel. He needed her to slow down, so he brought her a chocolate Ferrari with a unique vanity plate.

"Georgie, why does it read all M's?" she asked.

"That ain't m's, it reads *mmmmmm*, because I *know* that's how the car feel with all that ass in it," he cracked, slapping it just to see it giggle. "God-*damn*," he exclaimed, like it hurt.

And then came the kiss.

It happened like any other kiss shared between lovers, sandwiched between snuggles and laughter. But what made it different was the fact that Georgie had just Scarfaced a line of cocaine, as thick as a caterpillar from the surface of his mirrored tray. When he sat back, Niia, who was straddling him, giggled.

"You look like a pool shark."

"Huh?"

"Your nose," she replied, and before he had wiped it off, she had kissed it away.

It was a spontaneous act, but not one that she hadn't already been contemplating. She had been attracted to the twinkle of the little flakes since she had first laid eyes on them. It reminded her of the way the sun reflected off snow, the stuff you threw playfully and little kids made angels in. It was white, the color of purity, the color of heaven complemented with the shine and wink of a girl's best friend.

How could she not at least taste it?

She kissed it, and without hesitation, it kissed her back, numbing her lip and the tip of her tongue like a cool sensation.

"It's tingly," she giggled.

Georgie wiped at his nose.

"What, I had it on my nose?"

"It's..." Niia began, trying to find a word for the sensation. She smacked her tongue, but tasted only numbness. "What does God feel like?"

They looked at one another, and in that one glance had a whole conversation.

I want to. Do you want me to? Because I will if you hold my hand.

Why not? I'm your man, I can protect you from anything. This shit can't touch me. How can it touch you?

She picked up the mirrored tray and the short metal straw. She leaned over the pile and saw the reflection of her eyes in the tray. They held the cat-eyed expression of curiosity.

She inhaled like she was taking a breath of fresh air.

"Baby steps," Georgie cautioned.

But she had already fallen down the rabbit hole, and it felt like…

*Time keeps on slippin, slippin, slippin
Into the futurrrrrree*

Her senses exploded and it felt like she could hear the very pulse of the universe, but it was only her own heartbeat in her ears. She sniffed again, this time face first like Georgie did all the time.

"Now you've got it on your nose," he chuckled, using his thumb to rub it away.

He might as well have touched her clit. Her whole body sang out like *oooooohhhhhhh!* Goosebumps overtook her flesh, her nipples hardened and throbbed, her pussy salivated and blood shot through her veins like lava over ice, chilling her until her teeth chattered.

Ge – Ge – Georgie, don't…move," she hissed, cumming just from the feeling of sitting on his dick as she straddled him.

When he sucked her nipples, she thought that she would explode.

"Georgie, fffffuck me," she trembled.

Coke went flying one way and their bodies went rolling another way. Niia got on her knees and elbows, spreading so wide Georgie could see the pink of her creamy center.

"My pusssssssy is on fire!" she growled.

He plowed into her with one powerful thrust after another, penetrating her over and over again.

"Deeper Georgie, oooooohh deeper!" Niia squealed.

Every forward stroke put out the fire and every back stroke re-ignited it, making her beg for more, teetering on the edge of insanity. She wanted him so deep—impossibly deep—like the feeling she might get if he just crawled up inside of her and jumped up and down. Georgie leaned back, making the curve of his dick hit the sensitivity in her spine that spread the sensation throughout her whole body.

"Ohhh Georgie, I feel you all over!" she moaned.

"Cum!" he demanded, his voice deep and commanding, like a shaman priest, his dick beating out the rhythm of a voodoo spell, calling for the spirit. "*Cum*."

It started in her fingertips, in her ear lobes, the tip of her nose and her throat, building speed as it raced lower, rumbling like a runaway train, along the contours of her curves until it took the breath from her lungs and the voice from her throat. She froze, mid scream, and released the spirit all over Georgie's dick, her thighs, his thighs as well as the silk sheets bunched beneath them. Her body, still frozen, thrust in mid-air before it fell like a filet to the bed, boneless and jellied.

"Don't touch me," she whispered over and over.

It was love at first sight.

Into the futurrrrrre ....

"Georgie. Are you listening to me? Are you high on something? This is very serious," his lawyer Abe stressed to him.

"Yeah, I'm listening, I'm lookin' right at you," Georgie replied.

But it didn't look like he was looking at Abe, it looked like he was looking right *through* him. He and Niia sat there glass-eyed, like a black Raggedy Ann and Andy: numb, totally blitzed.

They hadn't slept in almost three days. They had flown from L.A. to Chicago to do a layout for *Savoy* magazine, then on to New York. Since Niia's career was about to really blast off, they needed to hire a full-fledged team instead of operating with the skeleton crew that Georgie had inherited from Alphonse. While in New York, he got a page from Skye, reminding him of the IRS.

"I'm not gonna forget," he assured her.

"I don't know, seems like it's real easy for you," Skye deadpanned, then disconnected before he could reply.

He went straight to see Abe.

"Why did you wait so long," Abe exclaimed.

"I got caught up in managing Niia; I'm managing Skye, plus I'm doing hair everywhere, but trying to open a string of salons. I mean shit," Georgie explained.

"Georgie, the IRS doesn't care if you had open heart surgery on your *ass*. Their attitude is, fuck you, pay me!"

"So that's why I'm here."

Abe shook his head and sighed hard.

"Georgie, this isn't candy money we're talkin' here. You mean to tell me you're running through *millions* and haven't paid *any* taxes?"

Defensive and irritated—especially since Abe was blowing his high—he squirmed in his seat and replied, "I don't know Abe, I thought they took it out already."

"Who are *they*?"

"The IRS, the government; I mean damn, if I knew, what the hell would I need you for?"

"To bake a cake."

Georgie chuckled, relieving tension.

"Seriously Georgie, they can seize your assets, freeze your accounts, or worse, throw you in jail. The IRS always gets their man... so look, gimme a few days, *maybe* I can straighten this thing out, okay?"

"Hey, that's why you get paid the big bucks," Georgie winked as he and Niia stood.

Abe stood and they shook hands.

"And please, for Christ's sake Georgie, pay taxes! Mrs. Akimbe, very nice to meet you. Take care of my guy over here, will ya?"

"I will," she smiled sweetly.

When they got to the elevator, Niia turned to Georgie and asked, "What did he mean throw you in jail? Can you go to jail for zees taxes, Georgie?"

He waved it off.

"It's nothing baby, believe me. Just shit they tell people to scare 'em up."

She pushed up on him, leaning her body against his and straightening his tie.

"They better not, because then I'd have to break you out," she simpered seductively.

"Oh yeah? How you gonna do that?"

"I have my ways."

"I'm sure you do."

"Besides, what would I tell your son?"

"We ain't even gotta," he began, before what she had just said hit him over the head. He looked at her, wide-eyed. She nodded excitedly, the smile making her face glow.

"You mean?"

"I mean!"

Georgie lifted her off her feet and spun her around, making her giggle like a little girl. He kissed her, then embraced her tightly, singing "If this world were mine…"

Georgie was on top of the world.

The birth of a child is a milestone in any man's life, giving him another reason to breathe. It both humbles and exalts you at the same time. He couldn't wait to see Niia grow both full and round, symbolizing the growth of their bond. Sometimes, he could look into her eyes and see the future, but then the light would shift and he would see only his own reflection. As promising as tomorrow seemed, there was still the allure of today. Georgie and Niia were young and living the fast life. Runways stretched from coast to coast and continent to continent, bridged by the smooches of air kisses, the popping bottles, bubbles, bubbles, endless bubbles cascading down cups that runneth over.

They inhaled life, scarfing it down with greedy abandonment because Georgie believed himself invincible and Niia believed in him invincibly, which rendered her invincible too. Their delusions were grand in scope, tragically weighted on wings as the sheer speed of their flight was bound to melt away, drip, by drip, by...

"Don't let it drip on your dress; hold your head back," he instructed Niia as blood ran from her nose.

She was sitting in front of her vanity mirror. He was looking at her through the mirror, standing behind her in his tuxedo.

"It doesn't hurt," she snickered, her voice nasally because she had her nose pinched with a towel.

"It's not supposed to, it's a coke bleed," he chuckled.

They were on their way to a roast being held for Jon Peters, the man whom so many in Hollywood told Georgie that he reminded them of. He had to admit, he was looking forward to meeting a man who started as a stylist like him to become the head of a million dollar studio. Everything was fine until Niia's nose began to bleed.

"Ma believe me, this batch we got tonight is fuckin' fire. You don't have to sniff so much to fly. All I did was a two and I can't feel my toes," he chuckled.

She laughed as she checked to make sure there was no blood on her face.

"I thought it was just me. Is it hot in here?"

Georgie went over and stepped into his shoes. When he turned around, she was standing up. He couldn't help but just look at her and admire her beauty. The white chiffon silk, off-the-shoulders gown, beaded with Swarovski crystal cascading from breast to floor, and matching crystal beaded mules, complimented her smooth, chocolate skin.

"Damn Ma...you're beautiful. You're like a fairytale princess," Georgie remarked, solemnly.

"Georgie, stop. You're going to make me cry and ruin my makeup."

"Okay, okay, I forgot that pregnant women are emotional Want a pickle?" he cracked, grabbing his dick at her.

She laughed, but not her usual laugh; it was more of a nervous titter. The phone rang. He turned to the nightstand to answer it.

"Yeah? They sent the white one, right?"

"Georgie."

"Because everybody's gonna be in black ones. Okay, we'll be down. When it gets here, call me."

He hung up and turned to find Niia laid out on the bed.

"Ma, the limo's on the way, but if you start that shit, I'ma ruin your dress," he joked, checking his bow tie one final time in the mirror.

When she didn't get up, he walked over to her.

"Niia stop playin' Ma. Come on."

She didn't move.

He looked down at her face. Her expression seemed to be frozen in swoon. She looked like a sleeping angel, like she always did when he watched her sleep, except for one thing.

There was no glow.

In that moment, he played back and listened to what he had only heard before.

"Georgie," she had said.

Now, on replay he could hear the quiver of uncertainty in her tone.

"Is it hot in here?" she had asked and he could see soft beads of perspiration on her neck. Standing, she had felt a

sway, one that had made her sit down. Her skin felt clammy.
His name would be the last word that she would ever say.
The cocaine literally stopped her heart. Mercifully, she
only felt a slight pinch and then she was gone.

"Niia," he whispered, but deep down, he knew that it was
useless. When it finally hit him, his knees buckled.

"No…no…no please," he prayed, backing away. "Niia!!!"
The sound of his agony spurred him to act. He snatched
up the phone, dialing 911 furiously.

"I need an ambulance now! Please hurry, please!"

"Where are you, sir?"

"She's dying, please."

"Sir, where *are* you?"

"I – I don't know," Georgie replied, realizing that he didn't
even know his own address.

He never had a reason to. He simply drove to and fro by
route. He knew the street, but his anxiety made him forget
even that.

"Sir, I can't…"

"Trace the call! Trace it!" he barked, then let the phone
fall to the floor.

He paced once then mumbled, "That's it, movement; have
to keep her moving, moving, moving…" he repeated, like a
mantra.

Georgie carefully lifted her limp body up and pulled her to
her feet, wrapping her arms around his neck.

"Come on baby, just gotta move, the ambulance is coming.
Hurry upppp! Stay with me please," he begged, the tears
beginning to fall. "Dance! We have to dance; dance with me
baby, please…just dance with me once more," he sobbed.

He was eight-years-old again, dancing around his room
with his doll, wishing God would make her real, praying that
God would keep her real. Her voice echoed in his ear, how
she had said it for the last time.

Georgie *You said you would protect me.*

Georgie, *I trusted you.*

Georgie, *I thought you loved me.*

"Please God, I'm sorry baby, I'm sorry." His whole body wracked with sobs. "Just dance. Remember our song, *if this world were mi – ne, I would place at your feet all that I own, you've been so good…*"

He could no longer hold her up, and him as well. He slowly fell to his knees, laying her on the floor, his tears glistening off of the Swarovski crystals on her dress. He rested his head against her womb and he cried like he had never cried before.

Many of Black Hollywood's finest turned out to pay their respects to the African star that would never be. Ironically, even though Niia's death was news in Hollywood, because she was not well known, it failed to register a blip in the rest of the country. Even the *Los Angeles Times* only gave it back story status, basic boilerplate: the type of an article where only the names change.

African Actress Dies of Cocaine-induced Heart Attack

Eight million and one.

Being that American remained unaware, the rest of the world did also—namely Cameroon, and Niia's family. It would be months before they learned of her death, thanks to Alphonse, who relished the opportunity to beat her one more time.

For this reason, Georgie had her buried in Philly on the other side of his grandmother, right next to where he planned to be buried. He tried to console himself with the thought that if they couldn't be together in life, they would be together in death.

After the funeral, after the condolences, and even when the sun had begun to turn its back, Georgie stood graveside, with Stephanie right beside him.

"It was a beautiful service. Sidney sang like an angel," Stephanie remarked.

"Yeah," Georgie replied, but he had barely heard the song Stephanie took his hand and squeezed it.

"Baby, I know this is painful. I know it hurts, but in times like these when we feel weak, we have to trust in the Lord. He'll make it right because *He* can do anything."

Georgie looked at her, emotionless.

"Even God can't change the past."

"No, but *you* can change the future, Georgie," she replied, much too quickly to have processed his words. "Do you think you can do this again? Is this the person you want to be? No, is this the person you *can* be or is this just the person you *want* to be just because you *can*?" Stephanie questioned.

"This will never happen again," he said, with a grit in his tone that said it was his pride speaking.

"Don't you even *know* what *this* is? Because I don't think you do. No, matter of fact, I *know* you don't. But until you do, baby it *will* happen again," Stephanie answered and kissed him on the cheek.

She was the first to see Skye approaching. She hugged and kissed Skye then turned back to Georgie.

"I'll see you at home," she said, then walked away.

Georgie and Skye stood side by side as the cemetery workers approached with their shovels. He had seen when she arrived with Guy and had been aware of her presence the whole time. It comforted him like a warm hug, even though she kept her distance. She knew that she didn't have to stand beside him to be close.

After several minutes, Georgie said, "...I didn't even know how to tell her family that she's gone. I tried everything. I even reached out to Alphonse..." His voice trailed off and he shook his head. "I failed her, Skye. I wanted to bring her family to her, but I took her from her family instead."

The masked anguish in his voice made Skye fight to keep the tears hidden behind her shades. She wanted to finally tell him, she understood why he did it, but the words wouldn't come, because to do so would have been to make a mockery of the pain that she was still feeling, seeing the ring he was still wearing.

"Abe told me what happened. Did they freeze everything?" she asked.

Georgie nodded.

The IRS had seized all of his assets and froze all his bank accounts. All he had was a few scattered thousands, his jewels and the Corvette that Skye had bought him.

"I – umm – talked to Benny. I told him all about you back story, your whole Giorgio thing, the reason you had to leave Philly and he thinks it would make a great movie. He wants to talk to you about buying the rights," she explained.

"I appreciate that, Ma. Tell him I'll be in touch," he replied, giving her a grateful look.

She nodded, then began to watch the cemetery workers.

"Do you need money?"

"I'm good."

"No you're not," she giggled softly, pulling a check from her crotch and handing it to him.

He looked at it; it was signed but there was no amount on it.

"It's blank."

"I know."

They looked at each other for a moment before he said, "Thank you."

"Don't thank me. It's your severance. You're fired."

He chuckled.

"I can't blame you."

"At least until you get your head together, and Georgie,

you really need to. I do, too. This…Niia has made me look at my life. I've decided to get help for my problem. You should, too," Skye proposed, a hint of pleading in her tone.

"I'm the problem. Where am I supposed to go for that?" he replied, bitterly.

She turned his face to her.

"I'm getting ready to work on my next album. I'm going to get a little place in the Caribbean, something simple. Quiet. Come with me, okay? Let's just go away, you know, *breathe.*

Georgie looked into her eyes and in that moment realized how much he loved Skye, how much she loved him, but deep down, they could never be together.

He caressed her cheek, thumbing away a tear, and said, "Skye, I love you…so much, but right now, I can't be the man you need me to be. I don't know if I ever will. You don't deserve that, so I'd rather leave you whole than leave you with one."

"Georgie, I…"

"Me too, Ma. *Believe* me, me too!" he tenderly cut her off, anticipating her objection. "Do you know how sick I'm going to be seeing you walk away? But Ma, it's for the best. I'll let you go before I burn off your wings."

She wanted to ask him, if he were her could he watch her walk away? If he were her, could he be the man *she* needed him to be? She wanted to say, Anya's not coming back, I'm here! *Me!* She left you Georgie, but when are you going to leave *her?*

But she didn't. Instead, she pulled his lips to hers, one last time, smiled into his eyes and said, "Poor Georgie…all I ever wanted was to hear you say my name."

The slight furl in his brow told her he had no clue…

"I hope you find what you're looking for, Georgie," Skye remarked, no longer able to keep the tears shaded, as she backed away.

"You too, baby…you too," he replied, and even though it took everything in him, he managed to turn and walk away.

Georgie couldn't see.

He was staring into the emerald green eyes of actress Vanessa Lauren as she sat in the stylist chair in her dressing room, but he just couldn't see.

"So what do you think?" she asked, playful flirtation coloring her tone.

"I think you're beautiful, but umm, what would you like me to do?"

"I was hoping you'd surprise me. Everybody says you have magic hands. Go see Giorgio, he can see what other stylists can't imagine," she giggled.

That was Georgie's gift. To be able to look at a woman and see not only the way she was, but who she could be. But since Niia's death, he couldn't focus on the vision.

He looked at her again, cocked his head, walked behind her, lifted, felt and played with her hair, but…nothing.

"Ma…I'm sorry. I can't," he admitted.

Vanessa looked at him sympathetically.

"I understand. I know about your loss. I'm sure it took a lot out of you. Rain check?" she winked.

He smiled.

"Sure, and it ain't even gotta rain."

But Vanessa was just the beginning. At first, Georgie thought, just a little more coke, just a few more drinks and he would get back what he had lost, only to find himself getting lost in it. Slowly, word got around that Georgie had lost his touch, and the calls became fewer and less frequent, drying up faster than a puddle in an Egyptian desert.

"Fuck hair," he mumbled, removing the parachute for a free fall, the bottom of the bottle fueling his bravado.

Two days later, he called Benny. The next day, Benny sent someone to see Georgie. The first thing he thought was, Pamela Anderson. That's who she looked like with voluptuous breasts and tapered, slender hips. She wore eyeglasses and a suit made for business, but underneath he could tell that she was anything but.

"Georgie, so nice to meet you. I'm Heather. Benny sent me?" she said as she stepped inside.

Georgie shook her hand then closed the door behind her.

"Yeah okay, I'm glad he did."

She smiled appropriately.

"Can I get you a drink?"

"Whatever you have is fine."

He returned with two wine glasses and a bottle of Zinfandel. He handed her a full glass.

"So what's the word," Georgie asked, sitting down across from her on the couch.

"Well...Benny says he absolutely *loves* the story! He says he definitely wants more detail, but from what Skye's already told him, he's sure he can get a mid-sized budget approved," Heather explained.

"Music to my ears. Who's gonna pay me?" he quipped.

"I'm not sure, but you know Benny, he'll definitely swing for the fences."

"Tell him I want Will Smith; he's from Philly too. I mean, he ain't as fly as me, but that would be asking the impossible, huh?"

They laughed.

"Confidence. I like that."

"Glad you approve," he sipped, offering a refill that was readily accepted. "So what's the numbers we're talking?"

"Benny says fifty thousand and ten percent net."

"Dah dunt chhsssss," Georgie said, providing the rim shot motioning as if he were playing the drums to her punch line.

"And for my next joke…"

"No joke, Georgie. Benny says it's a helluva offer. You're free to call him if you like," Heather suggested sweetly.

Georgie chuckled.

"Come on Ma, I've already negotiated three movie deals, one for Skye and two for my wife and everybody knows net stands for nothing ever tabulated," Georgie quipped, with irritation building under his chuckle.

Heather sensed it, too.

"Maybe you should call Benny."

Georgie sipped his Zinfandel. He knew that Benny was lowballing him because he knew Georgie was in a bind. He knew that if he was still with Skye or Niia was still alive, Benny would be offering twenty times as much. In Hollywood, perception is everything, and Georgie was perceived as a bloodied swimmer in a sea of sharks.

"Why'd Benny send you anyway? Who are you, his lawyer?"

"No. I'm Benny's assistant."

"I see."

And he did. He downed his drink.

"Stand up."

She looked at him, taken aback. A nervous titter escaping her lips.

"Excuse me?"

"You heard me, stand up," he repeated, without emotion.

Heather finished her drink.

"Now take off your clothes."

She didn't protest. She just looked at Georgie, a subtle, knowing smirk playing across her lips. When she reached up and unpinned her hair and let it fall softly over her shoulders, he knew exactly why Benny had sent her.

She was a part of the deal.

She undressed, taking off everything until she stood

naked, tan and succulent, the sun cutting through the room and slashing warmly across her silicon bosom and shaved pussy.

"Should I leave the shoes on?" she grinned seductively.

"No," Georgie replied bluntly.

She stepped out of them, reluctantly. He could tell that without them she felt more vulnerable. He wanted her to.

He stood, filled his glass and approached her slowly.

"Get on your knees."

Slowly, she lowered herself to the floor. He stood over her, eying her with a look, which she couldn't read. It made her nervous. Georgie put the glass to her lips. She parted them just enough to drink it, and drank it all.

"Now do that to my dick," he smirked as he pulled out his dick.

She opened her mouth and lolled out her tongue, seductively. Georgie put down the glass and held his dick to her. He rubbed the tip over her lips and cheeks then slapped her with it; that shocked, titillated and made her giggle.

"So you're the cherry on top, huh?" he quipped. "Open wide, I'm a big boy." She did. But instead of filling her mouth with flesh, she felt a warm, salty golden shower.

"Ahhhh!" she gagged, spitting the piss out and recoiling.

"Don't move! Don't *fuckin'* move!" Georgie bassed, never touching her, but his commanding voice was enough to ensure total compliance. He pissed in her face, on her hair, in her mouth. Tears and piss mingled, running down her cheek, he neck and off of her enlarged nipples.

"Still want to be the cherry on top?!" he laughed menacingly. "Huh? Still want to be a part of the deal?"

All that she could do was sob, shoulders wracked.

He shook his dick in her face, wiping it on her lips, then picked up his glass and refilled it. She started to get up.

"Did I tell you to move?" he asked coldly.

"Please…"

"You will; ain't that what you here for? Now bend over," he commanded.

"I – I – I want to go," she sniffled.

"Go where, huh?! Back to those fuckin' corn fields?" he laughed. "Back to fuckin' Nebraska, or is it Oklahoma? You think I don't know your story, you sexy bitch? Don't you know sexy is a dime a dozen? Now bend your sexy ass over!"

Slowly, she bent, positioning herself on her knees and elbows. Georgie walked around her slowly, dropping his pants and pumping his dick until it was semi-erect. He got behind her, resting his drink on her ass and plunging into her pussy.

She sobbed harder.

The sex was the closest thing to consensual rape since the apple dropped. He fucked her like she was a nut rag, faceless and meaningless, except for the point he was making. When he felt himself cumming, he pulled out, nutting all over her ass and back, wiping his dick off along the crack of her ass. Then he stood up, pulling up his pants. Now she was crying uncontrollably.

"Remember this, sexy bitch. Remember! Don't you ever forget and pretend you don't know what you are! What we *all* are," he barked, standing over her.

The contempt in his voice curdled her spirit like mildew and wilted her sense of self like a dying rose. She curled up on the floor in the fetal position, broken.

Georgie looked down at her and the hate began to lift. The echo of her incessant cries shattered his coldness.

"Heather," he sighed, "Heather…I'm sorry…I'm sorry. You didn't deserve that. Benny did, but you didn't."

She kept crying. He scooped her up and carried her to the shower. He turned the shower on and began washing her back.

"Why – why did you do that?" she sniffled.

"Shh, it's over, Ma. Just let me clean you up."

He ran the shower, treading her hair with his fingers, rubbing the water over her with caring caresses.

"You're very pretty."

"Thank you," she replied, the warm water soothing her wounded self.

"Your hair is dry though; who does your hair?"

"Huh?"

"Who does your hair."

"Just – just a salon."

"No, no, no Ma, don't just go to *any* salon; find one that fits *you*. Get to know them. Finding a stylist is like finding a man. They should bring out the best in you, make you feel good about yourself, you know?" he said, massaging her scalp and washing her hair.

"O - okay."

"I'm serious Ma, because I can smell the cheap shit in your hair. Your stylist must have sold her soul to the Koreans. You're too beautiful for that. When you bring the contract back, I'ma do your hair, get a better conditioner, show you what to look for, okay?"

Finally she smiled and Georgie rattled on like what had occurred earlier never happened.

He sat in the living room while she finished washing up. She came out with a towel wrapped around her. He was sitting there quietly, his hands tented in from of his face, tentatively.

"Ummm, I'm going to…go," Heather announced.

Georgie could tell that she was reluctant, that she really didn't want to leave.

"Okay."

"Unless," she replied, allowing her voice to trail off in innuendo.

"No, you should go…before he comes back."

She knew exactly who *he* was. She began to dress. Once she took off the towel, he allowed his eyes to travel slowly over her body. For the first time in his life, he looked at a beautiful woman's body and he felt what he had never felt before. Nothing.

When she was dressed, she turned to him and held up the bottle of conditioner that he had given her.

"Thanks, Georgie. I'll – um – see you with the contracts."

"No doubt. You can let yourself out."

She did. He sat. He didn't move. He thought. He watched the shadows on the floor getting longer…weaker…dimmer, until they disappeared and he sat silhouetted by the darkness and the glimmer of a street light outside the window.

Someone knocked.

"It's open," he called out, without yelling.

A short, Spanish dude walked in.

"Georgie?" he asked, with uncertainty, squinting into the darkness. He could just make out a figure seated in the armchair.

"I called you yesterday," Georgie replied.

"Yeah, but you never asked for heroin before, too. I had to make a few calls. Why's it so dark in here?"

"Ain't no lights on."

"Yeah, I can see that."

"Then don't ask no stupid questions. You got the shit?"

The guy—paranoid by trade—had never seen Georgie this…dark. He was always funny, charming, accessible. Now, it was as dark as a confessional. The room felt claustrophobic.

"Yeah, yeah, here we go."

They exchanged money and product.

"Let yourself out."

"Hey Georgie, be careful with that heroin. It's China

White."

"Hector, are you a dope dealer or a doctor?"

Hector walked out. The only sound was the occasional passing car, the hum of electricity and the ticking of a clock into the future. Georgie knew he needed light, but for what he planned on doing, electric light seemed too naked, too revealing. He needed the cloak of darkness. He cut on the TV to a random channel and used the light to dump out the cocaine and heroin on the back of Skye's album cover, but quickly regretted it. Her eyes seemed to bore into him.

Poor Georgie, don't let the world love you to death.

He knew what she meant now.

We are all performers, and the world is a stage. Just shoot for the moon; some settle for stars, but when potential becomes expectation, to not live up to one means to disappoint the other. First impressions become only impressions, and when you cease to impress, you cease to be. That is the death that the world loves.

He grabbed a deck of cards off the stereo speaker and began to mix and shuffle the cocaine and heroin into one substance. He noticed that both cards were kings of hearts, and he wondered how until he remembered that it was a pinochle deck; Niia had been trying to teach him the game.

Niia.

"Georgie."

The way she said his name for the last time still haunted him. He could still hear it every time someone called him. Her voice and theirs a duet, so sickening until he wanted to change his name to a language nobody knew, nobody spoke, nobody *understood*. So that nobody would call him again, *ever*.

Fffffff!

He took a hit of the mixture from the edge of the card. The coke he knew but the heroin was strange to his system and went straight to his stomach. It tasted like onions, raw but tasteless and then like a tsunami, it rose within him to great heights and surged up out of his throat in waves of vomiting that drove him to all fours. When he finally got his composure, he grabbed a bottle of gin to rinse the taste of vomit from his mouth, then spat it out on the floor before taking a healthy swig. The heroin had him mellow and the cocaine had him wired, speed balling…falling, riffing. Georgie, the king of hearts shoveling the mixture, inhaling it all.

"Goddamn!" he roared, as he heard hymns about Jesus looming overhead.

He had been subconsciously aware of the sounds of the preacher's voice, but at first it was only background static that came with the light of the TV, like the buzz of a fly comes with the smell of a grill. But flies – like preachers – drone on and on, emboldened by the sound of their own being, building momentum or seeming to do so as our tolerance loses its mooring, and then you explode.

Georgie exploded.

"What, you trying to tell me something?!" he screamed at the ceiling. "Huh?! Don't send nobody, talk to me! *You* talk to me!" Georgie ranted. "Stop hiding!!! Here I am; where are you?!" Georgie screamed, holding his arm out like Jesus on the cross.

"You're a fuckin' *coward*, whispering to muhfuckas in their sleep, squealing muhfuckas like a thief in the night! Take me! Youse a goddamn coward, you only take the good ones because you know a nigga'll give you hell! You need some help?! Huh?! Is that it?!"

He grabbed the gin bottle and poured it over his head, baptizing himself in alcohol.

"Now take your best shot. Where's your lightening bolt?!" he barked, then all of a sudden, his nose started to bleed.

He tasted it as it ran over his lips. He put his hand to his nose then looked at the blood on his fingertips. He laughed hysterically.

"A nosebleed?! That's all you got? Parlor tricks?" he laughed again. "Fuck you! Send me to hell, muhfucka; I'm used to it."

Georgie sat down to his pile, sniffing until he fell asleep... waiting.

He woke up the next morning, head banging like a slam dance, his throat raw with futility, his mind still frazzled and trapped. He had to get out. The apartment felt stuffy, the air stale and stilted. He got up and stumbled groggily out of the door.

When he reached the street, he headed for his little red Corvette. He felt his pockets for his car keys. He had left them upstairs. Mind frazzled, mind with a mind of its own. Random thoughts began to play in his head, like one of those old reel to reels that you might find in a box at someone's yard sale.

He decided to walk, too lazy to go back. The afternoon sun was bright. People were everywhere. They recoiled from him like he was a slice of darkness left over from the night before, reeking of vomit and alcohol, expensive designer clothes worn as carelessly as a vagabond's tattered garments.

"Fuck you staring at?" he mumbled inaudibly, self-consciously. A police cruiser drove by slowly, eying him, looking for a reason to lay him down. He stumbled on. Georgie came to a small park, the kind little kids play in and get abducted from. He sat down, the movie of his life still playing in his head.

He couldn't stop the endless loop, reminding him over and over again. He sat with his head in his hands, his head going boom, boom, boom, his heart going *bump-bump-bump*, his mind began to wander…

His first memory was the taste of candy, watermelon flavored Now and Laters. His grandmother had died, Stephanie had given them to him to shut him up. The picture of his father in his mother's room, only alive in his smile. "Get nasty with it," dancing, laughing, growing, becoming. Out of nowhere, the bullets ripped… The pain. Denise. The pleasure. Release.

"Am I next?" Her smile. Her arms raised, embracing new beginnings…chasing the sun.

Skye blowing smoke in his face, casting her spell, still unbroken.

Niia…

Niia…

Niia…

"As happy as a little girl on Christmas Day."

"If this world were mine…"

Just dance please; just one more time…

"Is this the person you can be or is this just the person you want to be because you can?"

Say my name…

Fifty thousand – peanuts.

Don't forget and pretend you don't know

Whowearewhoweallare!

Takemetakemeyoucoward.Jesssusdon'tlettheworldloveyouto death.

Georgie Porgie Georgie Por…

He felt like screaming, "Stop this thing, I want to get off!" but he gritted his teeth and then heard, "Are you sick?"

He looked into the face of a little blond girl, face full of freckles. She looked like a ray of sunshine with a tooth missing.

"What?" he replied, trying to focus on externals.

"You're sick. My daddy is a doctor. Do you need him to fix you?" she asked with the confidence of a child who believes that her father can fix anything, even the broken, stinky man in the park. It was the voice of unshakable faith.

"Sydney! I told you about talking to strangers," her mother scolded her, pulling her away.

"But Mommy, he's sick; we have to tell Daddy!"

It was then that Georgie notice she was carrying a small teddy bear. She held it out to him with a smile more precious, more redemptive than even God's forgiveness and let the teddy bear fall from her hand. Georgie watched her until she disappeared from view, then went over and picked up the teddy bear.

He sat on the grass, knees up, his arms rested across them, looking at the teddy bear. He felt the breeze of a second wind blow though him and then like a sprinter finally realizing that he was in a marathon, got up, headed home... and took a shower.

CAPTAIN SAVE A HOE

iiKane CHAPTER **17**

"My name is Georgie and I'm an addict."

"Hi Georgie," the choir sang.

Georgie's ear cringed, *so* not wanting to hear the clichéd response that he knew he would get. That is why it took him three days of considering before he joined the group. For three days after the experience in the park, he just stayed in his room. Going to rehab had seemed like the answer in the shower, but *being* in rehab didn't seem like it was an answer at all. The whole place looked like the set of *One Flew Over the Cuckoo's Nest* warmed over. All that was missing was the ass gowns. Everything was so sterile, so...clinical, so...dead that he wondered how one was supposed to get one's life back in a morgue.

He could have gone to one of the expensive rehabs, one of those "celebrity retreats," as the euphemism goes. But he didn't want the industry to know that he had a problem, and besides, he knew there were more drugs in there than on the street—and more expensive too. So he just signed himself into what was available, but he was beginning to regret it.

Until he saw her.

She was sitting Indian-style in a hard plastic chair known to waiting rooms worldwide, her sandals on the floor in front of her. She had the prettiest feet that he had ever seen.

Slender but tantalizing, with just enough space in between her toes that his tongue could dart in and around, and she was wearing a toe ring. He couldn't really make out her figure because she was wearing loose fitting grey sweat pants and an oversized, red and green t-shirt with the image of a powerful Black fist on it. Her face was hidden by her dreadlocks, salon neat, long and slender and they dangled like jungle vines as she sat, head bowed, reading a book.

She must have felt him staring because she lifted her head just enough to peer through her locks at him. Her cat-eye glaze had him pinned, thinking of Brazilian rainforests, a panther glaring through the trees and vines, *daring* him to come into her jungle. *Welcome to the jungle.*

He lost his train of thought.

"Georgie," Mrs. Stevens, the group facilitator said, calling him back from the aroma of cacao.

"Yeah…I'm a stylist. I've done everybody's hair, all the stars, Skye, Sidney, are there…"

"Ain't no stars in here," a fat Black dude named Leroy huffed.

Georgie took his hate in stride, shrugged and said, "I don't know, maybe we're all stars, you know, just trying to get our shine back."

"That's a very good way of looking at it, Georgie." Mrs. Stevens complimented, but Georgie was already back in the jungle.

"I'm sorry Mrs. Stevens, but excuse me. Excuse me," he repeated, ducking low to peer through the trees.

The panther peeked.

"We're in group and I think you're being very rude," Georgie remarked. She rolled her eyes and went back to the book. Georgie's hand shot up, finger pointing like he was in kindergarten and had to go to the bathroom.

"You don't have to raise your hand," Mrs. Steven

reminded him.

"Oh okay, but I think that she's being very unfair. I mean, we're supposed to be sharing, but I feel like she's hoarding the energy and it makes me uncomfortable."

The panther sighed hard, closed the book and looked up. She pushed her locks back, hitting Georgie with the full force of her beauty. Her name should have been mahogany because the brown hue had a deep reddish tinge, like there was a fire blazing within, just below the surface.

"Okay, you want me to share? I think you're an arrogant…"

"Hold up, hold up. What's your name?"

"What?"

"What are we, strangers in a train? This is group; you know, it's my name is…"

"Eanan."

Georgie looked at her.

"Is that your first name?"

"No."

Georgie's hand shot up again.

"Mrs. Stevens, red flag, *red flag*! *I* gave my first name, Leroy gave his, Veronica gave hers, so I'm not comfortable with her withholding hers," Georgie complained.

"In group, we only have to share what we're comfortable with," Mrs. Stevens reminded him.

"I understand that, but how do we know she's not a serial killer or something? Like, wait a minute, didn't I see you on *America's Most Wanted?*"

Mahogany rolled her eyes and went back to her book.

The rest of the group went well except for Georgie, who was lost in the jungle. This time, the panther didn't peek, even though she *knew* he was staring. All that he could see were those sexy little toes whose ring he wanted to taste.

When group was over, he had to fight the impulse to get

on some grade school shit, snatch up her sandals and hold them out of reach until she told him her name. But he restrained himself.

"Excuse me, Miss. Can I have a word with you?"

She stopped and pinned him.

"I like your locks; they're real pretty. But who does 'em? They appear to be brittle; what do you wash them in, acid? I'll wash them for you if you tell me your name."

"Excuse you," she replied, pulling the loc that he was holding out of his hand, "but I can do them myself."

"Then grease your scalp? Take care of the new growth for you?" Georgie requested, all but begging.

She chuckled, exasperatedly.

"Why do you want to know my name so bad?" she asked herself and him at the same time. Then she stopped, cocked her head, looked and him, then a smile of understanding spread over her face. "No one's ever told you *no*, have they?"

Mystery solved, she turned and walked up the hallway.

"Ma, don't do my like that, hol' up," Georgie called out, then started up the hallway after her.

That is until a big body blocked his path. Her name was ironically Miss Killjoy and she was 6'4", built like a linebacker with big, dookie ghetto braids all over her head.

"Mills, you know the rules: no men on the women's hallway," she bassed, crossing her massive arms in front of her massive chest.

Georgie looked at her. Under her elbows, he could see Mahogany disappear into her room. He was vexed.

"Miss Killjoy...anybody ever tell you that you look like Shenehneh from *Martin*?"

"Mills, if you don't get the hell out of my face, somebody gonna have to get me *off* your ass," Miss Killjoy retorted with a growl.

Georgie went back to his room, grumbling.

That evening in the cafeteria, he waited to see her. She didn't show. Since he didn't know her name, he called her something else, then spent the rest of the evening talking to Skye and his mother on the phone in the dayroom.

"I'm proud of you, Georgie," Skye said, exhaling when he told her where he was.

"Well Ma, I guess you were right."

"I always am."

"Even when you're wrong, right?"

They laughed.

"It's good to hear from you, baby. How's your wings?" he smiled.

"I've got wind beneath them."

"That's good…oh, call Benny; he's got a check for me. Pick it up.

"Okay."

She paused.

"Georgie, can you have visits?"

He smiled.

"In a few more weeks. I'll let you know. I'd love to see you."

He could hear her smile over the phone.

"My baby's growin' up," Stephanie exclaimed when he told her.

"Then when you gonna stop calling me a baby?" he quipped.

"Never! You can be a hundred and one," she cracked.

"Ma, when I'm a hundred and one, how old you gonna be?"

"Thirty five!"

The both laughed.

Georgie went back to his room and fell asleep, trying to guess the name of the girl with no name, twisting and turning different combinations, like he was trying to open a safe.

By breakfast the next morning, he was practically obsessed. He couldn't think of anything else. When she didn't show, he seriously considered putting Miss Killjoy into a sleeper hold then going straight to her room. If she hadn't come to lunch, he had decided that he would.

When he spotted her, head bowed over her book, half-eaten order of fries and chicken nuggets in front of her, he felt like he was back in high school with his first crush.

He sat down across from her.

"Hello, girl with no name," he dimpled.

"Hello, boy with no business," she replied without looking up. He chuckled.

"I've got business, yours; can't you see I'm all in it? What are you reading?" he asked, eating out of her fries.

She glared at him then tilted the book up.

"*Their Eyes Are Watching God*, by Zora Neale Hurston," he read the cover. "Is it good?"

"If I could read it, I'd tell you," she quipped sarcastically.

He reached for another fry. She slapped his hand, but he ate it anyway.

"Tell me your name and I'll read it to you. Matter of fact, I'll sing it to you, in soprano, wearing a tutu. Just tell me your name," he whined, playfully.

She pushed her book aside, leaned across the table and replied, "*No*. No, no, no, no, no. If you've never heard it, now you have. Get used to it," she snickered.

Even though the word did irk him, he didn't let it show.

"Ma, it's one thing to tell me no because I deserve it, but another just because you can. Now tell me, do I deserve it?" he questioned, putting his hands on his chest, resting his elbows on the table and giving her the puppy dog look.

She couldn't help but laugh. She sipped her soda through the straw, then answered, "Okay...give me one reason why I should tell you my name."

"Give me one reason why you shouldn't," Georgie shot right back.

"Because I told you before."

Georgie looked confused, thinking that maybe they had met before.

"Huh?"

"A thousand times. Shouted it over music in the club, whispered it so I couldn't disturb libraries. I've told you casually over drinks and reminded you of it at awkward moments. But you keep forgetting it, keep lying to it, keep disrespecting it. So *tell* me, why I should tell you again, and why will it be any different?" she explained, her voice only subtly embittered.

Georgie looked her in the eyes.

"Ma, I'm not…"

"You *are* them," she cut him off.

Georgie got slightly irritated. "You don't even *know* me, how you gonna put me in the same box?"

She gave him a sour look.

"Because I can see your reflection in the wedding ring. *Playa*," she spat, as if to say checkmate.

Georgie dropped his head to bite back the response she was asking for and gave her the one that her unawareness deserved.

"My wife is dead, but the ring I'm never taking off, even if I get married again, okay? So don't call me that again. I may be a bull shitter, but I'm not a liar."

Her facial expression melted.

"I'm – I'm sorry. I –"

"No, don't worry about it. I probably would've made that mistake too. You are right about one thing."

"And what's that?"

"You have told me your name before," he smirked, "a long

time ago, you probably don't even remember. The night I whisked you out your cabin and begged you to run away with me, run away and follow the North star to freedom…or maybe it was on the slave ship, in another language, I called out to tell you to be strong, that we would endure…or maybe it was when I prayed to you in the Egyptian temple, saying your name over and over, or maybe…just maybe, in the beginning, I'm the one who named you," he concluded, taking her analogy to the ultimate beginning.

While he talked, his whole aura transformed in her eyes. She had him pegged as an arrogant pretty boy, who thought the world revolved around him, and just out for a piece of ass. But the way he took her thread of a thought and weaved it into a vision had her looking at him in a different light and wanting to explore his mind.

"Is that right," she said, giving him her smile for the first time, the one where the tip of her tongue appeared between her teeth.

"Maybe," he grinned, enjoying her smile.

"Then what did you name me?"

He ate one of her nuggets.

"Well, it definitely wasn't a flower; you're not a Jasmine or a Rose, definitely not a Lily—you're not that delicate. So then I thought about music; I love music. I thought maybe you were a melody, lyric, whisper," he chuckled. "Horny… to be honest, that's as far as I got before I started calling you some things you might wanna figure out. But I meant no disrespect; I was pulling your hair when I said it," he concluded, then dimpled wickedly.

She laughed hard.

"You don't pull any punches do you, Georgie?"

He shrugged.

"The moment we start lying, we start dying, so why waste time?" he replied, looking her in the eyes.

The eye contact lingered for a verse, then she said, "Well…when I tell you my name, *if*…I tell you my name, you won't forget it this time because you won't be able to get the taste out of your mouth."

Peaches came to his mind.

"Ma forreal, I don't even want to know your name right now because if it's this much fun getting to know you, I can wait another twenty years," he winked as he ate another then bounced with her soda.

Now, it was his turn to know that she was watching and not turn around.

When he got back to his room, he thought about the girl with no name. She had him intrigued. She was not only beautiful, but he was also interested in her mind. He couldn't even remember being with a woman who read, and if she did, she didn't tell him about it; the magazine didn't count.

He laid back, looking forward to seeing her again.

Just as he dozed off, he heard a knock at the door.

"Yo," he called out, jumping up to open it.

It was Nurse Killjoy.

"You got a visit, Mills," she gruffed.

"A visit? Who is it?" he frowned, confused.

"Go see for yourself," she retorted, then walked away.

Georgie thought about it as he walked out to the courtyard. It couldn't be his mother because she had said that she would be coming in two weeks. Skye, he thought with a smile. She had probably flown straight back to surprise him. Thoughts of Skye always made him smile. She would always have a special place in his heart. But that was true of many women in his life.

Except one…the one that he hadn't expected but was waiting on for his whole life. She had it all.

Anya…

Anya…

...Anya?

The courtyard was a small area with several benches arranged where they weren't too close to one another. No one else was there except her, standing in the middle of the yard.

"...Anya?" Georgie gasped, not believing his eyes.

"Hello Georgie, how have you been?" she asked, that smile he had fallen in love with embracing his presence.

She was beautiful. She had let her hair grow out and she wore it in an upsweep, bangs accentuating her delicate features. Her sexy curves had filled out even more to the point of stallion status.

Georgie wanted to devour her, but he couldn't will his legs to move.

"I can't believe this," he said, shaking his head, never having been so shocked in his life.

"Believe it," she replied, crossing the space between them and wrapping her arms around him.

The hug felt better than any orgasm he had ever had, more intimate than any moment that he had experienced. Reluctantly, after what seemed like a moment in eternity, he broke the hug, holding her at arms length, massaging her shoulders.

"How did you know I was here?"

"Yvette. Your mother told Michelle, Michelle told Yvette and Yvette told me," Anya explained.

Georgie frowned.

"You talk to Yvette?"

Anya lowered her head, then looked back at him and replied, "Georgie, I've been in L.A. the whole time. I told Yvette not to tell you. It's not her fault; she wanted to tell you, but I wouldn't let her."

Georgie's facial expression showed that he was trying to wrap his head around what she had just told him.

"You what? Anya, what gave you that *right?*"

Georgie was vexed as he paced away from her. He couldn't wait to see Yvette; he was going to punch her dead in the face.

"Georgie, don't be mad. Try and look at it from my angle. You were with one of the most beautiful women in the *world*. How could I have competed with that?" Anya stressed.

"You didn't. She had to compete with you," he shot back, coming over to her.

Anya nodded.

"I sensed that. When I saw her album cover, the cut of her hair, the frosted tips... Did she know about me? Did she know what you were doing?"

"How could she."

Anya smiled, knowingly.

Georgie shook his head. So many emotions had been bottled up inside for so long, he didn't know where to start, until he blurted out, "Why did you *leave* me, Anya? Why? What happened? That night was so beautiful, and then you just leave in the middle of the night?" he questioned, his tone revealing his wounded pride.

She went to him, took his hand and they sat, side by side, on a bench.

"Georgie, we hadn't known each other long enough for me to be feeling what I felt. Something had to be wrong, because only lies came that easily," she explained, then smiled at him. "And you were so young, so fine, so *you*, I – I refused to believe, because it would've *crushed* me to find out otherwise."

"But it was *real*, Anya."

"Still Georgie, you weren't ready to love me and I wasn't ready to be loved."

"Anya, it's *still* real," Georgie remarked, lowering himself to one knee, holding her tiny hand in his.

She looked at him with tears brimming.

"No Georgie, you're still not ready."

"Ma, I was ready the first time I laid eyes on you," he replied.

"Georgie, how can you commit to me when you're still wearing another woman's ring?" Anya asked, running her thumb over the band,

He dropped his head.

"She's…dead, Anya."

"I know," she responded, tilting his head to look at her. "But if I'm going to do this Georgie, I have to be the only woman in your life, in your heart, mind, body and soul All of you, Georgie, because all of me is worth no less."

Georgie took a deep breath, and looked down at his band. He would always love Niia, but his love for Anya was greater. He was willing to give it all up to have her in his life. Slowly and symbolizing much more, he removed the band and put it on the park bench.

"I love you so much, Georgie," Anya sobbed, wrapping her arms around his neck.

He stood up, lifting her off her feet. She wrapped her legs around him too, kissing him deeply and tonguing him lustfully.

"Don't ever leave me again, Anya," Georgie cried, tears running down his cheeks.

She kissed each and every one away. "Never, baby, never! I promise!" she exclaimed. But her voice sounded far away.

Georgie looked at her. "Huh?"

"I said never, baby, never!"

Now it seemed as if she were on TV with the volume turned down.

"Anya, I can't hear you," he said, anxiety creeping into his voice.

He thought he was going deaf. Anya looked at him,

knowingly.

"Just know, wherever I am Georgie, I will always love you."

"What are you saying?!" he screamed, panicked.

"I'll always be here."

"Anya!"

"But it's time to let go."

"Anyyyyyyaaa!"

"I love you, Georgie."

And then he woke up.

It was all a dream.

He was still lying in his bed. It had felt so real. Her embrace, her breath in his face, the softness of her lips. But the only thing that had been real were the tears. They had drenched his face and they were still coming. It was like he couldn't stop them, so he didn't try. He let his heart have its one last cry before he let go. Georgie finally sat up and wiped his eyes. The sun was disappearing. The sky was the color of blackberry molasses…one of the things that never change.

. Deep down, he had always known that he would see her again, he just didn't know when or how. Now that he had he could finally exhale, even if it had only been a dream.

He started to go to the bathroom when he noticed something at the foot of his bed.

It was the girl with no name's copy of Zora's book. He smiled and picked it up. She must have snuck past Nurse Killjoy. She was showing him that she could reach him at will.

"Never underestimate a woman," he chuckled.

He went to the bathroom, pissed, washed his hands then caught his own reflection in the mirror. His eyes were still red-rimmed and tracks of tears still glistened in the bathroom light. But he didn't feel in any way self-conscious. It was a face of a man who loved and that is the manliest of all.

As he walked out of the bathroom and turned on the light to read, he thought to himself, *is it better to have loved and lost or to have never loved at all?*

He laughed and let the thoughts drift into oblivion because he knew that there was no answer. For once you have loved, you can never forget, but if you have never loved, then you will never know how much you truly have to lose.

Also Available From
VODKA&MILK

The Purple Don
Solomon

Revelations:
The New Scriptures
Solomon

They:
Want You Dead
Solomon

Trap Kitchen
Malachi Jenkins &
Roberto Smith
w/ Kathy Iandoli

Animal 4.5
K'wan
Write 2 Eat Concepts

Captain Save-A-Hoe
iiKane

Cham-Pain
iiKane

Commissary Kitchen:
My Infamous Prison Cookbook
Albert "Prodigy" Johnson
w/ Kathy Iandoli

Hoodlum 2
The Good Son
K'wan
Write 2 Eat Concepts

**All The Wrong
Places**
G.I.F.T.D

The Infamous
Solomon

Quantum Assassin
Chainworld
Matt Langley

MOVIE